A STRANGE
HABIT OF MIND

A STRANGE HABIT OF MIND

A CAMERON WINTER MYSTERY

ANDREW KLAVAN

THE MYSTERIOUS PRESS
NEW YORK

A STRANGE HABIT OF MIND

Mysterious Press
An Imprint of Penzler Publishers
58 Warren Street
New York, N.Y. 10007

Copyright © 2022 by Andrew Klavan

First Mysterious Press edition

Interior design by Maria Fernandez

Library of Congress Control Number: 2022906673.

Cloth ISBN: 978-1-61316-351-1
Ebook ISBN: 978-1-61316-352-8

10 9 8 7 6 5 4 3 2 1

Printed in the United States of America
Distributed by W. W. Norton & Company

This book is for Brian and Amy Anderson

"But there is neither East nor West, Border,
nor Breed, nor Birth,
When two strong men stand face to face,
though they come from the ends of the
earth!"

—Rudyard Kipling, from
"The Ballad of East and West"

PROLOGUE

Help me, he wrote. Then after that—nothing.

The music and the lights from the clubs below pulsed through the walls and windows as he lay despairing. The throbbing bass lines, the pounding melodies seemed to lend an aura of hostility to the shifting flashes of white and red and yellow that bathed the shadows all around him.

Somewhere out in the world, he knew, women were dancing. Their shapes electric. Their movements sinuous. Their nakedness-in-motion setting off a spark of life in the dead eyes of the men watching them from their stations at the bar.

But all that—the girls and the lights and the music—all that was of another time, the time when he was still alive, when he could see and hear and breathe, before this terror had swallowed him and filled him and closed around him like ocean water. That's all there was now: terror like ocean water. He was drowning in it, drowning in terror.

Sprawled on the sweaty bedsheets, he peered dully at the words he had tapped onto the text screen of his phone.

Help me.

Was there any point in pressing *send*? Would the man receive it? Would he answer the call? Would he come? And, if he came, could he save him? How could he? How could anyone save him?

Adam's thumb caressed the button that would dispatch his words into the ether. It would be like praying, he thought. Useless, like praying. What was the point?

But he never answered that question. He never made a conscious decision at all. He just pressed the button on impulse and off went the message into the empty air.

Help me.

For some reason, sending the text gave him a burst of fresh energy. He rolled off the bed and walked to the window. He stood staring down at the broad boulevard three stories below. The music from the strip clubs hammered against his chest. The lights from the signs flashed on his face.

Best Girls.

All Nude Girls.

Girls Girls Girls.

He ignored all of it. He watched the wide avenue, watched the cars passing this way and that, searched the cars with his hollow eyes.

For a second, he dared to entertain a little hope; a little. His message had been sent—sent to the one man who had ever done a decent thing for him, or tried to. Maybe the man would come. Maybe he would find a way to help him. It could happen.

But the very next moment even that little hope was gone.

A car had come into view from his left. It moved slowly in the heavy traffic beneath the blinking strip club signs. It was a fine silver car, a sleek Tesla 3. A car he knew well. How he'd loved it once. Its sharp lines seemed slashed out of living metal. It looked like some so-cool rocket from the future smoking into this present darkness. He could remember sitting in the passenger seat, awe-struck at the interior quiet and the dazzling dashboard array. "Wow! Wow!" he had murmured—partly to flatter the proud driver, sure, but partly because—wow. Wow.

Adam gazed sickly down at the car. He swallowed bile. The car was Death. It was his death, coming for him. Rolling with slow certainty through the traffic, nearer and nearer.

Adam made a little whining noise as the terror and inevitability of what was about to happen engulfed him again. He shuddered helplessly. Now, in a trance of fear, he turned from the window and walked directly to the apartment door and then directly out. He went to the end of the hall, into the stairwell, still in a trance. He climbed up the fire stairs. Pushed through the heavy door at the top. Stepped out onto the roof.

He was barefoot. He was wearing nothing but jeans and a soiled orange T-shirt. It was cold out here, really cold, but he didn't care. He didn't think to care. He couldn't feel the cold. He couldn't feel anything, neither regret nor simple sorrow. He didn't even know that he was weeping now, the tears streaming down his cheeks as he reached the edge of the roof and stepped up onto the low ledge at the border of it.

Crying, he glanced up briefly at the sky. The city lights had washed it clean of stars. It was just blue-blackness. Blue-black emptiness above and the flashing signs below.

Best Girls.

All Nude Girls.

Girls Girls Girls.

What a crap life he was ending. Maybe it was just as well he missed the final, unpleasant irony of it: the fact that as he stepped off the ledge, as he plummeted sick with misery past his apartment window toward the unforgiving pavement, his phone—the phone he had left lying on the bedsheets—was buzzing, the name of the caller appearing on the screen.

It was the answer to his texted prayer: *Help me.*

It was the name in which he had put what little faith he had.

Cameron Winter.

PART ONE

THE GHOST TOWN
OF DESIRE

The first man I ever killed was my best friend. My only friend, really. The only friend I'd ever had up to that time. You'll remember I was the classic poor little rich boy growing up. Raised by my German nanny Mia—far more than by my mother, who was busy with other things. I was privately tutored. Introduced to other children only as an after-thought at prearranged playdates and lavish birthday parties at elaborate venues—museums, amusement parks, giant toy stores, and whatnot. My mother would refer to these children as my "friends." But I never knew them.

And yes, yes, I feel guilty complaining about such things, the world being what it is, so full of suffering and so on. But each man's suffering is his own, you know, which gives it a special flavor, the taste of reality that other men's suffering can never have, no matter how much worse it may be.

Anyway, I'm the one paying for the therapy, so I'm the one who gets to complain.

I was lonely, growing up, for all my privilege. That's the point I'm making. All my heart's affections went first to Mia, as a proxy mother, and then to Charlotte, her niece, two years my senior and beautiful beyond believing, sweet and solemn and maternal herself. My first love.

So we're now in the period after I lost Charlotte, after she disappeared and began to become what she became to me, what we English professors call an eidolon: a phantom and an ideal, the ghost of my desire. Once she was gone, she acted in my life sort of like the green light in Gatsby's: a symbol of the thing I wanted most and had almost had, a Polaris of yearning that promised to lead me on, but instead bore me back ceaselessly into the past.

I returned to university. My social life was reduced to a series of brief encounters: weekend relationships with women who only had in common the facts that they were female and desirable and not Charlotte. They liked me, most of them. Loved me, one or two. But I couldn't give them anything of myself, not truly. I was unfair to them, I know. Not uncaring or anything. Never unkind. Just unfair.

It was a difficult time, a lost time. I knew I needed something, something more than these unhappy pairings.

So I took up martial arts. Karate, specifically. To work off all the energy and anger. And I discovered poetry at that time too, the English Romantics, which is now my specialty. That helped as well.

It was in karate class that I met Roy Spahn. My first friend. The man I killed.

He was only a few years older than I was, but he had a poise and calm and authority I could only aspire to. A black man. Half black. His father was black. He had a white mother. He was tall—at least a head taller than I am. Very lean and long-legged. He could kick you in the face from halfway across the room. A very impressive martial artist.

He was a black-belt second dan. Earning his living teaching at the dojo, but still undecided in his ambitions, still looking around for what he wanted to do with his life. He was a very skilled fighting instructor but, more than that, he was excellent at explaining the spiritual discipline that underlies the art—the inner stillness, the focus, the yin and yang of it, male fist into female palm. That was the stuff I needed to hear right then. Something to believe in. A way to think and to be.

And it turned out I had a talent for it. For fighting, I mean. Strangely enough, despite my soft upbringing, I had always been a bit of a hard character. When my parents finally sent me to school in my teens, I was always the guy who took on the bullies. Mostly I did it because I had this Charlotte eidolon in my head, always watching me in my imagination, and I wanted to be a hero in her imaginary eyes. But still. I was good with my fists. And now, it turned out, the whole karate ethos suited me.

Roy picked me out of the class from the first day. From that first day, I was always the one he'd call on when he wanted to demonstrate some takedown or technique. He'd even spar with me sometimes—which was a joke, at first. I was a beginner. He was expert and cobra-quick with inches of reach on me. From whatever direction I came at him, that's where he was, and I was on the mat the next second.

But he was a good teacher, and I was there to learn, all in, fully focused. I got better. And one day my moment came.

We were sparring, the two of us. The class watching us, surrounding us on the mats. Roy looped one of those uncannily fast kicks at my head and I somehow managed to duck under it, move in on him, and plant a fist in his floating rib.

The class gasped with surprise. And Roy—he didn't take it well. Invincibility was part of his persona as a teacher. He couldn't afford to be shown up by a mere beginner. So even as he lost his breath and staggered, he elbowed me in the mouth, hard. Gave me a good old-fashioned fat lip, with blood spattered on my chin and everything. We stood there glaring death at one another for a moment. Then we both started laughing.

We went out for a beer together after class, him and his sore rib, me and my swollen face.

He picked up the tab. He said, "Sorry about the lip. I couldn't let you get away with that in front of everyone."

"No, of course not. I should have thought of that. If I had, I'd have seen the elbow coming."

"You couldn't have stopped it."

I laughed. "So you say."

5

Roy had a terrific grin, a real klieg light of a smile when something genuinely tickled him. "We're done sparring, I'll give you that much," he said. "In public anyway."

"Really? Am I that good?"

"Oh yeah. Better. One of the best I've ever seen, potentially at least. Mind you, you're not there yet, nowhere near, and I'll still be happy to kick your ass privately any time."

"You can try."

"Oh, you're going to be so sorry you said that."

And we went on from there, fast friends by the time the evening was over. My first real friend.

Roy was good for me, great for me. For one thing, we did spar privately after that, all the time. And he did kick my ass. But he taught me too and I improved quickly.

There was also this: the guy was magic with women. I never saw anything like it before or since. He drew them to himself like some secret song composed for the purpose. It wasn't ugly or predatory. He wasn't one of these types who appeal to girls by mistreating them or through some kind of calculated mental manipulation. I've seen that. I've seen it work too. But that wasn't Roy. He just liked women. He liked their company. He was interested in what they had to say and how they saw the world, each in her own way. They seemed to be able to sense that about him from clear across the tavern. Plus he had the looks and the charm and the high-watt smile and all that. The women swarmed him, and there were always extras, always a few willing to settle for second best. I couldn't go into a bar with him and go home alone.

I learned a lot from him on this score. Watching him, watching the way he was—it really helped me. I was still sore-hearted over Charlotte. I still am today, as we know. But Roy taught me to stop looking for her in other women and to take each girl as she was, for who she was. That made things better for me somehow. It upped my sanity level, as much as was possible at any rate.

Roy also encouraged me in my scholarship. He took it seriously. He didn't dismiss it as precious or irrelevant or highfalutin. It was very encouraging, especially since all my professors had gone off on some theoretical-slash-political tack that had nothing to do with anything I cared about. That approach alienated me completely. But Roy—he wasn't a literary sort himself, but when I talked about the poetry I loved he could relate it to the Eastern philosophies he studied. It made for great conversations that went deep into whiskey bottles and long into the night.

After a while, though, I came to notice this one area of our relationship where there was—I won't call it friction, because there was never any anger between us, even when we disagreed—but just a growing focus of attention. It was like a slow whirlpool that kept pulling us back to itself, so that we talked about it more and more as the months went on.

It wasn't about race, not specifically, but that's where it started. Very early on, maybe even during that first beer we had together, I noticed there was a racial component to Roy's thinking. He wrestled with how to identify himself, being half one thing and half another, as he was. His black father had deserted the family when Roy was young. His white mother raised him and worked hard to give him a middle-class life and a good education. He had grown up in mostly white neighborhoods. But, of course, he still wore his color on his face, and it's always a political issue in American life anyway, so there was that side of it too.

And very early on—it started during that first conversation in the bar—he began dropping these offhanded references to various racial difficulties he had encountered in his life. He would make a remark, or more often tell some anecdote in which race played a part. About a woman who showed fear when he got into an elevator with her because he was black, or a teacher who made an unfair assumption about his abilities. That sort of thing.

I must have rolled my eyes at some point without meaning to because Roy reacted. He made a show of dropping his jaw.

"You don't think that happens?" he said.

"Can I be honest with you or do I have to worry I'll walk out of here with a black eye to go with my fat lip?" I asked.

He gestured at me with his beer mug. "Honest. Go ahead."

"It bores me, Roy. It feels like a power move on your part. You keep slipping these subtle little racial woe-is-me signals into the conversation and what am I supposed to do about it? Watch my tongue? Curb my ideas? Tiptoe through the minefield of your sensitivities? That would give you control over what I'm allowed to think or say, wouldn't it? I have no interest in that. All God's children have troubles in this world."

"Oh ho," he said. "How many millions did you say were in that trust fund of yours, golden boy?"

"Many millions. Many, many millions. But I've got my sorrows, same as anyone, and I'm not asking you to pat my head or give a damn. If you don't like the country, there's a plane leaving every couple of minutes. Personally, I think we're both lucky to be here."

I can see the look on Roy's face even now as I'm telling you this. He blinked and raised his eyebrows and dropped back against the tavern bench and gaped at me as if I'd confessed to a crime.

"You're a patriot!" he said in wonder. "Is that it? Are you a patriot?"

I hesitated. I felt embarrassed. It wasn't something a college student was supposed to be in those days: a patriot. It was too corny, too old-fashioned. It lacked nuance, doncha know. But when I thought about it, it seemed to me, you sort of had to be at least a little patriotic, given what else was out there in the world.

Finally, at a loss for a response, I quoted poetry at him. Walter Scott: "Breathes there a man, with soul so dead/Who never to himself hath said/This is my own, my native land!"

That was the beginning of it. It was like one of those sore spots you get in your mouth sometimes and you can't leave it alone, you keep coming back to it, rubbing your tongue over it again and again. A little at first and then more and more, we would return to the subject. Not the subject of race or patriotism specifically, though we sometimes approached it from those directions. But it was more general than that. It was more about—I don't know what to call it exactly. Commitment. Action and belief. What could a man justifiably do in the world and for what reason? That was what Roy had been trying to figure out when I met him, and as we talked about it, I realized that that was what I was trying to figure out as well.

"It seems to me a man gets hemmed in in the modern world," Roy said to me once. "The wilderness is gone. We don't even go into space anymore, not really. There are no secret places left. No room to move in an original way, a dangerous way, a way suitable to a man."

"In literature," I told him, "there's always this moment in time, this remembered moment in a country's past when men were men and they could show bravery and do violence in service to the common good. The Trojan War. Knights in armor. Cowboys in a gunfight on the streets of Laredo."

"Rescuing damsels in distress."

"Exactly. Paving the way for civilization with their swords and guns. Who even knows if it was ever real? Probably not, and certainly not the way they tell it. You put too much faith in that sort of story and you end up like Don Quixote, charging at windmills, pretending they're giants."

"Yes! Yes!" Roy leaned over his beer mug at me. "Sometimes I think, 'Well, maybe the military . . .' But then I wonder: is even that real anymore? I keep imagining myself gunning down some fifteen-year-old tribesman in some backward hellhole we have no business being in, or getting my legs blown off by some cave dweller's rigged device—and for what? It just seems like war for war's sake, at this point."

"Distress without the damsel."

"Right. Right."

These conversations always seemed to wind down into unsatisfying semi-resolutions. We would cloak the problem over with youthful cynicism. We would declare that it was all a fool's game, and there was no adventure left, no cause worth dying for, no damsels, no distress. Then, a few beer nights later, we'd be right back at it again, going over the sore spot, unable to leave it alone.

Then—then finally—one day—one night it was, actually—we were in the dojo together after hours, just the two of us, working it off in a full-on brother battle hand-to-hand, really going at it like giants in an ancient epic, Gilgamesh and Enkidu, cities laid waste around us, the forest leveled, trees snapping off at the trunks on every side, falling with a crash, the sweat flying off our faces, our hands and feet in a blur of motion, slashing, kicking, grappling, wrestling, back and forth across the mat, a massive man-dance of make-believe destruction, each of us all there.

Then we broke. Panting. Bent over at the waist. Hands on our knees. Done.

And Roy lifted his face to me and said between breaths, "I think I found something." I couldn't speak. I just waited to hear more. "There's this guy," Roy said. "There's this guy I think you should meet."

"What guy?" I panted. "What are we talking about?"

"He's like, you know—what's the word? A recruiter."

"A recruiter? You mean, like, for the military?"

"He heard about me somewhere. Me and the dojo. The kinds of things I teach. He approached me."

"What kind of recruiter?" I asked again. I had managed to straighten up now. I walked to the wall. I reached down and pulled my towel out of my fight bag, where it lay on the floor. I mopped my face with it. "The army? Marines? What are we talking about?"

Roy had also straightened, hands on hips, on the sides of his black belt. "No. Not the military. He says it's more, like, intelligence."

I remember I felt a sort of charge go through me. A quick little electric buzz. Intelligence—the secret services—I hadn't thought of that before. Neither of us had.

"You mean, like, spying?" I said. "Like the CIA?"

"Not the CIA. I don't think so anyway. He just says it's a division of intelligence."

Our eyes met across the mat and I could see we both were feeling the same thing now: a fresh sense of possibility.

"That's what he called it," said Roy. "The Division."

1

Cameron Winter paused here, staring into space. Margaret Whitaker studied him. For several long moments, they sat facing one another in a brown silence.

It was impossible for Margaret not to think of it that way. Brown. Tan. Bland. Everything in her office was like that: the desk, the walls, the rug, the chairs—even the framed photographs—a sunset, wildflowers, a trail through the woods, even the atmosphere. They were all serenely colorless. The idea was to keep things neutral, to create a sheltering aura of tranquillity amidst the tumult of the world. The snowy white February was at the windows, but here in her office there was peace.

That was the idea anyway. Winter's story had shaken that brown world up a bit. All that male energy—the testosterone-fueled drinking bouts, and wolf hunts and man-to-man combat. The tale had left Margaret rather breathless. She was sixty-seven years old, after all. A bona fide old biddy, she thought, suppressing a smile. There was only so much of this sort of thing her poor heart could take!

She had allowed Winter to fall into the habit of delivering these long monologues during their therapy sessions. She wondered now about the wisdom of that. Was it an innovation in technique on her part? Or was she letting Winter take advantage of her fascination with him? Hard to know. He had been coming to her for only a couple of months but their relationship was already extraordinarily complicated.

Some of it was just the standard therapy stuff: the transference of the client's feelings onto his therapist. Winter had been, for all intents and purposes, a motherless child and Margaret was obviously now a mother figure to him. There was something sweetly innocent about the simple trust with which he had begun to reveal his secrets to her. He was obviously yearning—and had been yearning for all his thirty-some-odd years—for a mother's sympathy and acceptance and forgiveness and love.

Well, there was a lot to be forgiven.

The first man I ever killed was my best friend.

Goodness me! Margaret thought. (She had a droll streak. You needed one in the psychotherapy business.)

It was on her side, though, that the relationship got really problematic. Her countertransference with Winter was multifaceted, to put it mildly.

For one thing, she worried she was a little too willing to accept the maternal role in his life. Ever since she'd started seeing him, she found herself meditating often on her failures with her own son, now a lost soul living far away. Was she trying to correct the mistakes of her past by mothering Winter?

And then there was this: she could play mama with him for all she was worth but it didn't change the fact that she also found him incredibly attractive.

At her age, she was hardly likely to spontaneously combust into lusty flame, but she wasn't dead yet either. She couldn't help noticing he was a very handsome man. What's more, he had the type of looks she had always found particularly appealing. He had sensitive, intellectual, even ethereal features, framed by longish, wavy, golden hair that fell around his ears and gave him the appearance of an angel in a Renaissance painting. He dressed like the college English professor he was, with wire-rimmed glasses and cable-knit sweaters under patched tweed jackets. But at the same time, his broad shouldered, slim-waisted frame was clearly muscular. He moved, even when he was sitting in the chair, with an Asiatic grace and self-control he must have learned as a practitioner of Japanese martial arts. And she liked all that. She found it an exciting blend of qualities.

But what disturbed her more than anything was the violence in him. She could see it in those controlled movements of his. She could see it in the slight swelling of the first two knuckles on each hand. That must've been the result of his karate training: punching wooden boards and doing push-ups with his fists pressed into concrete, and so on. And of course there was the violence of the stories he was finally beginning to tell her. *The first man I ever killed . . .*

And then, too, there was the violence of his passions. In his quiet way, he was full of passions. Grief and sorrow. An urgent yearning for beauty and for love. And guilt—lots of guilt—guilt on a grand scale—the sort of guilt you found in the final act of a Shakespeare play when the ghosts of the dead rose up to accuse their murderers. Once, not so long ago, he had cried out to her—softly, but with genuine anguish: *I've killed people, Margaret!* And before she had had time to consider her response, she heard herself say to him: *Yes, dear, I know,* in a tone that implied, *There, there, darling. It's all right now. There, there.*

She sensed he was going to need a lot of *there, there*s.

All this violence agitated her because it was part of what she found so attractive in him. If she was honest about it, it thrilled her. If she was even more cruelly honest, it cast a cold light back on her own marriage. Her husband had been a mild-mannered fellow therapist. Their long life together, from its beginning to his death, had been neither happy nor unhappy, but comfortable and intellectual and essentially passionless. Brown.

In short, her sessions with Winter were slowly reducing her to a great big puddle of emotional mess. And yet for all that she truly wanted to help the man. That was her job, for one thing. Plus she liked him. From his civilized demeanor, from his love of literature, from the clear light of old-fashioned manly virtue in his blue eyes, she could tell he was a person of quality. He may have done terrible things, as bad as he said. But she could not bring herself to think he was irredeemable. She wanted very much to help him forgive himself—and she knew she wouldn't be able to do that if she succumbed to a girlish infatuation with him, hoping his passion would rescue her from her dull, brown self.

She drew a deep breath. Whatever the complexities, the time had come for her to take back control of the session.

"You seem less depressed than when you first came to me," she said.

He blinked out of his fugue state and gestured mildly at her. "I guess you've worked your magic on me, Margaret."

She smiled slightly. "I'm glad you're feeling more hopeful. But I can't help noticing how often you still seem to focus on the past."

"Is that bad? There are things about my past I feel I have to tell you."

"It's not bad at all. It's just that I find your attitude toward the past very striking. You seem to have a powerful sense that you've lost something back there, something essential that can't be recovered."

"Do I?"

"It's a theme you keep returning to. There's Charlotte, obviously. As you say yourself, she seems to have become a symbol for all the feminine gentleness and nurturance you feel you missed out on during your childhood. Then there's these conversations you had with your friend Roy. All about the lost wilderness and the bygone days of knights in armor and cowboys. You missed out on those too. Even your love of English Romantic poetry—that's the eighteenth century, isn't it?"

"And the early nineteenth, yes."

"When the old world was dying."

"'There hath passed away a glory from the earth,'" Winter recited.

"Yes. That's it. You immerse yourself in all that nostalgia. As if you feel there was once a better time than this, a time you would've been more suited for."

Winter lowered his eyes. He smiled down at the colorless rug. He shook his head ruefully. "I come in here and tell you this story—this story full of blood and drama—and instead of asking me what anyone else would ask, instead of saying, 'What do you mean you killed your best friend?' you ask questions about—I don't know what—thematic subtleties."

"If you want my magic, Cam, you have to let me work my spells," Margaret said.

He laughed softly. He slowly raised his eyes. The look jolted her. The warmth of it, the childlike trust. It was so plain to see: he had surrendered himself to her. This handsome, civilized, and very dangerous male animal had given himself completely into her feminine care.

And it thrilled her. Too much, she thought. Too much.

2

For his part, Winter was exasperated with the whole therapeutic process. Sometimes, he felt Margaret was making him crazier instead of saner. Yes, she had worked wonders for him. He had been terribly depressed when he first came to see her. He felt so much better now. In fact, he liked and esteemed her more than anyone he had known in a long time. But whatever witchery the woman was practicing in that office, it had released an absolute circus of emotions inside him. Regrets and hopes and longings and painful insights were now pouring endlessly out of his heart like clowns out of a Volkswagen. As a result, he couldn't stop thinking about the therapist for ten minutes in a row. He had become addicted to the idea of her.

Later that afternoon, for instance, as he was right in the middle of giving a lecture on Wordsworth, he suddenly found himself thinking back to Margaret's remarks to him earlier in the day. He had been making his way through the poet's "Intimations of Immortality." Trying to convey some sense of its meaning to the slouching, dreamy, glum, and gormless students who had straggled into the lecture hall like refugees from the ruins of the American public education system. He had just reached the lines: *Whither is fled the visionary gleam?/Where is it now, the glory and the dream?* when his voice drifted off into silence. He stood on the lecture stage gazing into the middle distance. Margaret's words about the past, about his attitude toward the past, came back to him. A cascade of psychic connections started tumbling through his mind. The death of Wordsworth's mother. The loss of the poet's connection to nature. His own mother. Charlotte. Her disappearance. The irretrievable days gone by . . . *There hath passed away a glory from the earth.*

He came back to himself with a sense of panic. He had forgotten what he had been lecturing about. He blinked up at the dull-faced students in the tiered seats. He was about to admit he'd lost his train of thought. But just then, he noticed the clock on the wall. The hour was over. He was saved.

He briskly announced the reading assignments for the next lecture. He watched, still distracted, as the students tromped up the stairs to the lecture hall exit.

And he saw, standing beside the doorway, looking down at him, a woman, weeping.

It was Lori Lesser. The dean of student relations. A strange, neurotic person, in Winter's estimation. Her job, as he understood it, was to terrorize the students over their inevitable violations of the university's increasingly incomprehensible codes of speech and conduct. She went about this with the sort of grim, bloodthirsty dedication he usually associated with the Spanish Inquisition. Yet, notwithstanding, Winter always found her kind of appealing in some bizarre, mildly horrifying way. Forty or so, she had springy, unkempt red-blond hair and small, expressive features—the appearance of a fanatic, which struck him at once as both ferocious and oddly adorable. Under her consistently rumpled outfits, her figure was full and sensual. It made him think about violating the university's codes of speech and conduct himself.

Right this moment, though, as she stood at the top of the stairs gazing down at him, she looked only small and huddled and miserable, like a cat in the rain. She hunched inside her imitation camel hair overcoat. The tears streamed down her blotchy cheeks. The students hurried past her with nervous glances. There was always the chance she had come to denounce some of them for whatever unholy shenanigans they had undoubtedly gotten up to.

When the last student was gone—when she and Winter were alone together in the lecture hall—she heaved a tragic sigh and came thumping down the steps to him. He descended from the lecture stage to meet her, arranging his face in an expression of concern. He was concerned, actually. One way or another, Lori was always trouble.

She reached him. Looked up at him a long moment with overflowing eyes.

"Lori . . . ?" he said. "What's wrong?"

"Adam Kemp is dead," she told him. "He killed himself."

Winter expelled his breath. Well, that was a shock. Adam had texted him just two days before. Two words: *Help me.* Winter had called him back as soon as he received the message but there had been no answer. He'd been trying the number off and on ever since but had gotten no response. He had felt vaguely concerned, but suicide—that had never occurred to him.

"Ah, Lori," he said. She came close to him and he felt he had no choice but to hold her. She broke down completely, sobbing against his chest. "Now, now," he murmured. "It's not your fault."

It probably was her fault, he thought—at least partly. Adam Kemp had been a talented but troubled drama major at the university until last year, his junior year. Then, after a fairly typical weekend bacchanal, he had had sex with a coed. Afterward, the girl had decided she'd been too drunk to give knowing consent.

She had lodged a complaint against Adam with the Office of Student Relations.

It was the sort of offense Lori lived to prosecute, and prosecute it she did, the full Torquemada. Before she had even heard Adam's side of the story, she released a written statement to the student body, describing the incident in a way that made Adam sound like a predatory danger to every female within fifty miles of campus. Then she brought him up before an ad hoc administrative panel. He was not allowed to have an attorney present. And really, what could he say? The girl had been drunk, all right. So was he, but that didn't seem to count for anything. In the end, Lori had threatened to turn the matter over to the police if Adam didn't leave school. Which he did. Which was pretty typical of the way Lori handled these matters.

Winter had been the only member of the panel to stand up for the fool. No one else wanted to be seen defending a sex abuser. And Winter hadn't defended him. He thought Adam had behaved badly. But then, Winter was a man out of his time, an old-fashioned gentleman. He believed in walking a lady safely home if she was under the influence. That was the very objection he raised. These young people didn't live in a world of ladies and gentlemen. They were allowed to dress like slobs and curse like gangsters. To drink like tosspots. To tattoo and pierce their bodies like primitives. To listen to songs with animal rhythms and vulgar lyrics. They had no curfews, no chaperones, no guidance that applied to real-life male and female behavior. Indeed, they were told that gender was mutable and sex an irrelevance. And then the young men—only the men—were held to rules of behavior that would have been restrictive when Victoria was queen.

As far as Winter was concerned, both Adam and the girl had behaved exactly as you would expect young people to behave under such circumstances. They had gotten drunk and acted like idiots. If it had been up to him, he would have given them both a stern lecture on the connection between chastity and self-respect—mostly to cover up the university's complete failure to act in loco parentis as it should. Then he would have allowed them to return shamefaced to the study of whatever pseudo-knowledge they were wasting their parents' money on.

This, however, was not the Lori Lesser way. God was easier on the original Adam than Lori was on this one. Her final summation before the panel was a thunderous denunciation of the boy. If the girl had been too drunk to give consent, then how was their intercourse different from rape? And wasn't it just one more instance of the oppression of women by men down through the centuries?

The women on the panel were riled. The men were cowed. Winter was roundly condemned for his objections. And Adam left school under a black cloud of shame.

"I don't know, I don't know," Lori cried into Winter's now soggy sweater. "Maybe you were right. Maybe I was too hard on him."

"When did this happen?" Winter asked her.

"Two days ago, around ten p.m., they said."

"What did he do?"

She drew back from him—for which he was glad, because the press of her body was beginning to disturb him. She dragged her two hands down her cheeks to clear the tears away.

"He threw himself off the top of his apartment building."

Winter winced at the image. "Any idea why? Did he leave a note?"

She shook her head and sniffled. "Not that I know of. But apparently he'd been in trouble with the law recently. He'd been selling drugs, methamphetamines. The police had found a stash in his apartment. He spent a night in jail a week or two ago. But eventually the charges were dropped."

"You're getting this from the police, I take it."

She nodded, gazing up at him forlornly. "I contacted them when I heard about it. His mother called to tell me. She said . . ." She raised her tear-stained face to the ceiling fluorescents. "She said such terrible things to me, Cam. Such terrible, terrible things."

Winter felt he ought to console her, but he couldn't in all honesty. And anyway, his thoughts had already gone off in a different direction. Why, he was wondering, would a young man kill himself what must have been literally seconds after texting for help? Shouldn't he at least have waited awhile to see if he got a response—or no response? Of course, it was possible the boy had simply been irrational at that point. Still, it seemed strange to him. It seemed strange behavior that needed explaining.

Lori was gazing at him pitifully now. Her hands were jammed deep in the pockets of her overcoat. Her complexion was a sorry mess.

"You always said I was unfair to him," she said mournfully.

Yes, he thought, that was why she had come to him—to him specifically. She wanted absolution from the one person who had opposed her. If he declared her guiltless, that might counterbalance the accusations of the lad's mother.

"Well," he answered, as sympathetically as he could. "It's not you, really. It's the system that's unfair. The culture here."

But that didn't help. She was the system. She was the culture, its arm of enforcement. She began crying again, hugging herself and trembling. He stood there awkwardly, wishing he could bring himself to be kinder to her. And wondering: Why hadn't Adam waited a moment to hear back from him?

Then, she said miserably: "Oh, you think I'm to blame too." And she dropped down heavily into a seat in the first row.

Winter was growing uncomfortable. He knew that her guilt would soon shade into anger. He knew that could mean all kinds of trouble for him, trouble he didn't need.

Lori's feelings for him were—apparently—rather complicated. On the one hand, she had made it clear more than once that she was attracted to him. She had made several attempts to draw him into a relationship, all of which he had resisted. On the other hand, the faculty gossip was that his presence on campus rankled her. She felt he didn't belong here. She would've gotten rid of him if she could. She knew he had had an affair with a student once. It was before her time, back when the policy on such matters was more lax. The woman was happily married now and she and Winter were still friends. But, according to the gossip, Lori raised the subject often. She used it as an example of the appalling way men abuse their power.

More than that, she seemed to find Winter's very existence a sort of moral offense. His approach to his subject—the subject of English literature—was woefully antiquated. He did not go out of his way to include women writers or writers of diverse backgrounds. He did not explore the issues of race and gender. His only criterion was literary excellence, which he seemed to feel was an objective quality. And his only purpose was to explain to his students what the poets had been trying to express in their time.

Lori had fielded complaints about his attitudes from students and faculty alike. She had dutifully reported these complaints to both the dean and the chairman of the English Department. But despite the fact that Winter was only an associate professor and did not have tenure, no one seemed willing to engage with him.

All of which boiled down to this. He'd rebuffed her romanti-cally and offended her philosophically—and now he was refusing to absolve her of her possible role in a young man's suicide. To Winter, this seemed like a combustible combination. And Lori was a woman who, once inflamed, could be unceasing in her anger.

Considering this, he thought he should probably change the subject now, or better yet end the conversation completely. But he couldn't. The question kept niggling at him: Why hadn't Adam waited a few seconds to give him a chance to reply to his call for help?

"Did you know he was selling drugs?" he asked Lori. She sniffled and shook her head no. He perched himself on the edge of the lecture stage. "Neither did I. The last I heard from him, he was working at a small theater out in San Francisco. He had a girlfriend. He sounded happy actually." He murmured this last sentence more to himself than to her. He kept thinking back to that final text: *Help me.*

"You're just wrong, you know," Lori burst out suddenly. There was the anger beginning to rise. "I wasn't too hard on him at all. The university had to make a statement. You don't know what it's like for women in this culture."

"I'm sure that's true," Winter said absently. He was barely lis-tening to her anymore. When he finally did bring his attention back to her, he could see her tear-stained face was beginning to flush with rage. He decided his wisest move would be to make a run for it.

"Listen, I've got to go. I've got a meeting," he lied. He stood up. He put a hand on the shoulder of her imitation camel hair overcoat. "Don't torture yourself about this, Lori. Adam made his own decision." That was the best he could do for her. But as he climbed back on stage to gather his books, he added, "I'll try to find out more about it."

3

Cameron Winter had a strange habit of mind. He sometimes slipped without warning into a silent state akin to meditation. His points of view and his opinions vaporized. All that remained in his consciousness were shifting patterns of events and personalities. Often, when he returned to himself, he found that a new sense of some situation had arisen in him. Motives and actions that had before been puzzling to him suddenly became clear.

He had used this quirk of his more than once to untangle problems, avert catastrophes, and even solve crimes. Sometimes, just hearing about some circumstance or reading about it in the news—a kidnapping once, a disappearance, most recently a murder conviction that did not quite hold together—he was struck with an inner certainty that the secret truth of the matter would reveal itself to him where it had remained hidden from others.

He felt that way about the suicide of Adam Kemp. But the problem here was: he couldn't be sure if the feeling was genuine or if it was merely a reaction to guilt. Because he did feel guilty. He kept asking himself if there was something more he could have done to keep Adam from such an ending. He knew there probably wasn't. It was probably irrational even to ask the question. But he did ask it. And he needed to put the matter to rest.

He gazed out the window of the jet's first-class cabin. The winter fields of the Midwest slid away below him. San Francisco waited in the mist ahead. He thought of Lori Lesser. He felt sympathy for her now, even for her anger at him. Obviously, she felt guilty about Adam's death as well, and it was easier for her, far less painful, to rage against his, Winter's, attitudes than to examine her own actions. Suicides were always a mess like this. They left such a wreckage of hearts behind them, like tornadoes leave debris. Poor Lori. Poor Adam. Poor everyone.

He found the state of the city appalling. As his car traveled from the airport into the Mission District, he watched the graceful and imaginative skyline give way to filthy streets of wind-blown litter and homeless encampments under boarded storefronts. Among the long rows of canvas tents on the sidewalks, madmen and addicts slumped in the jumble of their belongings or shuffled through the gray weather like living piles of rags.

The car's driver, sick with bitterness and disgust, kept up a running commentary. "This was a beautiful city once," he repeated over and over again.

Winter remained silent. He watched through his window as an old woman bared her bottom to the wind in order to relieve herself on the sidewalk. The driver was right. It had been a beautiful city once. He wondered for a moment if what Margaret Whitaker noticed in him—his yearning for an irretrievable past—was more a problem of history than psychology. Maybe something essential really had been lost to time.

The car stopped in the shadow of police headquarters. It was a standing slab of black glass, a dark carbuncle on the face of the avenue. It looked as if the architect had built a gravestone to mark the city's death. Here lies San Francisco.

The detective who met him at the front desk—Inspector Solomon Raines—was a man about his own age, closing in on forty. With one glance, Winter judged him to be a once-decent man gone sour. Among the police, he knew, there were many such cases these days.

"Let's walk," Raines said.

Winter took this as a good sign. Raines wanted to get away from the department so he could speak freely.

Out in the cold, they strolled shoulder to shoulder toward the piers. Winter kept his gloved hands in the pockets of his brown shearling coat. His ivy cap was tugged down low on his brow against the weather.

"You were his friend," Raines said. He was a thickset black man with a round face hard as a stone, short-cropped hair, and an aggressive mustache.

"I'm a college professor," said Winter. "I had Adam in a class. He was a talented kid."

"He was thrown out of school, though, wasn't he?"

"He slept with a girl when she was drunk. When they were both drunk." They exchanged knowing glances, the way men do when they discuss such matters with no women present. Winter shivered and hunched against the damp, biting cold coming in off the water. "You're certain about it being suicide, I take it."

"Yeah, yeah," said Raines. "There were witnesses. One woman saw him right before he jumped. I went up there myself afterward. No one pushed him. It was suicide, for sure."

"Any note? Any motive?" Winter had to look to see the inspector shaking his head no. "I understand he'd had trouble with the law recently."

"Possession of meth," said Raines. "Detectives executed a search warrant and found his stash under some sweaters in his closet."

Surprised, Winter glanced at him. Raines stared resolutely forward, his tongue planted in his round cheek.

"What's the penalty for possessing meth in California?" Winter asked. "A stern talking to?"

"Pretty much. If that. It's a misdemeanor. A violation of the Health and Safety Code. There's a fine. You can get up to a year in jail if you did something stupid while you were high, like drove your car over a group of schoolchildren. Something like that might be frowned upon."

"They issue search warrants for a health code violation? You search a man's apartment for that?"

Raines's shoulders rose and fell beneath his overcoat. "It wasn't my case," he said. "I just caught the suicide." After a moment, Raines added blandly, "Maybe they were going up the ladder."

"Bringing pressure on Adam in order to get to his distributor, you mean."

"Quint, they call him. The distributor. They call him Quintero."

"The Farmer."

"He's an unpleasant individual, there's no question about that." Raines was still staring into the distance. Still occasionally scouring his cheek with his tongue. It made the big mustache squirm around on his lip like some sort of angry caterpillar. "He likes to mutilate his enemies then set them on fire. I think that's still illegal in San Francisco, though I haven't checked recently."

"That is unpleasant," Winter said. "Did Adam roll on him?"

"Not that I know of."

Winter's mouth twisted. This wasn't making sense to him. "But they never charged him, did they? For the meth, I mean. They just held him overnight, then let him go."

Raines sighed loudly enough that Winter could hear it over the wind. "It wasn't a good night for him. He was in County Jail Three." Winter waited and the inspector went on. "You know how they say Disneyland is the happiest place on earth? County Three is not that."

"He had trouble there?"

"His PD claimed he was left unsupervised in gen pop. Raped and beaten. He threatened to sue the city."

"So they dropped the charges."

"I guess they figured he'd suffered enough for his crimes," Raines said drily.

Winter made a face. "Let me get this straight here. They pulled him in for nothing, for a misdemeanor. Then they threw him to the wolves in county where he was sure to be torn to pieces like the skinny, sensitive little white boy he was. Then they set him free—so now this maniac Quintero would think the cops had turned him, that Adam was let off because he'd named his distributor. So Adam was basically waiting at home for Quintero to drop by and mutilate him then set him on fire. That pretty much cover it?"

Once again, Raines's shoulders rose and fell.

"Well, what the hell?" said Winter with some feeling. "Did the kid forget his donation to the Police Benevolent Association or something? What the hell, Raines?"

They had reached the basin. Beyond the piers, the water was dark and turbulent under the roiling gray sky. They stopped their ramble and faced one another. Raines's eyes met Winter's.

"It wasn't my case," he repeated.

Winter shook his head. But he understood. The city was falling apart around them. Raines must've needed all his energies to fight the politicos who were making it impossible for him to do his job. He wasn't about to rat on his fellow police.

"What happened to Adam's phone?" Winter asked. Raines gave a derisive snort. Winter knew he had hit on something important. "Adam texted me just before he jumped. I called him back. Several times. No one picked up. Did anyone dump his phone to find out what was on it?"

"I logged the phone," the inspector said. "But it went missing."

"But did you dump it? Did you get the records?"

"It was a suicide, professor. There was no call for that."

Winter was about to make a snide remark: it's hard to find out what you don't want to know. But he stopped himself. What was the point? Raines was obviously as disgusted with the whole business as he was.

He decided to take a different tack. "I would like to meet this Quintero character," he said.

Raines laughed once. "You can't do that. He's a psychopath. He's a dangerous man."

"He has no reason to be dangerous to me. I can't hurt him. I'm just a college professor."

Raines made no answer. The wind came in hard over the piers. Winter shivered again. He looked out at the whitecaps. "It just seems like a hell of a thing, that's all," he said.

There was a long silence between the two of them. Then Raines said, "Adam Kemp had a girlfriend. Talk to her. Talk to Evelyn Shea."

Winter turned back to him sharply.

But by then the inspector was already walking away.

4

The theater where Adam had worked was called the Hall. It had a dingy entryway on Valencia Street, a broad avenue, now forlorn. Winter walked past a fast-food restaurant on the corner, then past a homeless man sprawled snoring on the sidewalk. Then he reached the theater.

The door was open. Winter went in. The cramped lobby was empty. There was a glass counter with a cash register on it. There were posters of old productions on the walls. He passed through a narrow curtain into the theater itself. It was shadowy in there, hard to see. But someone in the dark was reciting Shakespeare, of all things. So maybe even in San Francisco, Western civilization wasn't quite over yet. Not yet. But then civilization never was quite over until it was, Winter thought.

His eyes adjusted. A noble-looking young Latino was standing in pools of shadow on the dark stage. He was reading Macbeth's last soliloquy off a script.

"Life's but a walking shadow, a poor player that struts and frets his hour upon the stage and then is heard no more. It is a tale told by an idiot, full of sound and fury, signifying nothing."

With that, some light suddenly bathed him, first white, then red, then blue. Someone was in the lighting booth, running experiments. The set was a city street, a slum street, ruined like the streets outside. Winter thought it was remarkably well crafted for a small theater where money was probably tight.

As the various lights played on the stage, the seats remained in shadow. Winter saw the silhouettes of several people sitting in the audience, watching. One silhouette—a woman's silhouette—was standing in the aisle a little distance in front of him.

"I want more blue in the spot," she said into her phone. "I want to isolate him from the fill so he looks like the night moves with him. It's his personal darkness. He thinks he's describing the world, but he's really describing the state of his own soul."

When she stopped speaking, Winter said, "Evelyn Shea?" He knew Adam's girlfriend was the theater's set designer. Her shadowy figure turned to face him. "My name is Cameron Winter," he told her.

He saw her straighten. He heard her draw breath. "Oh," she said. "The professor. Of course." She spoke into her phone again: "Play with it. I'll be back in fifteen."

With that, all the theater lights came on and he could see her clearly. It was his turn to straighten, his turn to catch his breath. His brief moment of hope for Western civilization ended abruptly.

Evelyn Shea was a pretty blonde who had recently been punched in the face. The bruises were turning an ugly yellow. She'd covered them with makeup, but they were plainly visible and she knew it. She presented them to Winter defiantly, her blue gaze unwavering.

"We should go out in the lobby," she said.

Winter led the way. It was only a few steps, but in the time it took to take them his attitude toward Adam Kemp's suicide changed completely. Adam had always been a troubled kid. He was a small, arty boy from the hardscrabble northern hills. He had a thug of a father. He got bullied at school. He took to Winter because Winter was a manly man who loved poetry and wasn't sorry for it. Adam needed a role model like that. Getting tossed out of school had probably devastated him. And getting hooked on meth surely hadn't helped. It was a sad story, no question. But Winter remained a gentleman out of his time, and once a guy started beating his girlfriend, he lost all feeling for him.

In the lobby, he turned to face Evelyn. They stood by the cash register. The play posters looked down at them, the actors making dramatic faces as if they were commenting on the conversation below.

Evelyn really was lovely, Winter thought. Mid-twenties, maybe. Midwestern, he would have guessed. Cheerful, cherub features framed by a tangle of golden hair. Winter wondered if it took a lot of doing to get her hair to tumble in a pretty mess like that. He didn't know. She was petite, barely came up to his chin. Even though she was swamped in loose jeans and a baggy sweater, he could see her figure was fine.

"You're right, you know," he told her. "About Macbeth. He's not describing the world, he's describing what life is like once you detach yourself from the moral order. It's a smart reading."

She liked the compliment. She smiled brightly—then flinched so that he knew her bruises were still hurting her. "Adam always spoke very highly of you," she said. "You meant a lot to him. I guess you're here because you heard what happened."

Winter nodded, but he couldn't just ignore the bruises. "Did he do that to you, Evelyn?"

Her lips went thin. "It was stupid. He didn't mean it . . ." she started to say. But she stopped herself. "God. I can't believe that came out of my mouth." She pressed her hand to her eyes as if to hold the tears in. "I mean, it was the drugs, that's what did it to him. I'm not making excuses for him. Or maybe I am. I'm sorry. I'm very confused and upset right now."

"Of course. I understand," he said.

"Anyway. I'm sure you didn't come here to listen to my tale of woe."

"I did, actually. I'd like to hear it, at least. I'm trying to piece the whole thing together."

"Why he did it, you mean."

"Yes. He texted me for help at the last minute. I called him back right away but I guess he was already gone. I'm having a bit of a hard time with that, to tell you the truth. I'm worried I should've done more."

"No, don't blame yourself. He thought so much of you. You were a mentor to him. He said you were the only one who ever stood up for him."

Winter didn't answer. He didn't want to tell her what he was thinking. He was thinking maybe he'd made a mistake, standing up for him. A man who beat his girl. Maybe Lori Lesser had been right to play the Fury. Maybe she had seen the truth about Adam and what he would become.

"Do you mind?" he said. "Telling me what happened?"

"No. No. Of course not." She gathered herself to the task. Watching her, Winter felt something go tight inside him. Her delicate beauty—his sense of her in the theater—his sense that she was smart, creative, and capable—that she knew how to read Shakespeare—his whole experience of her—it did something to him. He could almost feel Adam's fist connecting with her cheek. He could almost feel it on his own cheek. It made him wish Adam were still alive so he could beat the daylights out of him.

"It started with this text I got from Pup," she said. "Pup—that's my brother-in-law Gerry—that's what we call him, Pup. He has all these contacts in Hollywood. He texted me to say he'd gotten me an interview with Jennifer Bick. She's a hero of mine. Big set designer for the movies and TV. Working for her would be my dream job. I was so excited. But when I told Adam . . . he was high. He started getting all paranoid about how I was going to leave him. He said Pup hated him and had only arranged the interview to get me away from him. Which wasn't true. I mean, Pup didn't like Adam, but he'd been wanting to get me this interview for a long time. I was the one who put him off. I didn't feel ready. Anyway . . . I'm sorry. I'm rambling."

"It's all right, Evelyn. Go on. Your brother-in-law arranged a big job interview for you, and Adam was stoned and became insecure. Go on."

She breathed deeply, determined to continue. She was clearly near tears, but still dry-eyed. She was good solid midwestern stock, Winter thought, ladylike but hardwood at the center. He liked her.

"He'd hit me before," she said, "but never like this, never this bad. I was actually afraid." Here, her voice broke, though only for a moment. She swallowed hard and steadied herself. "I was afraid he might really hurt me. Kill me even. I was on the floor. He was on top of me. He was so angry. He was totally out of control. He wouldn't stop. When he got off me, he was roaring like an animal. I didn't know if he was finished or if he was going to get a weapon, something to bludgeon me with."

"Jesus," Winter murmured.

"I literally crawled to the door, terrified he would grab me and drag me back. But he didn't. I got hold of the doorknob and pulled myself up. I got out. I ran. I went to my sister's. Molly—she's over in Marin. When Pup saw me, oh God, he was livid."

Pup—Pup was Gerry, Evelyn's brother-in-law, married to Molly, Evelyn's sister. Winter recited it to himself to keep it all straight in his head.

"He never shouts or anything—Pup," she went on. "He just sort of turns to stone. You can actually see it, especially . . ."

When she couldn't finish, he said, "Especially?"

"I was such a mess that night. I was sitting at the kitchen counter, sobbing. Molly was reaching out across the counter to me, holding my hands. She was telling me I could move in with them, with her and Pup. They're rich. They have this whole estate with guesthouses on it and everything. I never wanted to take anything from them. I wanted to be independent. But Molly kept telling me I should move in with them now. That I had to. To get away from Adam. And I said—I was a mess, I was sobbing—and I kept saying, 'Adam doesn't mean it. It's the drugs. If I can just get him off the drugs.' Pup was standing over us, listening. I saw Molly look up at him. And I looked up at him too. And he had that look. That look he gets when he's angry. Like he's turned to stone."

"What happened then?"

"I agreed to stay with them for a few days. I said I needed time to think. Molly said I couldn't go back. She said I was behaving like . . ."

She didn't finish right away. She stared into space. Winter waited. He already knew what she was going to say.

She blinked, coming back to herself. "Like a battered woman. Molly said I was acting just like a battered woman. Accepting it. Making excuses for my abuser. Talking about going back to him. But the thing is, he wasn't always like that. When we first met he wasn't like that at all. He was so sweet. He encouraged me. He loved my work. I just thought if he would get off the drugs . . ."

Evelyn shook her head quickly. Winter could see she was in a silent argument with herself.

"I listen to myself. It's like I can't stop saying these things," Evelyn told him miserably. "I know what I sound like but I can't stop. I don't know if I would have really gone back to him . . . Except I do know: I would have. If he hadn't gotten arrested, I would have gone back. I loved him. That's just the truth."

"So this was when he got arrested," said Winter. "While you were in Marin at your sister's."

She nodded. "All the next day, I was waiting for Adam to call me. I mean, I knew he would. I knew he'd feel bad about what happened. He'd apologize. He'd cry. He'd tell me he needed me. Beg me to come home. I spent the day looking at the phone, waiting for him to call. Wondering what I'd say when he did. But I knew what I'd say. I hated myself for it, but I knew I'd go back to him. I loved him. I couldn't help it. Only he didn't call. I waited all that day. I lay in bed all that night, watching the phone. But he didn't call. Then the next morning, just as I was getting up, that's when he called finally. He was . . ." Evelyn lifted her bruised and beautiful face to the lobby's stained white ceiling. "He was totally hysterical. I never heard him sound like that before. He was babbling. His voice was all high-pitched. He was crying. He said the police had come to the apartment, searched the apartment, found his drugs. He said they took him in. They threw him in jail like throwing meat to animals. He said the other prisoners did terrible things to him in there. He kept repeating that: 'Terrible things.' He kept saying, 'Tell your bastard brother-in-law to call off his dogs.'"

Winter narrowed his eyes at this. He had the sense that he had fallen behind her narrative. Like reading a mystery novel and suddenly realizing you've gotten caught up in the drama and missed the crucial clue. Winter was a hard man at his core, harder than most people realized. His mild academic looks threw them off. They saw the geeky sweaters and pullovers but missed the lethal control of the body underneath. They saw the wire-rimmed glasses but never understood the cold eye he cast on life, on death. Yet, hard as he was, there was a true soul buried in him too and Evelyn's story stirred him. He felt for her. He felt involved in her mental struggle. He felt a new, dark anger against Adam and what he'd become. He felt himself in a state of moral confusion. Had Lori's persecution turned this damaged kid into an addict and an abuser? Or had he, as a mentor, failed to school the boy and hold him accountable for his behavior? Or was it some of both?

Listening to Evelyn, he had been so focused on his own emotional whirlpool that he only now realized he had overlooked the center of her story.

"Wait," he said. "Adam blamed your brother-in-law for his arrest? He blamed this . . . Pup? This Gerry? Why? How could it have been his fault?"

"Adam always blamed Pup for everything," Evelyn told him. "He was always ranting about him. Whenever he read about him in the news, he'd go off on these long tirades. The drugs made it worse, made him paranoid, like I said. He was convinced Pup was out to get me away from him."

"Was he?" Winter asked.

She made a gesture of uncertainty. "I confronted Pup about it. After Adam called that morning, I went upstairs to Pup's office."

The sound of Adam's voice on the phone had unnerved her. It was so high-pitched, sob-raddled, hysterical. Even with the bruises on her face still throbbing, she got caught up in her boyfriend's distress. When the conversation was over, she went to her brother-in-law's office on the mansion's top floor. She found him enthroned in his leather swivel chair. The windows on every side of him looked out on the rolling landscape of his estate, the cliffs, the bay. The early sun bathed him in its pale light.

"They're the police, Evelyn," he told her. "I don't control them."

"He says you sent them after him. He said they were doing this for you."

"Oh, Evie, for crying out loud. He's a drug dealer. What's he going to say?"

She didn't know what to believe. Her own mind was so at odds with itself, it was making her feel sick to her stomach. Adam had pinned her to the floor. He had smacked her and punched her until her ears rang and the world seemed far away and she feared for her life. And now here she was pleading for him and hating herself for it and doing it anyway as if some demon had gotten inside her and taken over her mind. But she went on.

"Just tell me. Did you send them, Pup? Did you send the police after him? Did you tell them to put him in jail like that?"

He swiveled away from her plaintive gaze. He stared out the window at the distant bay. He shook his head. "He beat my sister, Evie. My sister-in-law. But you're like a sister to me. You're my family. And what he did was a crime, even in San Francisco."

"I didn't ask you to do that," she said. She was angry on Adam's behalf. "That's not what I wanted."

He swiveled back to face her, fierce. "Life doesn't work that way. We're none of us who we are by ourselves. We're all of us what we make of each other and what they make of us."

"Oh!" She hated when he was like this, when he went gnomic on her. It was a bad, pretentious habit he had. She was too upset even to try to make sense of his pseudo-mystical utterances. She had no clue what he was talking about.

"Please, Pup!" she begged him.

"Please what? They're the police, Evelyn. What can I do?"

"You can call them off. You have influence."

"I have some influence. There's a limit."

She continued to beg him wordlessly with her grotesquely swollen face. Her blue eyes filled with tears of compassion for the man who had beaten her.

"He just turned to stone again," Evelyn told Winter, standing in the theater lobby. "He just said again, 'He beat my sister.' Pup is like that. His family fell apart when he was young. Family's very important to him now."

Winter was still scrambling mentally to catch up. The story of Adam's suicide had become to him like a tree in the mist, a complex shape obscured by a cloud of his own emotions. He kept feeling his way along one branch or the other—Adam's text, his own response, Lori Lesser's guilt and anger, the actions of the police, this psychopathic gangster Quintero, and now Evelyn—Evelyn and her brother-in-law.

For a moment, standing there, he was lost to himself. That strange habit of mind had a hold of him. His emotional mechanisms stopped. His reasoning stopped. His opinions went away. There was nothing but that tree in the mist.

Then he was back. The mist was gone. He saw clearly now. There were many branches to the story tree but only one trunk. All the branches grew out of that one trunk.

"Who is this brother-in-law of yours?" he asked Evelyn. "This Gerry, this Pup? Who is he?"

Evelyn looked surprise. "Oh! Didn't you know? Sorry. I always assume people know. All the publicity about him marrying my sister. I just assume . . ."

"Who's your sister then?" Winter asked her.

"Molly. Molly Shea. Molly Byrne. The Cinderella Girl, they call her."

Winter let out a noise of astonishment. The Cinderella Girl. Of course—of course he knew of her. No depth of intellectual distraction could have wholly sheltered him from the endless interviews, and feature stories, and blah-blah-blah of journalistic commentary about her.

Evelyn said, "She's the nobody from nowhere who married the famous billionaire Gerald Byrne."

5

Gerald Byrne.

Alone in his hotel room that night, Winter murmured the name in wonder.

Pup, he thought wryly. *Pup!*

Propped against the headboard of the gigantic hotel bed, his laptop balanced on his thighs, he smiled a quirky, cynical smile. "Pup" was the sort of name a four-year-old girl gave to her stuffed poodle. *Come on, Pup, let's have tea.* Whereas Gerald Byrne was nobody's poodle. His personal wealth was larger than the gross national product of two thirds of the nations on the globe.

Pup!

Winter could crack wise about the "many, many millions" in the trust fund his father had created for him. He knew he was rich by most people's standards. Given his more or less modest way of life, he actually was rich in the sense that he wanted for nothing. He had no extra houses, no private jet. He wasn't one of those men—it was almost always men—who became obsessed with their collections: wristwatches, race cars, sports memorabilia, and so on. He sometimes felt he ought to collect something truly valuable to him, like first editions of eighteenth-century literature, but he never got around to it. He never would. Once, in his childhood, after he'd carelessly broken an expensive camera, his father had scolded him: "You have no respect for things." It was true. Inanimate objects bored him. Cars, guns, houses, watches, even rare books. They didn't interest him at all. This was his dirty little secret. When he gathered with the guys for whiskey and cigars and they started discussing the 1973 Dodge Challenger one of them was restoring in his garage, Winter would silently recite poetry to himself to keep the ennui from killing him where he sat.

So yes, he was rich in the philosophical sense of having all his little needs fulfilled. But he wasn't really rich, not rich-rich. Not like Gerald Byrne. This stuffed poodle Pup was a walking kingdom. He was one of the princes of the world.

Here he was now, on the video playing on Winter's laptop. A youthful, tall, willowy figure. A little too thin but fit and nimble. With one of those long biblical beards men grow when their heads can no longer contain their self-regard and it simply flows out of their chins all the way down to their sternums. Also a black ponytail. Also a purple flower tattoo on his neck. Also a ring in his nose. Oh, how original and eccentric he was!

He was giving a speech to his fellow princes in one of their princely Swiss gathering places. He was pacing the stage with the headset in his ear *comme il faut* and the microphone running along his cheek *de rigueur* and similarly arrayed in other French phrases that signaled the authority of his billion-dollar wisdom. His talk topic was spelled out in three-dimensional letters, which by some video magic were projected onto the air behind him: *The Good World Project.* This too made Winter smile his wintry smile.

"To silence the voices of hate that divide us—this is not controversial, this is simply the right thing to do. To direct the resources of all nations toward humanity's shared objectives—this is not controversial. It's the right thing to do. To heal the planet from the wounds inflicted on her . . ."

But by this time Winter was no longer listening. He was using his expert research skills to call up whatever he could find about the man: biographies, features, interviews, exposés. Constructing a three-dimensional portrait of him in his own mind.

There were a lot of articles—a lot—about Evelyn's sister Molly. Molly Shea now Molly Byrne. The Cinderella Girl (and also a person in her own right, the journalists unctuously assured him). But Winter bypassed those for now. He'd get to her later.

For now, it was Byrne he wanted. Pup. Forty-two years old. The son of a minister from the northern reaches of the Midwest, only a state line away from Winter's university. He had had a strict religious upbringing but "childhood tragedy" had put an end to all that. He described himself as a mystic now.

"When you confront the mind of the universe, you discover it's within you and outside you at the same time," he told one reporter.

No doubt, Winter thought. With that many billions, he supposed you could tell the press any idiot thing. Who would disagree with you?

Byrne was a vegan. He did yoga for an hour every day. He hosted retreats in the Oregon woods with other celebrated characters. He took a power walk every sunrise along the cliffs of the Marin headland.

With his prophet-like beard blowing in the sea breezes and his eyes trained on a vision of the future only he can see, he strides along the Coastal Trail with his single bodyguard struggling to keep up, a familiar sight to the joggers and tourists who pretend to ignore him.

Give that wordsmith the rest of the day off, Winter thought.

Byrne had founded a charity for underprivileged children, the Fairy Tale Fund. He had enlisted his fellow gazillionaires in his signature brainchild the Good World Project. He was known to drop six-figure gifts—anonymously and without fanfare—on the obscure and worthy. For instance—and here was something that made Winter sit up on the bed and take notice—many police officers wounded in the line of duty had quietly received hundreds of thousands of dollars from Byrne. So had many families of officers who'd been killed.

You have influence with the police, Evelyn had said to him. And the hysterical Adam had cried, *Tell him to call off his dogs.*

Where had all Byrne's bajillions come from? Here was the story he told reporters.

As a child, he had been fascinated by—mesmerized by, obsessed with—natural patterns. It was an odd mind-set in a little boy, he realized later. For a while, he had even wondered whether he was on the autistic spectrum. But he was beyond that sort of thinking now. Now, his mind was at one with the universe—or at two with the universe, Winter thought, depending on whether the universe was within him or outside him at the time. In either case, Byrne no longer believed in what he called "diagnostic fictions" that "pathologized the human spirit." *Autistic* was not a meaningful distinction. The fact was: he simply loved discerning patterns. It just was the way he was.

His father had been the pastor of a nondenominational church called Grace in the Wilderness. It was not in the wilderness. A majestic stone palace of a place with a fine, square English tower, it stood on the intersection of a grassy residential street and a broad commercial avenue in the southwest corner of Minneapolis.

Pastor Byrne was a quiet, serious, scholarly man with a degree from Antioch Theological Seminary. He specialized in intellectual sermons that centered on historical and linguistic exegeses of scripture. He was also a warm and charming church leader. His congregation both respected and loved him.

Every Sunday, little Gerald, dressed in a miniature suit and tie, would attend the church's eleven a.m. service. He would sit in a front pew beside his nervous, birdlike mother. He would listen to his father's sermon. He would watch the way the sun shone through the church's stained-glass windows, the way the light shifted over the course of the service from the scarlet sky above the risen Lazarus to the rich blue sea on which Peter walked toward Christ to the angel white robes of the children on the savior's knee. Patterns within patterns, kaleidoscopic. The light, his father's words, the scriptures, God's creation. To little Gerald, it seemed a wonderful and intricate perfection, world without end.

Then, after his mother killed herself, he decided all that was crap.

Gerald had always found his mother puzzling. Why was she forever in motion, so anxious, so fraught? Why was she never silent, but always twittering like a sparrow about the length of his hair or a sock that had gone missing or the need to call a plumber to unjam the kitchen disposal? It was strange to him.

All the same, he loved her—very much. He loved the way she made things pretty: put flowers on the windowsill of the rectory where they lived and knitted yellow sweaters for him and hung the greenery at Christmastime on the mantel over the fireplace and along the church walls. He loved how she put food in front of him, sweet cereal at breakfast time and hot soup in cold weather. These were the patterns of her love for him, the designs of her heart written into his daily life.

The rectory where they lived was an impressive stone manse set back from the road on the lightly wooded acreage behind the church. It was two tall stories high, and then three small rooms on a third story with their dormer windows rising at the edge of the slanting red roof. Friday, the thirteenth of October, when Gerry was seven years old, there was a lightning storm that woke him from sleep near midnight. He went to the window in his blue plaid pajamas and watched the forking flashes etch their designs on the face of the billowing black clouds. Fascinating. Even chaos had its patterns.

In the two interviews in which Byrne told the story of this fatal night, he described the events as if he'd witnessed them himself. But Winter had called up photos of the rectory, and there was just no way the child Byrne could have seen what happened directly from his room, or from any room. He must have imagined it later.

His mother—he said—had come to the central dormer on the story above him. She had stood fidgeting there a long while, her head tilted, as if she were listening to a voice in the wind and thunder. Suddenly, her anxious quivering gathered into a central point of tension. She clasped her hands over her heart. Then, with a hoarse, raving cry, she threw her arms outward and shattered the dormer glass with her pale, white, nervous fists.

Bleeding, she forced her way through the jagged wreckage. Slithered like some wild lizardy creature out onto the roof. She climbed to her feet and stood at the edge of the gutter. The rain-paled blood ran in rivulets down her bare cheeks and her bare arms. Her bedraggled hair was plastered to her face as she raised her eyes to the forks of blue-white electricity that stabbed across the black night.

Then she spread her arms as if to take flight and tumbled forward.

Here Winter paused in his reading. He lifted his eyes, unseeing, to the middle distance. He sat awhile in thought. He couldn't help but notice the coincidence: another suicide plunge off another rooftop, just like Adam's. But after a few moments, he decided he couldn't find any other connection between the two deaths. Just because there was a pattern didn't mean it was significant.

Which was, in fact, exactly the conclusion that little Gerry reached in the tumultuous aftermath of the tragedy.

The police looked into Mrs. Byrne's suicide, with the help of the vestry and other church officials. It quickly came to light that Gerald's father had been carrying on affairs with three of the lonely housewives in his congregation. There had been an abortion. A misappropriation of church funds. There had been an ugly scene in a motel beyond the city limits: an angry husband had broken in on a wild debauch involving some unmentionable desecration of the cross. Pastor Byrne, the husband said, was cackling drunkenly as the desecration took place.

According to church procedures, all these sins were read aloud from the pulpit one Sunday morning by the assistant pastor. Gerald's father was then publicly stripped of his pastorship.

Little Gerald attended this solemn ceremony. Dressed in his miniature Sunday suit, he sat beside his aunt in the front pew. As his father's transgressions were denounced before the congregation, the child lifted his eyes and watched the sunlight move from one stained glass window to another, one scriptural scene to another. He was still mesmerized by the patterns of light and motion. But he saw now: they were the creations of his own mind. His mother was dead. His father was corrupt. There was no God. The patterns were meaningless.

Pup's family fell apart when he was young, Evelyn had told Winter. *Family's very important to him now.*

By now, Winter was wholly immersed in the story of Byrne's life, so he was startled when his phone buzzed. The readout told him it was Inspector Raines of the San Francisco police. Winter picked up.

"You still want to meet with Quintero?" Raines asked him.

"Yes," said Winter. "Yes, I do."

The meeting with the murderous gangster was arranged for that very night.

6

Sitting across the table from the sadistic psychopathic drug dealer, Winter remembered a nineteenth-century memoir he had read in the original French. A thief, forger, and wannabe poet named Lacenaire, convicted of a double murder, had penned his life story in prison while waiting to be guillotined. *Memoirs, Revelations and Poems*, the book was called. It was of some minor literary interest because there was reason to believe Lacenaire's exploits had inspired Dostoyevsky in the writing of *Crime and Punishment*. They were also the basis of a famous French film, *Les Enfants du Paradis*.

A line from the memoir came back to Winter as Quintero grinned at him with a self-conscious display of wickedness. Working from memory and according to his own translation, the line ran: *There is something that lessens the horror of a crime when one sees the criminal—who has been depicted as a monster—is just like any other man.*

In his experience, Winter had not found this to be true. For him, the fact that a murderer was "like any other man" was no more than an obvious and trivial detail. It did not lessen the horror of what he'd done in the least. Through the centuries, eloquent killers like Lacenaire had entranced academics and artists and other intellectuals with this sort of nonsense. They had sold them on the notion of murder as a rebellion against an unjust society, murder as a metaphor, murder as a form of self-expression. But then most academics and artists and intellectuals had never killed anyone. Winter had. He'd killed plenty of people. Murder wasn't a rebellion. It wasn't a metaphor. It was an atrocity. It haunted him. It was the reason he was spilling his life to Margaret Whitaker. He wanted her to wash the blood from his hands. He was desperately seeking relief from his guilt and self-disgust.

When he looked across the table at Quintero, he saw nothing but a rank thug preening, a lowlife eager to peacock his savagery in order to impress the mild-mannered academic Winter seemed to be. But all Winter could think about were Quintero's victims. Mutilated, engulfed in flames. Extinguished. No man is a metaphor to himself.

"Man, you must be the whitest human being I have ever seen in all my life," the gangster said. "You're like a snowman. Three scoops of vanilla with legs."

The other gangsters, Quint's underlings, grinned and chuckled and nodded. Well, of course, they would.

Winter was eager to get past these preliminaries. It was now the final hour of a long day. He had awakened at dawn in the Midwest. Had flown to the coast. Had met with Raines and Evelyn and had begun his research into Gerald Byrne. Now, as midnight neared, he was sitting in a tavern-like room, three floors above street level. It was all dark wood and rectangular tables. The windows behind the gangster gave Winter a fine view of the Golden Gate Bridge illuminated against the blue-black background. Most of the tables in the place were empty. Only these three tables by the windows were occupied by men and their bottles of beer.

Winter was at the middle table of the three. Inspector Raines was sitting beside him po-faced. Quintero sat across from him, his back to the glass. The grinning underlings—four of them—were seated two and two at tables to his left and right. There was a bar and there was a pretty Hispanic girl standing behind it, washing glasses no one had used.

Quint—Quintero—the Farmer—the violent terror of the infamous Drug Corridor D that ran up the West Coast from Mexico to Canada along the I-5—was a substantial Latino gentleman with a bald head and a mustache as aggressive as the mustache of Inspector Raines. It was a room full of aggressive mustaches, in fact. It was like there had been some kind of competition Winter hadn't been invited to join.

Quint was dressed in a shiny black silk shirt, unbuttoned up top and the cuffs rolled back so Winter could see he was all tattoos underneath. He had a medicine ball of a belly, but the muscles of his arms and shoulders bulged impressively through the sleek material. Winter, expert in the martial arts though he was, would still not have liked to fight this man. He decided not to mention he found shiny silk shirts sort of girly.

"How do you even go out in the sun with that white face, man?" Quint went on, milking the hilarity. "You burn right up."

Winter smiled politely. Raines's round face continued stony. Quint glanced at the inspector and decided to move on.

"So what you want? Exactly. You some kind of professor, is that right? Professor of Advanced Whiteness?"

"English Romantic poetry, actually," Winter said.

"Oh man. Man," said Quintero, sitting back in his seat, slapping the table lightly with one open hand. He glanced at his companions. "Well, go on! Recite me some poetry, man. I like poetry. Roses are red, right? Let's hear me some of that shit."

Winter took a sip from his beer bottle. Then, in a quiet, steady voice, he said: "I met a traveller from an antique land . . ."

He then went on to recite Percy Bysshe Shelley's "Ozymandias" in its entirety. The sonnet told of a broken statue in the desert, the majestic head sinking into the sand.

". . . And on the pedestal, these words appear: My name is Ozymandias, King of Kings; Look on my Works, ye Mighty, and despair! Nothing beside remains. Round the decay of that colossal Wreck, boundless and bare the lone and level sands stretch far away."

Quint had only been taunting Winter and had not expected he would actually recite. Surprised, the gangster fell silent for the length of the sonnet and listened with some seriousness. The other thugs took their cue from him and listened too. When Winter was done, the room was quiet. Quint nodded and frowned as if judiciously impressed.

"Look on my works, ye mighty, and despair!" he told his henchmen with appreciation. And to Winter he said, "I like it. King of kings, Homes."

He tilted his bottle toward Winter. Winter returned the toast. He suspected Quintero had missed the poem's underlying theme, but so it goes. You can lead a horse to water . . .

The important thing was that Winter had passed some sort of obscure test. The taunting phase of the discussion was over. He would now be treated with a modicum of respect.

"So what can I do for you, Homes?" Quintero deigned to ask him. His eyes kept flicking toward Raines as he spoke. Winter could see that Raines's lithic cop stare had some power over the gangster. A good cop in a bad city, Raines might have been the one man left in California Quintero had reason to fear.

"A friend of mine killed himself recently," Winter said. "Adam Kemp, his name was."

"Sorry for your loss," said Quintero.

"He threw himself off a building in North Beach."

"I think I heard something about that."

"Inspector Raines here investigated," Winter went on, pointing his bottle at the stone-faced Raines. Raines remained stone-faced. "There's no question it was suicide. There's no crime involved. It is what it is."

Quint made a gracious gesture. Winter was making it clear he had come in peace. This underlying theme, at least, the gangster did understand.

"I'm curious though why he might have done it," Winter said.

The gangster made a face. Shrugged. How should he know? "A man makes his own arrangements with death, Homes."

"No doubt. But I'm wondering if Adam had any reason to think—to be afraid—that you might have been angry with him."

Quint straightened in his chair and placed all five fingertips of one hand against his chest: *Angry? Me?*

"He'd been arrested a few days before and released without charge," Winter said. "I wondered if maybe that made you think he had begun to work with the police. To work against you, I mean."

Quint considered a moment, his eyes moving from Raines to Winter, from Winter back to Raines and back to Winter.

"You want to know this why?" he asked.

"It's just the sort of thing a man wants to know when his friend kills himself," Winter answered. "What was on his mind. What motivated him. As I say, there's no crime here, no harm, no foul. Adam made his own decision."

Again, the Farmer considered. "Unlikely," he said finally.

"Unlikely that . . . ?"

"If I knew this Adam Kemp. If I heard he was arrested and the Barneys let him go. It's unlikely I would think he was working with them."

Winter nodded. "That's what I thought. At first, it occurred to me you might think that, but it really doesn't make sense, does it? The penalty for possession is pretty much nothing here. The penalty for betraying you might be high." Quint made a vague flourish with his hand—vague, but not meaningless. "Adam was a smart guy. So are you. I don't think he would have been stupid enough to turn on you, and I don't think you would have been stupid enough to believe he had."

Quint tilted his bottle in appreciation of the compliment. He took a swig. He came out of it with a loud, "Ah!" Then he said, "Of course, if a man stole from me, that would be different. That would be a problem. At any level, that would have to be dealt with."

Winter took a slow breath. He felt a little chill in his stomach, a chill of something like fear. But it was not fear of Quintero.

"Stole from you," he repeated softly. "How exactly would something like that happen?"

Quintero wagged his head. He glanced at Raines. "Hypothetically?"

Raines gave no indication of having heard the question or of being alive at all. Winter answered for him: "Hypothetically. Of course."

Quint frowned. Considered. "Maybe if someone was useful to me, a sort of nobody that nobody paid attention to. Respectable. White. I might call upon him from time to time to hold something for me out of the way."

"Money, say."

"Or product. Hypothetically."

"Right," said Winter. "And if there were, say, a discrepancy—a difference between the amount he was given to hold and the amount he returned to you—is that something you would necessarily notice?"

"Not necessarily. Not right away. In all the hurly-burly of a busy life."

"Plus it would hardly be worth worrying about him stealing from you, would it? Because it would be such a foolish thing for him to do."

Quint nodded gravely.

Now, to go along with the chill in his belly, Winter felt a sour taste in the back of his throat like curdled milk. He tried to wash it away with another sip of beer. It wouldn't wash. "But if you received a tip . . ." he said.

"Then I would take it upon myself to investigate," said the gangster.

"Even if the tip was anonymous."

"It well might be."

"Anonymous."

"Absolutely."

"And if you received such a tip, you might—what?—go to this man's apartment, say."

"There aren't that many places to hide a stash in a small apartment. Speaking for myself, I'd look under the floorboards first thing."

Winter took another slug of beer, a long one, polishing off the bottle. It gave him time to think, time to imagine the rest of the scenario. He set the bottle down on the dark wood of the table. He glanced at Raines beside him. The inspector's expression had not changed in the slightest.

"So it might be," Winter said, "that someone would return from, say, a night in jail and find that his secret stash, his stolen treasure, was gone."

"It might," Quint answered.

"And so this person might deduce that his theft had been discovered."

"That could happen. I could see that happening."

"And then there'd be nothing left for him but to wait for you."

"There'd be no point in running," Quintero said.

Winter nodded slowly. The chill in his belly had gotten chillier. The taste of curdled milk in his throat was stronger, worse. He was done here. He pushed back from the table and stood.

"Thank you very much, Mr. Quintero," he said. "I appreciate your hospitality and your help."

Quint received Winter's thanks with a stately bow of the head. Majestic, Winter thought, like a king of kings.

"I liked your poem, Homes," Quintero said.

7

The chill in Winter's belly persisted—both the chill and the taste of curdled milk in his throat—as he continued his research on the plane ride home.

These symptoms worried him. The magical therapeutic skills of Margaret Whitaker had relieved him of the worst of his depression, but he knew he was still emotionally fragile. His past lay heavy on him. The killing. The disappearance of Charlotte. His long years of loneliness. And his loneliness now. Margaret had opened him up like a patient etherized upon a table. She had exposed the guilt inside him, the guilt and the yearning, the yearning for redemption and a yearning for love as painful and obvious as the bleat of some boy-faced pop singer mincing his way through a third-rate song. He felt vulnerable. He felt weak. Which was the last thing he needed given what Quintero had told him, given how Adam Kemp had died, given his growing suspicions about Gerald Byrne, given the depths of peril into which he was about to submerge himself.

The jet headed east. The ruins of San Francisco faded into the marine layer behind him. Ahead lay a white field of elaborate cumulous designs like cloudy kingdoms. He went on with his research, tapping at his laptop keyboard. The chill in his belly, the taste on his tongue persisted. He knew they were symptoms of fear. He was afraid. He was afraid of Gerald Byrne.

There was no official biography of the tech titan. The books that had been written about him were fast-money work, slapdash, not worth reading. The few people who actually knew Byrne personally and spoke publicly about him were circumspect when they weren't downright dishonest. No one wanted to insult such a person, not with his mountains of money and his vast social influence both here and abroad.

So the best source of information on Byrne, Winter came to feel, was Byrne himself. Interviews in business and technology journals. The occasional appearance on a discussion panel. The occasional speech, plus some video chats and podcast conversations. It was enough to occupy a four-hour plane flight. But how reliable was it? How much could he trust Byrne's version of his own life?

Not much. Winter remembered an exchange he'd had with Margaret a few weeks before. He had quoted from a letter of the poet John Keats: "A man's life of any worth is a continual allegory—and very few eyes can see the Mystery of his life." Margaret had replied, "Maybe a man's life becomes an allegory when he tells it. It does work like that, you know. We reveal ourselves in the stories we tell." Maybe so. But Byrne, Winter decided after an hour of research, had a way of telling stories that hid as much they revealed.

His mother's suicide, for instance. That had to have been catastrophically traumatic. The exposure of his father's corruption had to have been shattering. But that's not the way Byrne spoke of it in his interviews.

"It was a difficult time," he said mildly on one podcast. "But we had a very soft landing."

In one sense, this was true enough. During the course of his ministry at Grace in the Wilderness, Byrne's father had forged strong connections with the state's wealthy business people and powerful politicians. These allies were there for him in his hour of need. Mere weeks after he left Grace church in disgrace, the ex-pastor was quietly installed as the head of the communications department of a major East Coast pharmaceutical company specializing in the manufacture of antidepressants and other psychotropic drugs. He moved to Philadelphia, taking his son with him. Within a year, he was married to the socialite daughter of a former state governor. Though the governor had spent a year in prison in connection with an influence peddling scheme, his family was still welcome at the best homes on the Main Line. Young Gerald grew up among people of wealth and power.

Winter reflected on this for a few moments, gazing out the window at the mountainous clouds. *We had a very soft landing,* Byrne said. But had he? A seven-year-old? Had he really? How had he come to understand his mother's death? How had his father explained his behavior to him? The affairs, the embezzlements, the desecrations? Had he made excuses or had he denied it all? What could it have meant to Gerald at seven—at eight, nine, ten, seventeen—to see his beloved mother destroyed by a Corinthian catalogue of sins, and then to see those sins go completely unpunished? Not just unpunished. His father had been rewarded with a good job and the acceptance and favor of the theoretically great and good.

"It was very sad, of course," Byrne said in one longish e-zine feature. "I loved my mother very much. But in a way, it was liberating too. I was always fascinated by patterns, remember. And I had had a tendency to see those patterns in the cliched theological context supplied by my father. Creation. Sin. Redemption. And so on. When that context fell away, I was set free to see that the patterns of reality were actually random and therefore limitless. They could be shaped into infinitely fresh configurations by the human mind. That was the beginning of my fascination with the possibilities of technology."

Winter laughed aloud when he read that. Obviously, it was nonsense of the purest ray serene.

How did you feel about the violent destruction of your moral and emotional universe, Mr. Byrne?

Well, it gave me an interest in technology.

Byrne had come up with his first successful program while he was still a student at MIT. Winter's understanding of computers was practical but not very deep. No matter how many times he read the description of Byrne's innovation, his mind acted as a sort of filter that turned the words to mist. He could never quite grasp exactly what the program was. As near as he could tell, Byrne had designed some sort of gizmo that monitored and repaired online security systems. Winter knew this was probably just a series of ones and zeroes, but he couldn't help but picture it as a little robot-like device traveling along wires, making repairs with its robot claws.

Whatever it was, it made the twenty-year-old Byrne his first smallish fortune, a mere hundreds of millions of dollars. With this in hand, he dropped out of school and headed for California.

There, over the course of the next decade or so, two things happened. The first was that Byrne used his fortune to create a new social media platform, which he called *Byrner*. Byrner rapidly became one of the dominant means of social communication in the world.

Winter used social media in his work. He could research on it, get news, and communicate with his students. But he didn't spend much time on it aside from that. He did realize, however, that for some people, most people, even famous people, even powerful people, their entire experience of the internet took place on social media. And for most of those people, Byrner was one of their platforms of choice.

So in the ten years after Byrne left school he became the master of a techno empire. He acquired the power to influence and direct and even censor the people who used his site. Thus he could control a substantial branch of the stream of information as it flowed around the globe. He also went from being a millionaire to being a billionaire and from a billionaire to a boogle-e-dillionaire, with wealth beyond the ability of the human mind to comprehend.

So that was one thing that happened.

The other thing was this. Byrne discovered that women liked rich men. Beautiful women. Celebrated women. Women whose nude scenes on-screen had formed the better part of his sex life before he hit the jackpot. They—the real *they*, with their real flesh really nude—were now suddenly willing to go to bed with him.

Before this, Byrne's social life had been intermittent at best. His pseudo-cool demeanor and his mystic utterances occasionally attracted a certain kind of lonesome and unpopular liberal arts major. There were plenty such girls haunting the coffee shops around the many universities near Cambridge. With a bit of effort and the judicious use of recreational drugs, he could occasionally liberate himself from involuntary celibacy.

But when he became a superduper-illionaire the game changed dramatically. Winter amused himself for twenty minutes by visiting various gossip and personality sites and finding pictures of Byrne with his arm around some of the most famous and beautiful actresses, models, and socialites in the world.

Then he pinched the bridge of his nose, squeezing his eyes shut. The research was beginning to weary him.

Shortly afterward, though, he came upon a long-form podcast interview that refreshed his interest. At the time of the interview, Byrne had recently stunned the celebrity-watching world by abruptly putting an end to his libertine existence. He had become engaged to marry Molly Shea. Evelyn's sister. The "nobody from nowhere." The Cinderella Girl.

Byrne was clearly feeling pleased with himself, happy and loose. He agreed to record an hour-long conversation with a popular male podcast host. The host prided himself on being a foul-mouthed bad boy, blunt and vulgar on the subject of sex. Winter despised the host from the moment he first heard him, but he had to admit he drew something out of Byrne, something almost honest, something more than the usual mystic-autistic maundering anyway.

For a while after his success, Byrne told the roguish podcast host, sleeping with famous and beautiful women had become an obsession. He had bought a mansion in Beverly Hills and a penthouse in Manhattan in order to be closer to their watering holes. He had had professionals teach him how to groom and dress. He held exclusive soirees during which he adjourned to the bedroom with first one lovely guest and then another and sometimes another during the course of a single evening. Over the span of five years, he estimated he had been to bed with close to a thousand different women—an average of about four new lovers every week.

"I thought I was living the good life, the life we all dream of, all men dream of anyway," he said.

Winter gazed out at the fantasia of clouds as the podcast played over his earbuds. Byrne had a smooth, deep, gliding voice with a curious lack of emotional tone to it.

"It took me a long time to realize that I was actually becoming more and more unhappy," he went on. "When I was honest with myself, I had to admit that my chief pleasure in life was not the women I was with . . . I mean, I enjoyed it when I was with them, obviously. But my chief pleasure was the envy of other men. It lifted my spirits to imagine they wanted what I had, that they wished they were me. Aside from that, though, I was actually growing deeply depressed."

"Now hold on a second," said the podcast host. "You're banging a different starlet every other night, and it's depressing you? What the hell is that about?"

"They had just become shapes to me," Byrne told him, in what Winter believed was a rare moment of plain speaking. "We were doing these intimate things with our bodies, but I didn't feel that I was making genuine contact with them at all. The shape of them set off a chemical reaction in my brain and I became aroused and I took steps to produce another chemical reaction to satisfy that arousal."

"Sounds good to me!" cried the loathsome podcast host.

"Well, it satisfied some brain pattern that desired social standing and masculine achievement. And physical pleasure. But it was completely detached from who I was or who the women were. It was all just patterns reflecting patterns in an infinite regress, a hall of mirrors."

"Whatever," said the host. "Most guys would cut off their right nut for half an hour with one of these babes."

Winter winced at this but he kept listening. For once, he felt Byrne was speaking something like the truth.

"I felt totally alone," Byrne said. "Surrounded by shapes of women I didn't really know. I was stranded in a ghost town of desire."

Soon, Byrne said, he was waking up hungover, sick to his stomach and sick to his soul. He would stare at his haggard face in the mirror and reassure himself he was on top of the world. He was the man who had everything, he told his reflection.

But that just made it worse. Because he knew he was miserable.

He went to see a psychiatrist. She was a fashionable doctor with an office in Beverly Hills. He sat in a leather armchair and told her his tale of woe. She listened for about fifteen minutes. Then she prescribed a course of antidepressants.

"We'll start here and then adjust the dose as we go forward," she told him.

Byrne's fluid, confident, and strangely passionless voice continued. Winter could tell that this—this moment—was central to his personal mythology.

"I filled the prescription," he told the podcast host. "I went home with my little orange cannister of pills. I sat at my desk in my leather swivel chair, holding the cannister in my hand, brooding over it like Hamlet with Yorick's skull. Slowly—very slowly—the awareness dawned on me. If I unscrewed the cannister cap, if I shook a pill out onto my palm, if I placed the pill in my mouth, if I swallowed it, it would be like Persephone eating the pomegranate seeds in Hades: it would bind me to this hell forever."

Byrne delivered this monologue in a tone of dry irony. Winter, for his part, was impressed by the classical references. Hamlet, Yorick, Persephone, Hades. Somewhere between making zillions of dollars and bedding hundreds of starlets, the man had found time to read.

Byrne went on in the same ironic tone. "Ever since my mother died when I was a child, I had committed myself to a life without meaning. And now here I was. Essentially, I had come to this psychiatrist and I had said to her, 'I'm depressed because I'm living a soulless life. I'm not living as a human being. I'm living as if I were a meat puppet with a chemistry set inside.' And the psychiatrist's answer was: 'Well, take this pill. It will adjust the chemistry set and then you will be a happy meat puppet instead of a sad one.'

You see? She wasn't solving the problem, she was urging me to surrender to it. And so now, here I was, sitting in my chair with the orange cannister, trying to choose between two different versions of my life."

Winter was curious whether this revelation of Byrne's, his reaction to the psychiatrist's prescription, had had anything to do with his father's work in the pharmaceutical industry. He wished the podcast host would ask that question. But the host didn't, of course. Because the host was an idiot.

"Finally," Byrne said. "Finally, I just thought, no. No, I'm not depressed because of chemistry. That makes no sense. The chemistry is a physical analogue of a spiritual experience. I am depressed because I am not living as a man should live. I am not living as a man at all. And with that, I got up out of my chair. All the while, remember, I'm holding this pill bottle up in front of me, staring at this pill bottle. And I walked more or less blindly into the bathroom. I took the cap off the cannister—and I'm still brooding on this object in my hand as if I'm going to see through the orange plastic into some vision of a better life. And then . . . Then I just turned it over. Just like that. I turned the cannister over and dumped the pills into the toilet. And I flushed them down."

"Whoa," said the idiot podcast host. "Awesome. Awesome. What then?"

Even above the ambient noise of the jet engines, Winter could hear Byrne draw a deep breath and let it out in a long sigh.

"Then," he said, "in that moment, right then, the trajectory of my life changed forever. I thought to myself, if the patterns of reality can be infinitely transformed and rearranged by the mind of man, well, then I would begin a search—a quest—for that infinite freedom to make of the world not what was given to me but whatever I would. I would essentially re-create the universe in the image of my own soul." There was a pause and then he added: "Let there be light. You know?"

"Whoa," said the host. "Awesome. Awesome. I'd love to keep talking, man. But unfortunately we're out of time."

So the podcast interview ended. Winter drew the earbuds from his ears just in time to hear the pilot announce that the plane had begun its initial descent. He slipped the buds back into their charging case and snapped it shut. He continued gazing out the window as the jet sank through the spires of the cloud palaces and the view went white and misty.

The chill had returned to his belly. The taste of curdled milk had returned to his throat. Really, they had never left. He had been distracted by the interview and forgotten them, that's all. Now that his attention returned to them, he found they were worse than ever. He felt even more exposed than he had before. Even more vulnerable. He felt even more afraid—afraid of Gerald Byrne.

This was a formidable man. This man did not just dream grand dreams. He lived the dreams he dreamt into reality. Innovation, business, wealth, women, influence: what he set out to accomplish, he accomplished. Despite his mystical affectations and his fashionable sensitivities, he was an engine of indomitable will.

And this man—this indomitable man—had murdered Adam Kemp.

It was a perfect murder, too. Oh, maybe it wasn't murder in law, but that was part of its perfection. Adam had laid hard hands on Byrne's sister-in-law, and Byrne had engineered his death—his torture, his rape, and his death—just like that, like snapping a finger. One or two phone calls and it was done.

Winter brooded out the window. The plane continued its descent through the clouds toward the snowscape of middle America. The white expanse below mirrored the white expanse above as if, thought Winter, the obscure earth were reflecting the mysterious intents of heaven.

He thought of Evelyn Shea. The delicate beauty of her face, her bruises. He thought, *Maybe Adam deserved what he got.* Maybe it was only justice. Rough justice, but justice all the same. It would be easy to think so, anyway. It would be easy to tell himself that and let it go.

But could he? Could he let it go? Could he convince himself that Adam was Byrne's only victim? The only one who had ever crossed the leader of the Good World Project, who had ever angered him, who had ever violated the sacred spaces of his psychology?

I would begin a search—a quest—for that infinite freedom to make of the world not what was given to me but whatever I would . . . Byrne had said. *I would essentially re-create the universe in the image of my own soul. Let there be light.*

How many others had there been? How many others who were not part of the "good world," who were not good, who deserved to die?

How many other murders had Gerald Byrne committed?

That was the question. That was one question anyway. Another question was this: What was Cameron Winter going to do about it?

PART TWO

ETERNITY IS
A WOMAN

We went to see the Recruiter.

I don't know how to describe this experience to you, Margaret. In a way, it was absolutely hilarious. And in another way, it was—literally—deadly serious. It was both at the same time.

You have to understand. Roy—Roy Spahn and I—we were still basically kids, still boys. I was barely twenty. Roy was, I don't know, twenty-five at most. The two of us had been doing our karate together and sitting in bars and talking philosophy and picking up women and so on. We had forged a real friendship between us. And it meant the world to me.

But there was a sense in which it was all a kind of play, wasn't it? The karate was play fighting. The philosophy was play philosophy. It had no real-life consequences like real philosophy has. The girls were play relationships. We had this ache inside us to do something with our lives, to take action like men. But to do that, we needed to believe in something. And to believe in anything—to really deeply believe—terrified us. God? Country? Principle? Once we had a standard, we would have to live up to that standard. And what if we couldn't? What if we weren't real men at all? Just blabbermouths. Just frauds, playing at manhood. No. Cynicism and irony were our superpowers. They protected us from testing ourselves in the real world.

Even when we decided to go see the Recruiter, it was sort of a lark, a comical outing. The idea of "intelligence" was exciting. Joining this mysterious thing called "the Division"? In theory, it might be the answer to all our big questions. But we didn't seriously mean to do it. It was just a lark.

Then we met the Recruiter. And there was nothing theoretical or larky about him, that's for sure. The Recruiter was just about the realest, most serious thing I'd ever seen. Real as a cinder block. He even looked like a cinder block—like a cinder block come to life.

We met him in a small office over the Armed Forces Career Center. It—the center—was this little storefront in a local strip mall. There was a pizza parlor on one side of it and a nail salon on the other, and in the middle was the Career Center with a slanted roof and a single dormer on top. There was a big window out front. Two gigantic flags crossed in it: the Stars and Stripes and another flag representing the military branches, Army, Navy, Air Force, Marine Corps. Even the location was weirdly unreal. On the one hand, it looked so bold and serious. The military! What could be more real than that? But on the other hand, it looked like the place had been slapped up temporarily between the pizzas and the manicures. Like next week it would be gone and there'd be something else there instead. A tanning salon or something.

Roy and I went in like a couple of goofy kids. Nervous and silly. We spoke to the soldier at the front desk. We showed him the card the Recruiter had given Roy. The soldier led us to the back of the place and opened an unmarked door. There was a stairway. The soldier said, "Go right up." So we were going up to the room with the dormer window on the roof.

Roy led the way. He was looking back at me, giggling. And I was saying, "Ssh, ssh," but I was giggling too.

At the top of the stairs there was a little landing and a door. Roy knocked. There was no answer. He lifted his fist to knock again—and suddenly, the door was yanked open and there he was. This concrete block of a man. A black man, much darker than Roy. He was dressed in military khaki, pants and shirt, but without any identifying insignia. He was tall, as tall as Roy was, but broad across the shoulders and obviously muscular, stomach flat as a board. He had a big square head, shaved bald so you could see how flat it was across the top. His face was set in a frown, hard and utterly humorless. His eyes were so furious and intense they looked like they were going to shoot bullets at us.

We were instantly intimidated. Both of us. We sort of snapped to attention the minute we saw him.

The room was tiny. A cubicle. Totally empty except for the Recruiter's gun-metal desk, his swivel chair, and two straight-back chairs for us. There was one recruitment poster on the wall: a picture of men and women in uniform looking competent and grim. "Find Your Inner Warrior," it said. That was it. Plus the dormer window looking out on the mall parking lot—the mundane reality that suddenly seemed very far away.

The Recruiter leaned toward us with his dark hands clasped on the desktop in front of him. He looked at Roy. He looked at me. He looked at Roy again—he knew right away that Roy was the leader of us.

"Does the word 'undercover' scare you?" he asked. Like that, just that tone, that serious. No irony whatsoever. Not a hint of a smile.

I don't know what Roy was thinking, but me, in one part of my mind, I couldn't take it seriously. The man seemed like a parody of himself, a satire of a humorless patriot. But in another part of my mind, I felt I had suddenly been grabbed by a gigantic iron hand and was being dragged out of my ironical life into something entirely different, something foreign to everything I had known up to that moment. The whole situation seemed completely beyond my control.

In any case, neither of us answered him. Neither of us knew what to say.

"If that question is too difficult for you, too subtle, too nuanced, too fraught with philosophical complexity," the Recruiter said, "let me rephrase it in order to bring it down to the elementary level of your obviously childlike powers of comprehension. Would you find it at all uncomfortable to be surrounded by evildoers who wish your nation ill,

whose loyalties are not to any humanly recognizable good, but only to the commission of sadistic atrocities in the service of a nineteenth-century materialist error if not a seventh-century idolatrous corruption of the image of Christ our holy and all-American Lord? Would it disturb your equilibrium in the slightest to know that you had entered the company of these demonic homunculi under a false flag and that the merest slip of your tongue could reveal the deception to them and thus deliver you into an unimaginable agony of torture ending only with your slow death? Because if that sounds like good fun to you, you are obviously idiots or madmen and in either case the Division can't use you."

Afterward, we went back to Roy's apartment. Roy lay on his bed. I collapsed onto this leather beanbag chair he had. And we both just dissolved into uncontrollable laughter.

"Does the word 'undercover' scare you, Cam?" Roy kept saying. Then he would clutch his stomach and bump his forehead against the wall, giggling this crazy high-pitched giggle.

And I would say, "Is that question too difficult for your childlike comprehension, Roy?" And I would laugh so hard I'd fall out of the beanbag onto the floor.

Finally, we exhausted ourselves. We lay on our backs—Roy on the bed, me on the rug—gazing up at the ceiling, gasping for breath between the last outbreaks of laughter. Slowly, we grew quiet. Silent. But we went on lying where we were, gazing up at the ceiling.

Then Roy said, "I'm gonna do it."

I lay there silent a few seconds more. How could I answer him? What was I doing with my life? Nursing a broken heart for Charlotte? Constructing an emotional block that kept me from finding love with anyone else? Reading poetry? Look, I love poetry. But I was a young man. I was eager to do something, not just read. Was I a patriot? Did I even believe in a single word the Recruiter had said? Did I have any real understanding of what he would be asking us to do?

Looking back, it seems to me, I was just young and male and yearning for something I couldn't name. For life. For what I thought was life. Maybe if Charlotte hadn't disappeared . . . Maybe if she'd gone on being the Charlotte I knew . . . But—she was gone. And here I was, alone with all my yearning.

So I said: "Okay. Okay. I'll do it too."

Next thing I knew, there we were. It seems like that, anyway, when I think back on it. It seems like we spoke the words and were instantly transported into the service. And listen, there's stuff about this I can't tell you. I don't mean to be melodramatic, but it's for your own safety. The short version is this.

We started training with a branch of the military. No one knew we were any different than anyone else. Even we didn't know what was going on. We just kept our mouths shut and did what we were told to do.

First, we went through normal basic training. That was hard enough. But then we went on to another level. That was—beyond difficult. A genuine test of fitness and will. We ran so much—carrying such heavy packs—people's shins literally broke. They just fractured under them and they had to quit. We swam with flippers until some guys had to stop because their legs just wouldn't work anymore. We carried these logs along the beach. Half a dozen men with a log on their shoulders. Lifting it up over our heads and down again, up and down. Carrying it with our feet sinking into the sand. Carrying it on our knees. Doing push-ups in the sand. Crawling in the surf. They tied our hands and feet and dropped us into a pool and we had to somehow keep from drowning. They shot live rounds at us while we crawled through an obstacle course in the dark of night. We could see the tracers going over our heads. We could feel them pass. It seems to me now we never slept. It never stopped. It was constant. It was insane.

At first, all you could think about was not giving up. Then, as it went on, giving up was all you could think about. Surrender. Surrender was like this golden ring floating in the air in front of you. All you had to do was reach out and grab it and the pain would end. The drill instructors knew it too. They taunted us with it. "There's no shame in giving up," they'd say. "Just say the word and it'll all be over. You can go and have yourself a nice cold beer, a nice long rest." Like the devil in your ear, tempting you. Some guys did it too. They just broke. They grabbed the golden ring of surrender and just like that they vanished, they were gone.

But the taunting strengthened me. It filled me with defiance. I think the DIs knew about that too. They knew that some of us would dig in. And if you did that, if you didn't break but kept going, eventually you ran right through that golden ring of surrender that was hanging in the air in front of you. You ran through it and you came to a place beyond it, an open road inside yourself where there was no surrender at all anymore, not even the possibility of surrender. And after that, after you reached that place, you felt like you would never surrender to anything ever again.

That was the place where the irony died, that open road inside you. The irony, the cynicism, the arrogant superiority of our youth. All of that garbage was suddenly gone. Because now—now you felt . . . just . . . . indestructible. You felt like you were a new sort of creature entirely, a creature you barely dared to dream you could be but had always wanted to be, deep down: an indomitable animal of uncanny daring. A man.

And I was so . . . grateful. Grateful for what they had turned me into. You want to know how grateful? Well, there was—I always laugh when I think of this—but there was this crazy rumor that went around for a while—this rumor that they were going to issue each of us a puppy. They were going to let us take care of the puppy and learn to love it. And then they were going to order us to kill the puppy. To show how hard we were, how committed. Obviously, it was completely ridiculous. Nothing remotely like that ever happened. But if it had? I would've torn that puppy's head off with my teeth. That's how grateful I was.

Then, without warning, it was over. We were taken out of it. Me and Roy and two other guys we barely knew. Just like that. It was shocking. Here we had become part of something. A living unit. Ready to die for our leaders. Totally committed. Then one day, first thing, zero dark thirty, we were rousted out of bed. Told to climb in the back of a truck. Our bags were already there, all our belongings, already packed. And they drove us away. And that was that.

We sat there, the four of us, staring at one another. We didn't say a word. We were just in shock. Disoriented. We drove for hours, absolutely silent. It was as if we had woken up to find our lives up to that point had been a dream.

Eventually, the truck stopped. We got out. We were at the end of a dirt road in the woods. We grabbed our gear and hiked in even deeper until we reached an encampment in the middle of nowhere. Structures among the trees. Barracks. A mess. A clearing, roped off like a fighting ring, surrounded by a circle of towering trees. The Hemlock Cathedral, they called it. Because the way the sunbeams poured down through the trees made it look like a holy place, like the inside of a church.

And there in the center of that hemlock church, glowing under those beams of light, there stood the Recruiter.

That was another shock, to see him again. To find him there. Like discovering an ancient statue in a forest. There were other men too, other trainees, all of them in street clothes. Twelve of us altogether. No women. There were women in the Division, but they trained separately, as we found out later.

They took our uniforms and issued us street clothes as well. That felt stranger than anything. We had just forged these new indestructible identities as part of a living unit, and now it was as if they had taken those identities away, as if they had said, "You're no longer who you are. We are about to make you someone else."

Which was more or less what they proceeded to do.

The whole tenor of our training changed after that. We had to reorient, reshape our ideas of what it was we were learning. The Recruiter was at the center of all of it. Teaching us new methods of self-defense in the Cathedral. Beating us black and blue in there. Walking among our desks in the classroom. Lecturing us endlessly.

We didn't laugh at him anymore, I'll tell you that. The days of laughing at him were gone, gone with our irony. Every word he spoke made perfect sense to us now. He was the leader we wanted. Needed.

To be fair to the man, he really was a lot more subtle than Roy and I had given him credit for. He had a streak of irony himself—only it was true irony, too deep for children like us to see at first glance. The crazy things he told us in his lectures—about the way the world worked, the way the country worked, the way the government worked—well, they really were crazy but they were also true, and over time we began to suspect that he knew that, that he understood he was taking us into a level of geopolitical understanding and action where insanity and reality were impossibly intertwined.

He was a more subtle psychologist than we had understood at first also. He knew exactly how to play us—just like he'd played us in that little room at the top of the recruitment center in the mall. He knew exactly where our weaknesses were. Where to probe for fault lines, to see if we would break. And over the next few weeks guys did break. You'd wake up and there'd be an empty bunk in the barracks next to you. And you couldn't say exactly why the guy had zeroed out. But then you'd remember some exchange between him and the Recruiter. And you knew that had had something to do with it.

I mention all this because of the way he treated Roy—Roy specifically. That's what I'm trying to get at. Aside from the Recruiter, Roy was the only black guy in our group. But Roy, remember, had a white mother and he was light-skinned. I'm not going to try to unwind all the *complexities of that. What do I know about it? But the Recruiter played on it. He harped on it all the time.*

"Half," he was always saying. To Roy, I mean, specifically. "You can't be half committed. You can't be half patriotic. Half your mind is no good to me. Half a man is worse than no man at all." It was constant. There was never a racial angle to it, not openly. But it was always directed specifically at Roy. With me, for instance, it was different. With me, it was always, "Professor," or "Poetry Boy." He'd say, "Intellect alone won't save you at the midnight hour, Poetry Boy." That sort of thing. But with Roy, it was always "half." Half, half, half.

To be honest, I didn't completely understand what was going on at the time. Roy was just my friend, my big brother, my mentor, my sensei. Black, white, whatever. We're all American mutts, in the end. But the Recruiter wouldn't let it go. He kept at it. Half, half, half. And it got to Roy. It got to him.

After four weeks in the encampment . . . Cathedral Station, we called it. After four weeks at Cathedral Station we were finally given leave. They drove us into this small city nearby. And, of course, all I could think of was finding a girl.

So the first night, Roy and I went into a bar together. Sat together at a table like we always did. But for once, I got lucky first. We were talking. Like always. Or he was talking. I was hardly listening, I was just scanning the room, looking for women. And my eyes hit on this cute, bouncy little blonde. It was as if she had been waiting for me. As soon as our eyes met she gave me this bright smile. Like a spotlight going on. Like sun through the clouds. Roy was right in the middle of a sentence, and I just said, "Gotta go, brother. See you later."

Nan. That was her name. It's nearly twenty years ago, but I remember every moment I was with her. If a doctor had written me a prescription for her, she could not have been more perfect for that moment. Cheerful. Silly. Generous with her affections. Nothing but soft places on her. The girl was a walking vacation.

So in the morning, I went back to our hotel room, mine and Roy's. And I was whistling a happy tune. I'd had one of those wonderful nights you get in life sometimes. And I came through the door, and there was Roy, pacing back and forth in front of the window like a big cat.

And I said, "Man oh man, I just—"

And he decked me. Pow. Flashed to me clear across the room like he'd been shot out of a gun and gut punched me before I even knew he was there. And you have to understand. Roy and I had been fighting with each other since we met. Karate stuff. Sparring. Hard. Really going at each other. But this was different. We'd spent the last four weeks learning to strike in a totally different way, a much more focused, much more deadly way. So he took me off guard and hit me low and I dropped. Boom. Down on the floor. Stars and little birdies flittering around my head like in the cartoons.

And so help me, Roy came at me to stomp me. He cocked his foot. I thought I was going to the hospital. Maybe to the dumpster in the alley outside. And just out of desperation I slid one shoe behind his ankle and kicked him in the knee with the other shoe. So now he went down. And I jumped on top of him.

For the next, I don't know, fifteen seconds—four hours—three days we were rolling around on the floor, grappling with each other. And if I hadn't known better, I would have sworn my best friend was trying to kill me. We went somersaulting across the room. A bedside lamp fell over. The bulb imploded. The coffee maker vibrated off the bureau. Roy grabbed it and tried to hammer my skull with it. The cord ripped out and sparks flew above me. I just managed to twist the thing out of his hand.

All the while, the whole time, he was spitting curses at me—and not just curses—he'd gone totally racial. Calling me words I'd never even heard before. "You caulkie cricket-eyed ghost-faced goober!" I mean, it *makes me laugh now, but at the time, with him trying to rip my throat out, it wasn't all that funny.*

Well, Roy had taught me everything I knew. There was no chance of my ever beating him hand to hand. Finally, he pinned me flat. Knees on my arms. He rose up above me to strike some horrific final blow. I looked in his eyes. He was clearly intending to reduce me to dust and blood.

Luckily, he came to his senses. He hovered up there long enough for my life to flash before my eyes. But at last he gave a curse and climbed off me.

I slowly sat up. Feeling my face, my body for broken bones. Scuttling over to the wall so I'd have something to lean against while I quietly bled to death. And the whole time, Roy was pacing back and forth in front of me, cursing a blue streak, going on and on about me walking off with Nan the night before. And all of it still had this racial edge to it.

"I'm right in the middle of saying something to you, man! I'm right in the middle of talking to you soul to soul and you piddle off with some milky-assed Betty Crocker trailer trash ditzy white girl? Why? Was my heart too black to look at straight? You had to hide your face in her blondie-blonde curly hairs so you wouldn't have to see the coal-dark core of me?"

All this crazy racial stuff was just pouring out of him like that. And all the while he was pacing back and forth in front of me. I thought at any moment he might change his mind and leap at my throat to finish me off.

Finally, when I could move my jaw, I said, "You know, you're talking about the woman I love."

He stopped pacing. He gaped at me—in wonder, as if I'd just landed from Mars. And he started laughing. He started shaking his head and laughing. He sank down onto the bed. Holding his head in his hands. Making a noise—I couldn't tell if he was laughing or crying anymore. I'm not sure he could tell.

I started laughing too, even though it hurt like hell. I just leaned back against the wall and shook with it.

"You can forget your invitation to the wedding, I'll tell you that," I said.

He said, "Save you from having a colored section."

I rolled my eyes. "For crying out loud, Roy. What the hell? What the hell is it with you all of a sudden?" Then it struck me. I said, "Wait. Is this about the Recruiter? You're not letting him get to you, are you?"

He was sitting slumped on the bed, shaking his head, staring at nothing like he'd just regained consciousness and wasn't sure yet where he was. "Half, half, half," he muttered.

"Oh, don't pay attention to that stuff. He's just playing with you, man. He's just testing you"

"I know that."

"He does it to all of us."

"You think I don't know that?"

"Well, take it out on him next time, would you?"

"I would. But he'd kill me."

I laughed. It hurt my battered ribs. "Ow," I said.

Roy finally turned to me, focused on me. "So you had a good night, huh."

"A classic. One for the books. I wish I could pack her up and take her back with me."

"I heard you singing when you came in."

"I'd still be singing if you hadn't broken my damned jaw."

He snorted. For one more second he looked normal. Copacetic. He looked like the usual Roy.

Then his face just sort of collapsed. He had an expression on him I don't think I'd ever seen before. Like a little kid in a crowd who suddenly looks around and realizes he's lost his mom.

"It's just . . . I keep thinking about where they're going to send me," he said.

I said, "What do you mean?"

He said, "I'm the only black guy."

I shrugged. "It's just the situation right now. It's a question of blending in with our environments."

"That's exactly what I'm talking about," he said. "Who am I gonna be fighting? Who am I fighting for?"

"What do you mean?" I said again, more forcefully this time. "You're fighting for us. For the good guys. The Stars and Stripes. The moon landing. The app store. We talked about all this."

"Did we?" He sighed—like all the bad air was coming out of him. He shook his head. "What are we doing, Cam? What're we letting them turn us into?"

I made a dismissive noise. Waved him off. I didn't want to hear it. I liked what they were turning me into. That sense of becoming indestructible. I loved that. You know how there's always a shape in your head, a shape of something you're supposed to be, something you were born to be. There's that shape, and then there's the shape of who you actually are, a different shape. And the distance between the two shapes, between who you are and who you were born to be, that's where all the discomfort is, all the shame, all the sense of being not quite right, never quite good enough. The Division—the Recruiter—all the training—they were closing that space in me, they were bringing me and who I was supposed to be together. I loved that. The Recruiter—see, he had my number too. I didn't want to be Poetry Boy. Or the Professor. I wanted to be this guy, the guy he was turning me into. I loved that.

"What have we done, Cam?" Roy said to me. "What the hell have we done?"

But I didn't want to hear it.

8

As he was finishing his story, Winter stood up out of his chair. He had never done that in one of their sessions before. He moved to the window. He stood there with his hands in the pockets of his slacks. He stared out at the snowy street below, a short stretch of storefronts and taverns ending where the state capitol stood domed and majestic against the great lake and the gray sky.

Margaret Whitaker could not decide whether he'd walked away from her to work off some nervous energy or because he was trying to escape her steady gaze—or both. Probably both, she thought.

She let him remain standing a few moments more. Then she said, "Come and sit down now, Cam."

It touched her the way he obeyed. Coming back to his chair without hesitation, without objection, without even a wry smile. Like an obedient child. That was how much he trusted her now.

This was another trait in him that attracted her: the completeness of his affections. When he gave himself, he gave the whole thing, nothing left over. That's why he could not get over Charlotte: because he had loved Charlotte without reservation. It was why he hadn't been able to hear Roy's doubts about himself and his place in the world. He had made Roy his big brother and that was the end of it from his point of view. And he could not entertain Roy's doubts about the Division either. Because that decision had also been made and that was it. It was over as far as Winter was concerned. Once his heart was given, the thing was done, and done completely. There was no nuance to his devotion.

And now—now he was devoted to her. She felt the burden of that responsibility. She felt the pressure not to fail him. Him, whom she loved—or would have loved had they not sailed past one another on the unforgiving sea of time.

"This man you call the Recruiter," she said when he was seated across from her again. "You seem to have come to like him, no? You seem to have come to respect him quite a lot."

Winter did not meet her eyes. He nodded thoughtfully, gazing at the brown yet somehow colorless carpet. "I did. Like I said, there was much more to him than I thought at first."

"And Roy—your friend Roy—what about him? It seems as if your feelings toward him were changing too."

Winter made a circular gesture with one hand, as if he were trying to pull the right words out of the air. "Roy was . . . he was more at odds with himself than I'd realized. There was something about him that wasn't . . . that wasn't whole somehow."

"Half, half, half," said Margaret gently.

"I don't know," he said. "Maybe this is naive, but I don't think it was about race. Not really, not deep down. To be honest, I think race is almost always a cover for something else, a diversion from what's really going on. I know that's not a very popular opinion nowadays but it's what I think."

"I think the important thing for you is that you were shifting your loyalties to some degree. Up to now, Roy had been your mentor, and now you were shifting your loyalty from him to the Recruiter."

Winter lifted one eyebrow, as if he were considering the idea for the first time. "You mean that's why he attacked me. Because he felt he was losing me to the Recruiter."

"I wonder how that affected him, feeling uncertain about himself as he was."

"So then I'm right, aren't I? It wasn't about race. Because the Recruiter was also black . . . Oh, wait, I see."

"As you say, the Recruiter was more 'whole.' That's why you were turning to him."

"Well, right. That's what I meant about race being a symbol."

"Well," said Margaret, "a lion may symbolize strength but it's also a lion. Symbols are not just what they symbolize, they're also the things they are."

"But I . . ." Winter's tone was defensive. "To be fair to myself, I couldn't spend all my time worrying about Roy's problems. I had my own journey to make too, after all."

"That's right."

"I was only twenty."

"Exactly."

"I needed to become whole too, I think. And Roy . . . Roy, in the end, couldn't take me there. Because he wasn't whole himself."

"But the Recruiter was."

"He was. That was the point about him. His wholeness. Roy and I laughed at him when we first met him because he seemed to take himself so seriously. Then we realized—at least I came to realize—that he didn't take himself seriously at all. He didn't have to. Because he was so completely who he was. We thought we were ironic, but he was irony personified. He was both himself and the joke about himself. I've never met anyone else like him. Yes, he was a whole man, and he also realized that being whole was comical in a broken world."

"So he was the one—not Roy—who could mentor you on your journey into adulthood."

Winter nodded.

"And how was he doing that exactly, Cam?" she asked. "What was it he was teaching you? Specifically, I mean."

She was touched again by the childlike trust in his eyes. The childlike love. For the mother figure, she thought ruefully. Oh, why did she have to be so old?

"What are you asking me, Margaret?" he said.

She answered him gently—like the mother figure she was doomed to be. "We've talked about this before, Cam. About how sometimes a story is more about the parts you leave out than the parts you tell. The hidden meaning is in the silences."

He drew a slow breath. "And? What am I being silent about?"

"You haven't told me what you were doing exactly. There in Cathedral Station. Wasn't that the question Roy asked you after your fight in the hotel: 'What are we letting them turn us into?' What were they turning you into, Cam? What was the Recruiter training you to become?"

A change came over him as he sat there. It was very dramatic to see, like a special effect in a movie. One moment, he was her client, open, vulnerable, surrendered to the therapeutic process. The next moment he metamorphosed before her eyes and he was once again the man she had known when they first met, solitary, controlled, watchful, potentially deadly, the secret man who thrilled and frightened her.

"Do you make notes on these sessions?" he asked her.

Margaret nodded. "I do, yes. I have to, for legal and ethical reasons."

He nodded thoughtfully for a moment. Then he said, "Don't. Stop. Or make things up in your notes. Lie in them."

She started to smile but she didn't. Because he wasn't joking. And he wasn't being melodramatic either. He was serious.

Margaret suddenly felt nervous, as if there were a chill blue wind blowing through the warm brown room. She was—as she was so often and so painfully aware—an old woman who lived alone with a cat. She was not prepared to find herself in danger.

"All right," she said slowly. "All right, I understand."

"Do you?"

"Yes. I should be careful what I put in my notes."

"I try to keep everything vague," Winter said.

"I know. I recognize that."

"But it's not really possible, not completely. I'd be kidding you if I said it was."

"You're talking specifically about my question. Roy's question. What was the Recruiter turning you into?"

"Yes."

"You feel you should answer that."

"Yes. I feel I have to. If you're going to understand any of this, I don't see how I can hold it back."

"All right, then," Margaret said. She tried to keep her voice from trembling. She tried hard not to show him her fear. "What's the answer then? What was the Recruiter turning you into?"

After one more moment of hesitation, Winter said: "Well—obviously—we were training to become assassins."

9

Three days later, Winter stood on a clifftop as the cold morning dawned. Far below, the roiling ocean thrashed the rocks. High above, the last star faded and the night sky paled to a frigid white-blue. Winter shivered inside his shearling coat. The wind was bitter. His ivy cap did little to protect him. His ears and cheeks were scarlet with the cold. His lips were trembling.

He remembered the words of the adoring journalist who'd been allowed to accompany his hero—"Tech Merlin Gerald Byrne," as he called him—on one of his legendary sunrise power walks along these Marin headlands.

With his prophet-like beard blowing in the sea breezes and his eyes trained on a vision of the future only he can see, he strides along the Coastal Trail with his single bodyguard struggling to keep up, a familiar sight to the joggers and tourists who pretend to ignore him.

But Winter had been standing here half an hour and so far there was no Tech Merlin in sight. No tourists either, come to that, not in this weather. And only a solitary jogger had gone past him, dressed in sweatpants and a thermal shirt, seemingly oblivious to the arctic atmosphere. Must have been a trial lawyer, Winter thought, or some other kind of unfeeling beast. Aside from that, his only company was one lunatic red-tailed hawk shrieking like a demon as it tumbled wildly on the swirling wind.

A line of Wordsworth came to him: *Now the sun is rising calm and bright . . . /And all the air is filled with pleasant noise of waters.*

Like hell, he thought.

The white disc of the sun was rising like the pitiless eye of an Aztec god. The seizing, spitting surf at the base of the cliffs was beginning to glitter bitterly with the cold light of it. None of it was calm. None of it was pleasant.

The minutes passed. One red tower of the Golden Gate Bridge became visible over the hill behind him. The skyline of San Francisco—deceptively pristine and beautiful at this distance—started to gleam white against the trailing clouds and the blue sky.

And there, finally, long past sunrise proper, Gerald Byrne appeared, a small figure very far away.

Why was Winter waiting for him? He did not have a plan, nothing very specific anyway. He just felt the need to take the measure of the man, to test his theories about him against the living presence. Winter's guilt over Adam Kemp, his moral confusion about his role in Adam's descent into drugs and degradation, had made him feel uncertain. He had his suspicions about Byrne's role in the boy's death, but it was all such inward stuff. Imaginative. Without proof, without substance—not enough to act on. He felt if he could stand face to face with the man, look him in the eye, he might begin to believe his own suppositions. Or not. Either way, he would be able to form some idea of what to do next. Because if it turned out he was right he would have to do something. He could not simply let it go.

Byrne grew nearer, power walking along the narrow dirt track that wound out of the horizon. He went out of sight as the track dipped below the rolling rim of the hill.

Winter huddled in his coat. His teeth began to chatter. Byrne reemerged, much closer, just below him on the trail, but rising. Winter could make him out clearly now. His tall, lean figure was clothed in nothing more than a track outfit. No hat. His ponytail bounced behind him as he moved with determined vigor. His long beard waved in the winter wind. Even more of a savage beast than the trial lawyer, Winter thought. Impressively rugged.

Another figure came into view behind him. This was the "single bodyguard" the journalist had written about. But he was hardly "struggling to keep up." He was fit and agile, moving easily, turning his head now and then to give the area a professional scan. He wore jeans and a British commando sweater, olive drab, with epaulettes. He had a navy watch cap pulled down over his ears. Winter could not make out his face yet, but something about the way he moved struck him. He wasn't sure yet what it was, but it was something, all right. He didn't like it. It gave him a queasy feeling.

Byrne crested the hill. He saw Winter standing there on the path in front of him. He came to a stop. He grinned.

The bodyguard came up behind him. Also stopped. Also grinned. Winter could see now that the guard was Eurasian, classically handsome, with very smooth, youthful features, very bright eyes.

Winter's queasiness increased. What the hell was everyone smiling about? And what was it about the bodyguard that troubled him?

Byrne came forward slowly, casually, panting lightly from his exertions.

He said: "Cameron Winter, I presume."

If that was supposed to startle Winter, it sure enough did. If it was supposed to make him nervous, it did that too. He guessed Byrne was sending him a message. He guessed the message was: You cannot act in secret against so Merliny a Merlin of technological tech. If he was going to research Gerald Byrne, Gerald Byrne was telling him, Gerald Byrne was going to find out about it. Gerald Byrne saw all.

"You know me," Winter answered. It sounded lame even to him.

"Word gets around," Byrne said with his easy grin. "You know how things are nowadays."

Winter figured this was meant to make his mind race with possibilities. He figured this because his mind was, in fact, racing with possibilities. Was Byrne enough of a wizard that he could see right into Winter's computer and spy on his online searches? Or had he just heard about him from his sister-in-law Evelyn? A casual remark: *A man named Cameron Winter was at the theater today . . .* Winter couldn't be sure.

Byrne was now standing right in front of him—above him, too, because he was a good three or four inches taller. He was still smiling, relaxed and easy. Seemingly untouched by the cold while Winter shivered. His earring glinted in the morning light. Up close like this, Winter recognized the flowery tattoo on his neck. It was the ayahuasca plant, the source of a hallucinogenic tea used in South American enlightenment rituals that had recently become popular with Western seekers of truth and beauty. Winter's researches had not yet reached the ayahuasca portion of Byrne's biography. But he'd seen references to it, including images of the flower.

"I'm looking into the suicide of a student of mine," Winter said.

Byrne gazed off mystically at the glittering sea. His flowing, passionless voice was familiar to Winter from listening to the interviews. "So I understand. Adam Kemp. Sad story."

"I was one his professors at the university."

"Oh, I know who you are. You defended Adam when he was accused of abusing a young woman. Another young woman. Before my sister, I mean."

Winter didn't bother trying to argue the point. Whatever moral nuances there had been to Adam's behavior in college, they had been rendered meaningless. When Adam pinned Evelyn Shea to the floor and slugged her in the face, he became what Lori Lesser had accused him of being. It wasn't tender feelings for Adam Kemp that had brought Winter to the cliffs.

But he was annoyed, all the same—annoyed at the way Byrne had seized control of the conversation. Winter had tried to ambush him, and Byrne had turned the tables. It was irritating as hell.

On top of which, the Mysterious Eurasian Bodyguard Guy was enjoying the show a little too much. Grinning and nodding and laughing silently at Winter. Winter realized all at once what it was that bothered him about the way the man moved. It was the same way he, Winter himself, moved. The bodyguard had had some sort of similar training in the hilarious dark art of dealing death. He was an equal, then, a similarly dangerous man. So Byrne aside, Winter could not even muster a psychological advantage over the damned bodyguard. Grinning and nodding and laughing.

Byrne squinted mystically at the sparkling ocean another moment, then turned to look—and to look down on—Winter. "But you're more than just an English teacher, aren't you, Cam?"

Winter lifted his chin at him defiantly. "Am I?"

"Oh yes. Yes, you definitely are. You have an interesting way of showing up here and there at odd moments. Moments of trouble when there are mysteries to be unraveled. You rescue kidnapped women. You find missing children. You solve murders. You're an impressive gentleman."

Winter raised his shoulders against the cold. He sniffled. He was already tired of this game, tired of Byrne outsmarting him, intimidating him, getting the better of him. It was getting old. He was ready to play a different game.

"I have a strange habit of mind," he said. "Sometimes when things are murky to other people, they come clear to me. Sometimes when things are hidden, I can uncover them."

The two men's eyes locked, cold and hard. They stood silent atop the cliff as the wind blew and the ocean crashed beneath them.

Then Byrne smiled sweetly. The bodyguard behind him went on grinning.

"Is that why you're here? To help clear up murky things about Adam Kemp's suicide? To make the hidden things known."

"I think so," said Winter. "I think that is why I'm here."

"And yet it all seems very clear to me. A troubled young man steps off a roof and falls to his death. Maybe I'm being obtuse, but that doesn't seem murky in the least."

"The thing is—Ger," Winter said, because he didn't like the way Byrne called him "Cam." "The thing is, I think you killed him."

Byrne did not flinch at the accusation, not even a little bit. "Me?" he said.

"Yes. I think you engineered his death."

"Engineered his death," Byrne echoed quietly. "Oh my." Maybe Winter only imagined the hardening of his smile, the fire in the depths of his apparently peaceful eyes, the threat in them. Byrne glanced back at his Mysterious Bodyguard. The Eurasian went on grinning and nodding and laughing silently. "What a phrase, eh, Nelson?" Byrne said. Then, looking back at Winter—down at Winter—he said, "Just how did I manage to *engineer* Adam jumping off a roof by his own free will?"

The wild and bitter wind intensified, but only Winter shuddered. Byrne's long beard waved and his hair stirred, but he seemed otherwise unaffected.

"You reported Adam to the police," Winter said. "Not just for beating your sister-in-law, but for the drugs too. How else did the cops know the drugs were there? Evelyn wouldn't have told them, so it must've been you. You didn't like Adam. I'm guessing you'd already investigated him. Maybe you had your guy here search his place." Winter used his head to gesture at the bodyguard. *Your guy here.* "Maybe you sent the cops a photograph of his stash so they could get a warrant."

Byrne's gaze moved in a slow study of Winter's face. "'A strange habit of mind,'" he said again. "Good phrase. I like that."

"The police don't have many friends in a town like San Fran," Winter went on. "But they know you. You're the guy who sends six-figure gifts to cops when they're hurt or killed in the line of duty. When you told them Adam had beaten up your sister, you didn't have to explain to them what you wanted done. They knew. They gave Adam the full treatment, didn't they? Threw him in gen pop. Turned their backs while the thugs went at him, beat him, raped him. As far as the cops were concerned, it was just a favor for a friend."

Byrne gave a little huff of breath, a little shrug. "I'm sure you overestimate my influence."

"I doubt it."

"I did call the police, though. Like you said. That much is true. Adam beat my sister black and blue, so I called the police. What would you have done under the circumstances?"

Winter didn't answer. He didn't have a sister. He'd been an only child. But he knew well enough what he would have done if he did have a sister and Adam had beaten her. He didn't have the money or influence or even the imagination to rig it in some elaborate fashion like Byrne did. He would have just taken Adam to some lonely place and worked him over. He wouldn't have killed him, but he wouldn't have left much of him alive either, just rags of flesh and bits of bone. Then he would have hoisted his sister over his shoulder and carried her off to his elfin grot. Locked her in a high tower in the fairy tale woods. Left her there until she grew her hair long enough so some handsome prince could climb up the braids and rescue her. Then he would've beaten the crap out of the handsome prince by way of a warning. Then he'd have attended their wedding, casting dark glances at the prince the whole time just so the prince wouldn't forget.

"Why does she call you Pup?" Winter asked suddenly. "Evelyn. Your sister-in-law. 'We call him Pup,' she told me. Makes you sound like some kind of stuffed animal. What's that about?"

"It's a pet name," said Byrne, monotone, deadpan. "It's short for puppy dog. It's what my wife calls me. Because I'm so bouncy and affectionate."

Winter laughed. Shook his head. "Well. The thing is—Pup," he said. "It was enough already. Getting Adam locked up. Beaten. Raped. That was enough. I wouldn't be here to quibble with you over that. That was fair payment for your sister. But you didn't have to tip off Quintero."

Byrne narrowed his eyes and pouted. "Who?"

"The man's a psycho. You knew that," Winter said. "You had to know what he does to people who offend him. Tortures them. Mutilates them. Sets them on fire. Dropping the word to a guy like that that Adam was ripping him off—that's too much. It speaks to me of something bad in a man, something twisted and bad, that he would do that. I mean, if a man would do that, what wouldn't he do? That's the question that keeps bothering me. If you would do that, what wouldn't you do? Puppy Dog."

Byrne stood quietly, still unaffected by the icy ocean wind—stood quietly looking down on Winter a long several moments, so long that Winter might have felt nervous again. Except he was done with being nervous.

"This—this habit of mind of yours," Byrne said. "It seems to me, really, it amounts to nothing more than spinning stories about people in your head. Inventing scenarios about a fellow."

"Well, that would be a character flaw, all right."

"It would. It really would. It would be a genuine mistake."

Winter shifted his gaze to the bodyguard. The bodyguard was still grinning. Still grinning, but not nodding anymore, not laughing. In fact, the grin wasn't even much of a grin anymore either. Just a collection of teeth really. Like a shark shows you before it rips you to pieces.

Byrne waited until Winter met his eyes again. Then he said, "The world has many problems, Cam. Poverty. Inequality. Dangerous levels of pollution. Climate change. I run a charity. Actually my wife Molly runs it for me. It's a charity for underprivileged children. It gives them a chance in life, a chance they wouldn't get otherwise. I run another project that's trying to redirect national economies to deal with all these problems, these problems that threaten society, that threaten the earth itself. The Good World Project, I call it."

Byrne's gaze was locked on Winter's. Winter wished he could keep from trembling. He didn't want Byrne to think he was afraid of him. He was just so damned cold.

"Adam Kemp abused my sister," Byrne told him. "He beat her, really brutally. You saw her later, but you should have seen her when she first showed up at our house. It was a terrible thing.

I called the police to report it—over her objections, by the way. Adam had her so confused, she wanted to protect him. But as you say, I called the police. What the police decided to do then—how they treated Adam—well, I don't know anything about that. They didn't tell me and I didn't ask. As for this Quintero character, I've never heard of him."

Winter's mouth quirked at the corner.

"I've never heard of him," Byrne repeated. "And I would be very troubled if anyone put it out there that I had. I called the police on a woman beater, that's all. If bad things happened to Adam after that, maybe I'm guilty of not caring very much. I didn't care very much. I don't care very much now. I have other things on my mind. More important things, like the things I mentioned, like poverty and children and the environment and so on. So. You're right. I didn't like Adam. He beat my sister. And I called the police. I wouldn't want anyone to say more than that."

Winter nodded. He was tired of playing eye wars with Byrne. He looked away, out at the roiling sea. He realized that he had gotten what he'd come for. All his suspicions had been confirmed. It was not a happy realization. It made him feel tired inside. Because it meant that this—this conversation, this man-to-man locking of horns—was not the end of anything. It was just the beginning.

He turned back to Byrne. Byrne exchanged another glance with his bodyguard Nelson. Byrne smiled gently. Nelson showed his teeth. Then it was back to locking eyes with Winter.

"You understand me, Cam, don't you?" he said. "You understand what I'm saying to you."

"I think we understand each other. Pup," said Winter.

Byrne inclined his head in acknowledgment and in goodbye. Then he power walked off along the trail.

Nelson the bodyguard walked off after him, but not before giving Winter a nice sharp shot in the shoulder with his shoulder.

Winter staggered where he stood—then he just stood, his hands in his pockets, and watched the water rising under the rising sun.

10

Winter had papers to grade on the plane ride home. He had classes to teach and meetings to attend all through the day following. It was not until evening that he had a chance to take up his research again.

It was dark as he headed across the campus, under the snowy, leafless trees, past the carillon tower and the Greek colonnade, to the building that students called the Gothic. It was a hunkering haunted monster of a place, arches and gables and towers, all gray stone. That's where his office was.

It was after hours. The building was empty. His footsteps echoed as he climbed the steps to his tiny cubicle on the second floor. He was asking himself: What was the point of this? Why couldn't he leave it alone? He remembered Evelyn and her bruised face, her lovely face under the tangle of yellow hair. Her small, fine, fragile figure. Winter probably could have circled her waist with his two hands. He pictured how Adam had pinned her down, pinned her arms to the floor with his knees so his fists were free . . .

He shook his head to chase the images away. Why couldn't he let this go? Adam was what he was, did what he did, made his choices. Plenty of men have beaten their women and gotten away with it. Adam was unlucky. His girl had a powerful brother-in-law so he paid a price. So what? Who cared? Why should Winter act the avenger for him?

And yet. Here he was. Climbing the Gothic stairway to his office. Here he had to be. Something compelled him. Not Adam. Not even the bit about Quintero, though Quintero was a clue to it. It was something else. Something more. Something deeper. Every word Byrne spoke testified to it. *Let there be light.* Winter didn't quite know what he was looking for yet, but he knew it was there. And he knew he had to find it.

Just as he reached the second-floor landing the phone in his pocket buzzed. He fished it out. He gave a little sigh when he saw the name on the readout: Lori Lesser.

"Hi, Cam. It's me, Lori." She was trying to make her voice sound clipped and professional. It wasn't working. He could tell she was upset. "Do you have a few minutes to drop by?" she asked. "It's very important that I speak with you." He was annoyed. He knew it was uncharitable of him, but he couldn't help it. He had been waiting all day to get to his research, and he didn't like being interrupted. He hesitated. Lori said, "Please, Cam, really." Which made him close his eyes and suppress a second sigh. He could tell this was trouble. Lori was always trouble.

"Are you in your office?" he asked hopefully.

"No. No, I'm at home."

Of course she was. "All right," said Winter. "I'll be right over."

He killed the connection. He told himself to stop being such a jerk. He told himself to be nice. He did not feel nice.

The Neurotic Dean of Student Relations—that should have been her full official title as far as Winter was concerned—met him at the door of her small house about a block from campus. He could see at once she had been crying. Her eyes were red and puffy. Her cheeks were blotched. She wasn't trying to hide it.

She shut the door behind him. She started right in while he was peeling off his big coat.

"I just can't stop thinking about Adam," she said. "It really hurts me to know that you blame me for what happened . . . I can't sleep, Cam."

She bit off the final words before the tears could start. Winter was grateful for that. He did not want to get in a situation where he felt obligated to put his arms around her. She was dressed more elegantly than usual in a tan woolen skirt with a big belt and a green sweater, an outfit that showed off her figure. Winter was attracted to her and wanted nothing to do with her. He was sorry to be alone with her in her house.

She stood biting her lip and pressing one hand to her forehead. He thought she was waiting for him to comfort her. Or maybe he was flattering himself. He hoped he was, but he doubted it.

For lack of a better strategy, he drifted from the foyer into the living room. He dumped his shearling coat on a chair and plunked down on the sofa. He'd been here a few times before, for parties and other university functions. He was always surprised how prim and middle-class genteel the decor was. He always expected more pottery and political posters, but she kept that sort of thing confined to the kitchen. Lori trailed in after him.

"Do you want something?" she asked. "A drink? A glass of wine?"

Did he ever. He held his peace till she'd poured them both a Riesling. She sat down next to him on the sofa. She smelled nice, too. Only then did he realize he should have sat on the chair.

He lifted his glass to her. Drank. The wine was tart and lemony and good.

"I should have called you before now, but I didn't have time," he said. "I told you I'd find out more about what happened, and I did. Here's the thing. Adam's suicide had nothing to do with you. He'd gone bad, Lori. The drugs ruined him. He was losing control of himself. His girlfriend Evelyn—she's five-foot-three, a hundred pounds maybe. Sweet, smart, talented girl with a real future. She got an interview for a good job and Adam got jealous and beat the hell out of her."

Lori sat up straight. "What?"

"He knocked her to the floor and kneeled on her arms and slugged her in the face till she was all bruises."

"Oh my God, Cam. Oh my God!"

"Plus he stole money from a gangster and the gangster found out about it."

"Are you kidding me?"

"I'm not. He killed himself because the gangster was coming for him, to take revenge. That was the part I couldn't figure out. Why would Adam text me for help and then jump off the roof without giving me a chance to answer him? My guess is the gangster showed up, that's why. Time just ran out for him. It had nothing to do with you, Lori. It had nothing to do with either of us. He just went bad and things unraveled. You can let it go."

Lori sat holding her wine and gaping at the room. Trying to feed the new information into her emotional algorithm.

"So I was right," she said finally. "I was right to hold him to account when I did. Wasn't I? I saw something in him. His treatment of women."

Either that, or she'd hounded a troubled kid into addiction and violence, Winter thought. But who could ever tell about such things? Who knew how things would have gone if they hadn't gone the way they did? It didn't matter anyway. Not to him.

"He was a grown man," he told her. "He made his own choices. We all get dealt cards. We all have to play them. It's never fair."

She faced him. "Thank you," she said. "Thank you for saying that. Thank you for telling me this. It really helps."

He shrugged. "It's true, that's all. He took drugs and beat his girl and ripped off a gangster. He could have not done those things. He could have done other things instead. Then he'd be alive or at least we'd give a damn that he wasn't."

"I give a damn," she said earnestly. "I'm sorry for him."

"Well, suit yourself."

She smiled. The effects of her crying jag were fading. Her face was becoming its frantic, ferocious self again, strangely appealing in a postmodern way he couldn't quite account for. Inwardly, he shook his head at himself. He'd been alone too long, that was the trouble. Too lonely too long.

"You're a funny guy, Cam," she said.

"I endeavor to amuse."

"You say these things sometimes that make me worried about you, about where you stand. But you're really very protective of women, aren't you? In this old-fashioned patriarchal way, I guess."

"I tend to come down against punching them repeatedly in the face, all other things being equal."

"You're like a remnant of a past civilization. Like a mummy from the past that came to life in the new world."

He laughed in spite of himself. "I'm going to try to find some way to take that as a compliment."

"It is. I mean, I find it attractive anyway. That's probably not very politically correct of me, but I do. I really do."

Her eyes softened. Her nice smell enveloped him. His fingers itched to fiddle with that sweater. Winter could feel the erotic change coming over him, the change from a state of reality to a state of desire. Already, he was beginning to convince himself that he liked her even though he knew he didn't. He didn't like her or dislike her. He didn't feel one way or the other about her. That was the reality, but he was forgetting it as he sat there in his desire. He was beginning to tell himself that an affair with her would not necessarily be a disaster even though he knew it would necessarily be exactly that. In fact, even as he was drawn to her, even as he was tempted to put his wineglass down and pull her to him, even now, he could see the whole catastrophe that would surely follow. If he had sex with her, he would have to pretend to like her afterward. She was not a fool. She would know he was pretending. She would feel hurt. Her hurt would turn to anger. Whose wouldn't? As things were, she didn't know which she wanted more: to get him fired or to sleep with him. Once the anger set in, her choice would become clear. Getting him fired would become her crusade.

And here was the surprise ending—the secret Winter knew that Lori did not. If she really, truly set her mind to getting him fired, it would ruin her life. It would be she who lost her job, not him; she who lost her job and then became unemployable. Because a man like Winter didn't get hired at a university like this for his scholarship or his teaching skills. He had been hired because he knew things, things about the dean, things the dean wanted to keep hidden until the end of the world. For all his mild manner, the dean was a Machiavel, an expert politician. He had outmaneuvered many women like Lori. He had outmaneuvered more than a few men like her. So if Lori went on a crusade against Winter, before she even realized she had threatened the dean's position, the dean would destroy her. And then Winter would feel bad. He would feel it was all his fault because he had slept with her and made her mad. It would be a mess.

He set his wineglass down. "I should go. I have work to do," he said.

"Ca-am!" she said with a forced laugh.

"What?"

"Am I losing my touch here? I'm practically throwing myself at you."

He sighed. He stood. "It's not a good idea, Lori."

"Why not? You don't have to make such a big thing out of it. I just don't want to be alone tonight, that's all."

He mumbled something about the fact they worked together. It made him feel idiotic—to flee a seducer like this. He felt like a virgin fleeing a rake in an eighteenth-century novel. *I won't! You will! I can't! You must!*

Lori clapped her wineglass down on the coffee table. "Boy, you really dislike me, don't you?"

"Come on, Lori." It wasn't much of an answer, but what could he say?

"Am I really that unattractive?"

For a moment, he stood where he was, computing the various outcomes. He could walk out and inflame her hurt and anger against him. He could say, "Oh, all right," and grudgingly agree to stay, which would inflame her hurt and anger against him even more in the long run. Or he could pretend to surrender to his hidden passions and fall upon her with a series of romantic charades that would buy him about a week's fraught peace before she saw through them and it inflamed her hurt and anger against him to the nth degree. That last way, at least, he'd get to sleep with her before the real trouble started.

But no. He preferred to remain blameless in his own mind. The trouble would come, but let him not be the one by whom it would come.

He settled for a gallant-sounding exit line about how lovely she was and how it was difficult for him to do what they both knew was right and something something something—at that point, even he wasn't listening.

His last backward glimpse of her as he saw himself out was chilling. She was sitting with her legs crossed, her hand dripping from her knee with limp elegance. She was regarding him with what was supposed to be a detached and superior smile but was in fact a glare of smoking fury.

Somehow, he knew, she would come for her revenge.

11

He spent the rest of the night alone in his apartment, alone with his laptop, a delivery chicken salad, a bottle of scotch, and a crushing sense of solitude. He felt bad about the Lori incident. He felt he had been unkind to her. He could tell himself he had behaved impeccably. Technically he had. But he'd been unkind to her in his heart. She was right. He blamed her for her treatment of Adam. But his grudge was not with her. It was with the modern world. She was right about that too. His courtliness, his protectiveness toward women, his patriarchal whatever—he was a walking mummy from the past. And not even from the real past, but from a past he read about in books and imagined. His disdain for the modern world had become disdain for her and she saw that in his eyes and he was sorry for it. It was unkind.

After enough scotch, his self-reproaches devolved into sentimental self-pity. He hated that, but he indulged in it.

He found a photograph of Charlotte Schaefer online—his old crush. It was not the later Charlotte, not the Charlotte who had gone crazy after finding out about her father's dirty dealings with the Stasi during the bad old Communist days back in the old country. Nor was it the little girl Charlotte who had tended and mothered him when he was an even littler boy. It was peak Charlotte, the teenaged girl he had loved with a child's devotion and a man's passion. It was a picture of her as a senior preserved on her high school's website.

The photo was buried deep in the website's history files, but he knew how to dig it up. Every time he had found it in the past, he had promised himself he would never search for it again. But never mind. There she was. A serious and tender fraulein, impossibly beautiful, her rose-white features crowned with the corona braid that encircled her golden hair. She had a porcelain perfection and fragility that reminded him of the German statuettes that had decorated her mother's home when they were both children. But then, there had always been something old world about her, hadn't there? Something elevated and ladylike. Maybe that was why he couldn't let her go. Because she had the aspect of a maiden from those made-up days of yore in which his mind was mummified.

Where was she now? he wondered, as he always wondered. Gone without a trace, without a trail, even online. Sometimes he tried to convince himself that he should look for her, if only to make sure she was safe—safely away from that evil fascist gnome she'd been living with the last time he saw her. Sometimes he had the fantasy that he found her. That they came together. They married. They were happy. Then one day, she discovered his past, learned about the things he had done with the Division, the blood on his hands. For her, it would be a repeat of the trauma she had experienced when she found out about her father. She would never forgive him. And how could he stand to lose her a second time?

Reluctantly, he closed the website. *I was desolate and sick of an old passion*, he recited silently. He nursed his whiskey. *Yea, I was desolate and bowed my head.*

For the next few moments, he rested his head on the back of his chair. He looked up at the ceiling. His mind drifted. His boozy thoughts became fragmentary, tangled. He thought of himself with Lori. He thought of Lori with Adam. Adam with Evelyn. Evelyn with Gerald Byrne.

Men and women—they were no good for one another. Ladies and gentlemen—they were nowhere to be found. The world was out of whack. The time was out of joint. Did it matter to anyone but him, living in the literary past? Was something really wrong with the world, or was he just a mummy shaking his wrapped fist at the chaos he found outside his pyramid?

He sat up. He sipped his whiskey. He set it down. *Desolate and sick and I bowed my head.*

Now his fingers were on the laptop keyboard again. He was searching for Molly Byrne. Byrne's wife. The Cinderella Girl. Why? Why couldn't he let this go?

Then there she was: Molly. Article after article about her, all the articles much the same. Glossy features geared toward women readers. Gushing, glamour-riddled prose. The journos were eager to portray Molly as a strong, independent, accomplished woman. They went on and on about her work running Byrne's Fairy Tale Fund for underprivileged children, and so on.

But that was not the story their readers cared about, and the journos knew it. The women who read these articles wanted the other story, the real story, the story about "the nobody from nowhere who married the famous billionaire Gerald Byrne." How did that happen? How did she make such a catch? They wanted to dream themselves into her love story.

Two photographs—reproduced in almost every article—told that story better than words. One was a picture of Molly Shea, the drab secretary at the Minneapolis church where Byrne's father had once been the pastor. The other was a picture of Molly Byrne, wife of a billionaire. She was wearing a cobalt blue gown. She was smiling brightly as she strode across a stage to accept yet another award for her charitable works. She was an American duchess.

And yet, all accessories aside, she was not a beautiful woman, neither beautiful nor plain. She was simply normal and agreeable-looking. Short and full-figured—one could almost say *dumpy*, if one were unkind—with an appealingly open and friendly face under dull brown hair, limp in the first picture, curly and vibrant in the second after the high-priced stylists had gotten to it.

And here was another funny thing about her. Despite every effort by the journalists to present her as powerful and assertive—*independent, strong, accomplished*—she came across in interviews as modest, honest, unpretentious, and self-effacing. It was she, in fact, who had given herself her nickname.

"Really, there's nothing special about me, except that I'm married to Gerald," she said in one interview. "I was an ordinary girl living an ordinary life. And then one day I was the wife of a billionaire. Basically, I'm Cinderella."

She went on: "I guess Gerald had already had all the glamour girls. Believe me, I sometimes look at the pictures of him with all those actresses and models, and I think to myself, 'Wait. You had her, and you chose me? What, now?' But like I say, I guess he had tried all that and he was ready for something different."

In a rare TV chat with a famous talk show hostess, she was delightfully comic and self-effacing. "Believe me, even at church, he could have had any girl he wanted," she said. Winter liked her voice, a delightfully normal pipsqueak voice, cute and silly. "All the girls at church were after him. The more he ignored them, the harder they threw themselves at him. I used to joke that each Sunday, they would unbutton another button on their blouses trying to get his attention. If it had gone on much longer, they'd have come to church naked to the waist."

"But he chose you," said the interviewer. She didn't mess around with feminist counternarratives. She knew what the ladies in her audience were there to hear. She got right to the point: he chose you, Cinderella.

"One Sunday, after the service," Molly told her, "I was manning the cookie table, selling chocolate chip cookies I baked to raise money. I looked up and Gerald was just suddenly standing there in front of me. Of course, I knew who he was. Everyone at church knew. Normally, he was surrounded by a gaggle of women with their blouses unbuttoned. But now here he was. He'd come over to see me, me specifically. I couldn't have been more startled. And just like that, he asked me out. He said he found me very appealing."

When she said that—when she said "very appealing"—she clasped her hands under her chin and struck a silly ain't-I-appealing pose. And she really was appealing. She was as charming as she could possibly be. Winter found himself smiling as he watched her. The audience laughed and applauded. They loved her. Who wouldn't?

Winter sat back from his laptop. Hoisted his scotch again. Smirked at himself. Now, on top of everything else, he was jealous of Gerald Byrne. He hadn't been until now. He hadn't envied Byrne his money or his power. Winter had enough money. He'd never particularly wanted any power. But love? Here Winter was, nearly forty, alone in his apartment, mooning over a picture of a high school sweetheart. And Byrne meanwhile? Byrne with all his arrogance and his mystic pretensions. Byrne who had maneuvered Adam Kemp into suicide. Byrne had had the maturity and the good sense to walk away from Hollywood flash and win himself the devotion of this adorable creature, a woman of genuine quality, the Cinderella Girl, née Molly Shea. So here sat Winter, alone and lonely, gazing at her—at Byrne's wife—bitter. Angry. Jealous.

Maybe that was his true motivation, he thought. Maybe his half-formed suspicions of Byrne were fueled by envy and resentment. Maybe he wasn't looking to make things right at all. Maybe he just hated Byrne because he was successful at love. Maybe he wanted to destroy him for that.

This much, at least, was certain. Three days later, when he was sitting on the fifty-minute puddle-jumper flight to Minneapolis, there was a certain acid glee in his heart. He was heading to see Molly's family. He was going to question them about Gerald Byrne. And he knew full well that Gerald Byrne would hear about it. And he knew full well that Gerald Byrne wasn't going to like it.

Winter smiled grimly to himself, thinking it over. Thinking: *Oh, no. Puppy Dog wasn't going to like this one little bit.*

12

Molly's mother was named Annabelle. Annabelle Shea. She was a pleasant-looking woman, somewhere around sixty. She kept her hair light brown, a mass of curls atop a pale, open, pie-plate face. Bright brown welcoming eyes, dancing with home fires.

Winter found her in a pleasant suburb of the city, in a modest 1950s-era house of the type that used to be called a Rambler. One story, sprawling, with a low roof and stone facing. The snow was thick on the lawn but the driveway and the front path and the sidewalk corner to corner had all been shoveled clean—not by the neighborhood boys, Winter thought. Gerald Byrne had paid for professionals.

"Pup used to nag me about this place all the time," she told him, showing him around the living room. "He wanted me to come live on their estate in California, put me in one of their guesthouses so I could be near the grandkids. But I would always say to him: 'What's the point?' The guesthouse is there if I need it. I can visit any time I like. And I have grandchildren here too, you know, Little Jack and Susan, right nearby. Anyway, I'm used to this old place. It's where I lived with my husband, Dan. And I don't know—I don't like to be beholden. Finally, Pup gave up on that project. One Christmas, he just gave me the mortgage to this place for a present, wrapped up in a box, all paid off. I didn't ask for it, but I couldn't say no. Of course, it's nothing to him."

Winter had not explained to her the reason for his visit, not really. He had simply said he was a college professor and that he was interested in Molly's life and her marriage to Byrne. Mrs. Shea naturally assumed that he was writing some kind of article about her daughter. He didn't correct her. In any case, she seemed happy to talk to him. She was not hesitant at all.

"I knew I liked Pup the first time he came to visit. That was at Easter. I said to Molly, 'When are we going to meet this young man of yours?' I thought maybe she was ashamed to show us to him, us being so regular and all. But really, you know, it was the other way around, it turned out. She was afraid we would disapprove of him, that we'd think he was too high and mighty. And Brenda—that's my oldest—she was like that a little, just at first. She can be a bit suspicious of people, to be honest. I said to Molly, 'Why don't you invite him over for Easter?' And so she texted him would he like to come? And right away, he texted back and said, 'Oh yes. Of course. You're my girl, aren't you? I want to meet your people.' Just like that. You should have seen Molly's face when she read that. 'You're my girl.' She just turned scarlet with pleasure. We all had a good time teasing her about it."

Winter forced a sympathetic smile. Grudgingly, he had to admit to himself that Byrne had behaved very well here. He had not tried to steamroll the Shea family with his wealth and fame. He'd gone out of his way to win their approval, as any decent young man might have done.

He had come to visit for Easter. And at one point during the three-day weekend Byrne had found himself in the Rambler house alone. Molly had gone out to visit her sister and her niece and nephew. Mrs. Shea had gone to the supermarket. Byrne was reading a book when Mrs. Shea arrived home with a car full of grocery bags. The billionaire had rushed outside to help her carry in the groceries.

"He said, 'You go on in and start unloading and I'll carry in the rest,' just like that," Mrs. Shea told Winter. "Then when he was finished—it was so funny—he had this puzzled look on his face. He said everyone in the neighborhood was staring at him. And it was true. The neighbors had all come to their windows to watch him bring in my groceries. Next door, Lilith Johansson had her nose pressed to the window of her sewing room like she was looking at a goldfish in a bowl. And Robbie McMahon across the street—why, she just came right out on her front lawn with a cup of coffee and watched Pup bringing the bags in like it was a TV show. Poor Pup. He said to me, he said, 'Why is everyone staring at me, Mrs. Shea?' And I said, 'Well, dear, the fact is they don't see a famous billionaire bringing in my groceries every day.' And you know what he said? He said, 'Well, they're just going to have to get used to it, aren't they?' That's when I knew he was serious about Molly."

After that—after bringing in the groceries—Byrne sat with Mrs. Shea at the kitchen table. They drank coffee together. He shared his memories about his mother's suicide and the scandal at the church that was once his church and was now Molly's. He was manfully frank with her about his years of promiscuity and about the depression that had slowly crept over him during those years. He told her the story about the psychiatrist and the cannister of antidepressants he had flushed down the toilet. The message was clear: he was finished with that life. Mrs. Shea didn't have to worry that he would get tired of Molly and return to his glamour girls. He was done with them.

"We were all a little afraid he was going to come in here and sort of stomp around, you know, like a big shot. 'I'm rich and I can do whatever I want.' But he wasn't like that at all. He was sweet as pie, really."

Mrs. Shea's husband, Molly's father, Dan Shea, had been an attorney. They had had three daughters together, but he had died when the girls were young. That was the family tragedy. It had taken its toll on all of them.

"I had to raise the girls myself," Mrs. Shea told Winter. He and she were ensconced in the living room armchairs, cozy as old friends. Sipping coffee together, munching on vanilla crème cookies off a plate on the end table between them. "It wasn't easy, I don't mind telling you. Dan was a careful man, very responsible, so we had some insurance, and that helped. Then I got my paralegal certificate and I went to work for Dan's old firm, but oh . . ." She held one hand to heaven and rolled her eyes.

She had gone to work for Dan's former partner Lou Walsh. She had naturally thought he would be a friend to her. But no. Once she was working for him, the mask came off, she said. Walsh turned out to be a tyrant. A bully. And things only got worse after she repulsed his sexual advances.

"I couldn't believe it! When my Dan was alive, we used to go out to dinner with Lou and his wife Jenny. He was a married man! Well, I wasn't going to put up with any of that nonsense, believe you me," she said.

Walsh overworked her. Underpaid her. And though she couldn't prove it, she was certain he poisoned her reputation around town so she couldn't leave him and find work elsewhere.

"So I said to myself, I said, 'Annabelle, you're just going to have to put up with it, and that's all there is to it.' I had three girls to feed and get through college. What else was I going to do? Eventually, of course, it all caught up with him. With Lou, I mean. These things always do, you know. All the affairs. And lying to his clients, holding their settlements back from them, keeping some of the money for himself. It all came out, yes indeed. Jenny left him, took the kids. He almost went to jail! Finally, he had to leave town in disgrace. Then suddenly, what do you know? The other firms started to call me and hire me. So it all worked out for the best. Of course, by then anyway, it didn't matter quite so much, the girls were all taken care of. Except for Evvie. She's the Creative One. That's always a bit of a problem, isn't it?"

She proudly handed Winter a framed photo of her three daughters, Brenda, Molly, and Evelyn, oldest to youngest. Winter admired them. Brenda was the Serious One, she told him. She had married Jack Wallace and helped him turn his furniture store into a five-store chain with locations throughout the Midwest.

"Between you and me and the four walls, I think Brenda was really the brains of that whole operation," Mrs. Shea confided. "Though, of course, it's Jack who gets the credit. But they both work hard, the two of them. Which means more time for me with Little Jack and Susan. That Susan, I swear, is just the cutest little thing you ever saw." She showed Winter a photo of Little Jack and Susan. He admired them too.

Evelyn was the Creative One but also the Pretty One, everyone said so.

"Sometimes that can be a curse, though," said Mrs. Shea. "The boys were always around her like flies, and some of them not so nice. Well, she got all tangled up with that Adam Kemp boy out in San Francisco and enough said about that."

Molly was the Domestic One. "Right from the beginning, all that girl ever wanted in life was a husband and a home and lots and lots of kids running around her feet. It was her and her dolls, right from the beginning. Tea sets and toy ovens and strollers. She was practicing, you see. For as long as I can remember. But she had her boy troubles too. I guess there's no avoiding it nowadays. Things were simpler when I was a girl. You met a fellow and if you hit it off you got married and that was that, for better or for worse. Now . . ."

Molly had gone to school in Denver, Colorado. She studied art history. She said she was planning to teach. "But we all knew she was getting her M-R-S degree, there was never any doubt about that. And then she met Charles, and we thought, well, all that was settled. Which goes to show you. You never can tell."

This was the story Winter carried back with him on the puddle jumper home. The story of Molly and Charles Merriman. He thought about it as he gazed out the plane window at a pale expanse of February sky. Thin scuds of clouds drifted and dissolved along the horizon. That strange habit of mind came over him. His thoughts blurred. All his opinions and uncertainties faded into a sort of active emptiness. There was nothing left but the facts of the matter. The facts floated in his head like puzzle pieces, like a mental game of Tetris, shapes falling, interlocking, building into a grand design without his doing anything but gazing into space.

Molly had met her college boyfriend Charles Merriman in a class on American literature. He was a devout Evangelical Christian. He led Bible studies and sometimes manned an information table on the quad. "Do you know Jesus Christ?" he would ask his fellow students as they hurried by.

Molly had always been religious herself. The Shea girls were all churchgoing Presbyterians, and Molly was the most committed to the faith. She fell in easily with Charles's ideas. She was happy to adapt to them.

"She gave herself over to Charles with her whole heart," Mrs. Shea told Winter. "We always knew it would be like that, once she met the man of her dreams. Whatever he wanted, Molly would go along with it. I never saw a girl so devoted to anyone."

Charles had asked Molly to take a purity pledge, a promise that they would remain virgins until they were married. She had been happy to do it. She was proud that Charles wanted to. She believed it was the right thing to do, the biblical thing, and she didn't think she would have had the willpower to do it without his support.

"She was so in love with him, I can't even describe it," said Mrs. Shea. "It was always Charles this and Charles that, and Charles said this, and Charles believed that. That was so Molly. Like Ruth in the Bible. Whither thou goest . . . Wherever Charles went she was going to follow."

It was her older sister, Brenda—the Serious One—who first began to have her doubts about the relationship. Brenda had an eye for these things. She knew people. She paid close attention to their behaviors. And she had a "suspicious nature," as Mrs. Shea put it. After a few months she noticed that Molly's enthusiasm for Charles was taking on a frantic tone. It was too hot, too bright, she said. Her devotion had developed an undercurrent of panic.

"Brenda kept saying to me and Evelyn, she kept saying: 'Something is up with those two. Something is up.' We wouldn't listen to her." Mrs. Shea shook her head with regret. "We thought she was just being Brenda, you know. Brenda is always seeing trouble everywhere."

But this time Brenda was right.

One night, after a study session together, Molly accidentally took one of Charles's notebooks back to her dorm with her. Normally, she would have held on to it until she saw him at lunch the next day or maybe she would have called him to make sure he didn't need it in the morning. But this time—who knows why?—she didn't call. She just went to his dorm to return it. When he wasn't there, she didn't leave it for him. Again, who knows why? She traced him to a friend's house off campus. Brian, that was the friend's name. Brian's front door was unlocked. No one ever locked their doors in this college town. Who knows why she didn't knock before she entered? She didn't even call out for him once she was inside. She came down the hall and heard noises and opened a door and found Charles and Brian together in the bedroom. It confirmed what, at that point, she must have already suspected, deep down.

"He was one of those gay boys," as Mrs. Shea put it with a regretful shake of her head. She clucked her tongue. "And there they were right in front of her. Just like that. It was a terrible shock to us all, let me tell you."

It was more than that for Molly. For Molly, an entire cathedral of dreams tumbled to rubble in a moment. It was not so much the act she witnessed—though that horrified her—or the fact of Charles's homosexuality per se—though she strongly believed it was a sin before God.

"Well, it was just the dishonesty of it!" said Mrs. Shea.

Molly had loved this man with all the power of first love and now she knew: every single moment they had been together had been a lie. The purity pledge—it was just a dodge, wasn't it? The qualities she had bragged about in Charles—his sensitivity, his gentleness, his interest in her interests—they now seemed to her not virtues but signposts pointing to his dark secret. If he had just been honest with her, but no: he had turned her loving devotion into a humiliating joke.

There was even worse to come. Charles not only had been lying to her all this time, he'd been lying to himself as well. The tension between his religious beliefs and his sexual desires had been too painful for him to acknowledge. He could not face it. So he had tried to convince himself the desires weren't there.

When Molly discovered him with Brian, Charles was exposed not only to her but also to himself. He could not go on pretending. He might have adjusted to the reality. He might have decided to resist his desires and hold to his beliefs. Or he might have changed his beliefs, or he might have abandoned them. But he did none of these. He was emotionally shattered. He left school. He lost touch with his family. He ping-ponged between drug-fueled interludes of anonymous sex and guilt-ridden torments of religious mania. He went bad.

All this, as Mrs. Shea told Winter, Molly discovered later.

In the moment, Molly was shattered too. She left school too. She returned home, brokenhearted. She could no longer trust herself or anyone else. She could no longer muster her old sense of fun and silliness and devotion and joy. She became a mouse, scuttling from corner to corner. She huddled at home for months in her old room. Then for months after that she hurried from a studio apartment to her job as church secretary, head down, eyes on the pavement.

Only children had the power to brighten the soul within her. When she taught Sunday school, she came back to life again, merry-eyed and goofy and devoted as in the old days. The children adored her, and when she was with them it soothed her painful yearning for love and motherhood. The other church ladies saw this and pitied her. "Her fiancé turned out to be one of those gay boys, you know," they said.

Then along came Pup. One day she looked up from the chocolate chip cookie fund-raising table and there he was, standing right in front of her. He said he found her "very appealing."

Molly and Gerald Byrne's wedding had been a small, private affair, but there was no keeping it out of the news forever. Soon, the Cinderella Girl articles began to appear here, there, and everywhere. Molly became famous as the "nobody from nowhere who married the billionaire."

That's when Charles Merriman made his sinister return.

Despite the purity pledge—that promise of virginity—when Molly loved, she loved with passion. Her clinches with Charles had made her gasp and hunger for him. He, on the other hand, had been desperate to hide his cold reaction from both her and himself. In one of these breathless moments, he had convinced her to let him take photos of her in the nude. He told her this small sin would help him resist the greater sin. Secretly, he must have hoped he could teach himself to want her. In any case, she posed on the bed for him while he circled her with his phone camera.

"Well, sure enough, once he heard how Molly had married into all that money, up he showed, right out of the woodwork," Mrs. Shea told Winter. "He told her if she didn't pay him a hundred thousand dollars, he would put those pictures up on all these horrible websites for everyone to see. A hundred thousand dollars! Poor Molly. She was frantic. She could hardly bear to tell Pup the truth. But I said to her, I said: 'You've got to do it, Molly. That's what marriage is. It's honesty.'"

Winter gazed out the airplane window. All his opinions were silent. There was nothing in his mind but the facts falling like Tetris. Molly naked on her dorm room bed. Charles with his camera. The pale blue sky outside with small silver airplanes glinting in the distance. Scuds of clouds drifting and dissipating.

Charles gave Molly an ultimatum. Pay him his blackmail by Monday or face public humiliation. But that weekend he drove up into the mountains for a ski party with his friends. He lost control of his Toyota Yaris on a sharp turn on a snowy road. The Yaris sailed off the cliff and into space. It plunged down the side of the mountain. It crashed and exploded into flames on the frozen earth of the forest below.

The nude photographs of Molly were never found.

Winter gazed out the airplane window. He saw scuds of clouds. Silver airplanes. Naked Molly. Gerald Byrne.

In the silent expanse of his imagination, he saw the Toyota tumble down the mountainside. The Toyota exploding. Burning. He saw Charles Merriman locked inside. Screaming and shuddering as the flames consumed him.

13

It was three days later that Winter first laid eyes on Hannah Greer. He was drinking an afternoon coffee in the comfortable darkness of the Independent. It was a quaint café just off campus. An ivy-covered brick building, dimly lit within. A swirling paisley mural covered the walls, surrounding tables of stained wood.

Winter had his laptop open on the table in front of him. He had a croissant on a plate by his right hand. He was reading about Gerald Byrne's famous spiritual awakening through the use of ayahuasca.

Winter had no set beliefs about religion. Overall, he thought, the cosmos seemed an odd place and full of mystery. He entertained faith. He entertained skepticism. It depended on the day. But drug-induced mysticism never impressed him. LSD revelations, Navajo peyote ceremonies, that sort of thing—he dismissed it all. You could ingest a hallucinogen and see a cartoon mouse dancing on the ceiling, but that didn't mean the world was Disneyland. So why should you suddenly find faith if you swallowed the same substance and saw the face of God?

But this was Gerald Byrne's story, not Winter's. This was what happened to Byrne before he returned to his father's church in Minnesota. Before he met and married Molly Shea.

After he emptied his psychiatrist's orange cannister of antidepressants into the toilet, Byrne had gone on a spiritual quest. If money and success and beautiful women couldn't bring him happiness, what on earth could?

His father's corruption had soured him on Christianity so he read about Eastern religion instead. He hired a meditation coach. He explored the mental depths of nothingness. He learned the lingo of *dharma* and *satori*. But deep down he found it all pretty unsatisfactory.

Then one day in August he held a party at his mansion in Los Angeles. He and several of his Hollywood friends sat sunk in lounge chairs around the swimming pool. The California sunlight sparkled on the water. Beautiful women walked by in bikinis. Some went bare-breasted. Byrne and his friends watched them, passing around a reefer, lounge chair to lounge chair. They inhaled a particularly potent strain of Silver Haze from Holland. Byrne, as he recalled in one interview, was "baked out of my mind."

The man lying on the lounge chair beside his was a famous studio executive. Byrne would never name him, but Winter took a guess and imagined a short, hairy creature with a comb-over and a bowling ball belly. The famous executive told Byrne he had just returned from the Amazon jungle. He had used ayahuasca under the guidance of a shaman. It was, he said, a bullet train to the godhead, guaranteed.

Byrne summoned his personal assistant to the side of his lounge chair and instructed him to arrange the trip.

Just as Byrne was boarding his private jet to Brazil, Winter looked up from his laptop and saw Hannah. He had turned from reading the article to take a bite of his croissant. He was lifting the croissant to his mouth when he spotted her. His hand paused, the croissant in midair.

Hannah was sitting by the window on the other side of the shop. The gently falling snow outside made a sweet greeting card background for her. It seemed to set her apart from the chaotic modernity of the paisley mural. It seemed to frame her out of time.

She was lovely. A student obviously, twenty or so. Small and slender. Delicate, sensitive features. She had a black beret perched adorably on her gold and silken hair. A braid of her hair flowed out from the beret to lie upon her shoulder.

Winter finished bringing the croissant to his mouth and took a bite. This close to campus, there were plenty of attractive young women around. A gentleman trained himself not to leer at them. And Winter hadn't leered. It was just a glance. But he was aware at once that the sight of her had moved him.

There was something about the girl. For one thing, she was reading the selected letters of John Keats. Winter couldn't make out the title at that distance, but he recognized the cover of the edition. Even at a university, you could go a long time without seeing a pretty girl reading Keats's poems let alone his letters. Even the poems would have struck him like an arrow in the heart. But the letters . . .

And that wasn't all. There was the face like a cameo. The prim posture. The graceful figure in the vintage argyle sweater, the modest skirt down to the ankles. The archaic aspect of her, like a portrait in a museum: *Girl Reading a Book.* More than once, Winter had stood before just such a portrait and drifted into a reverie, hankering after a lady who'd been dead for ages, if she'd ever lived at all.

He turned back to the article on his computer screen, back to Gerald Byrne and his quest. But just before he started reading again, one more thought unsettled him: she reminded him of Charlotte. That's what it was. That's what had made him pause mid-croissant.

Where was he? The pool party. Smoking dope. The famous studio exec. Oh yes: Byrne began his trek to the Amazon.

Byrne flew into town on his private jet, but after that the going got tougher. A bumpety-bump jeep ride from the airport. A putt-putt boat up the river into the rain forest. A sweaty hike with two other billionaires, trudging away from the dock and into the trees, following a guide who spoke no English.

They came to a clearing. At the base of a raised hut with a straw roof the shaman was waiting. He was a pleasantly unpretentious Dutchman named Lucas. He called ayahuasca "the medicine," or simply "she." He told them the voice of Enlightenment was always experienced as feminine. Eternity was a woman.

After two days of spiritual preparation—lectures, ceremonies, prayers—he and the two other seekers gathered together in the chattering jungle dark of night. The hut was lit by candles set in a star pattern at the center of the floor. A native woman blew scented smoke over the participants where they sat cross-legged on the floor. She chanted in an unpleasantly whiny voice. A native man with pendulous breasts and a gut like the Buddha prepared the drug in a smoking vat, then passed it out to them in clay cups.

Byrne found the taste of the stuff grotesque, like drinking paint. Each of the seekers was given a bucket and boy oh boy did Byrne ever need it. He felt as if he vomited for hours and then had diarrhea and then vomited again. He was grateful when the shaman blew out the candles so he could crap himself silly in the dark.

"You are being purged," chanted Lucas in Portuguese.

"I didn't need him to tell me that," Byrne later told an interviewer with a laugh.

But then the medicine took effect. Byrne felt himself sinking away from the surface of his body and plunging into galaxies. He saw his childhood, still there, still alive in his inner infinity. He heard his father's voice. He saw his mother's face, which he loved so much. He lived his whole life again in minutes or hours or years. Then his own biography opened majestically, like a double doorway onto the stars. Enlightenment lay beyond and then . . .

What horror! A monster blocked the way. A tentacled, multiheaded, yet somehow very human beast with enormous fangs. Byrne, a child, was helpless as it reared up over him.

But wait! A Savior. Descending from galactic nowhere into his consciousness! Was it the Jesus of his childhood? Was it feminine Eternity? It was—it was both—and yet it was also Himself. The Savior seized the monster by the throat and hurled it from the door. The way into everlasting reality lay open before him. . .

"Excuse me?"

Winter had allowed himself to be swept up into the narrative of Byrne's epiphany, so he was startled by the voice speaking right beside him. He straightened and looked up. The blond girl in the beret was standing at his elbow.

"Are you Dr. Winter?" she asked.

"I am."

"I'm very sorry to bother you. My name is Hannah Greer. I just transferred here from Northwestern. I wasn't in time to register for your Wordsworth class this semester, but I wanted to tell you you're one of the main reasons I decided to come here."

"Ah. Thank you. That's nice to hear."

Winter was used to being fussed over by pretty young students. Girls—girls especially—tended to love his lectures. He never tried to take advantage of their admiration. He was a disciplined man with an antique moral code. He had had one affair with a student, a young woman named Victoria Nowak. It had arisen out of mutual affection, and it had ended in friendship. But it had violated that code of his, and he'd resolved never to let anything like it happen again.

And yet, close up like this, the presence of Hannah Greer washed over him like a wave. She seemed so much like Charlotte. Not in looks necessarily, but something. An aspect. An attitude. Her posture reminded him of her. And that slightly formal phrasing of her speech, as if she were translating her thoughts into English from another tongue. And her serious yet tender manner.

"*Wise Passiveness and Negative Capability* is the reason I became an English major," she said. "No one writes about poetry like that anymore. With that kind of insight."

The book had been Winter's doctoral thesis. It had been published by university presses both here and in England and it had developed a bit of a cult following. Like Charles Manson, he sometimes joked.

"Well, thank you very much," he said. "I'll be teaching Keats in the spring. I hope you'll sign up."

"Oh, I definitely will. I was just reading his letters." She pointed back at her table where she'd left the book. "His description of his meeting with Coleridge is wonderful. The reference to nightingales is so intriguing."

Winter smiled politely. He hoped she could not see how powerfully she affected him. If only she had been a little older, a fellow teacher maybe . . . If only she had been Charlotte herself.

"I give an entire lecture on that meeting," he told her.

"You don't really!"

He laughed. "No, I really do."

"That's very exciting to hear. I have so many questions about it."

She hesitated. He could see she wanted him to invite her to sit down with him. He would not do that.

"Well . . ." she said finally.

"It was very nice to meet you, Hannah," Winter said politely. "I'll look forward to having you in my class next semester."

She made a movement then—just a small one, very subtle. A little nod of the head while her hand tugged gently at the edge of her skirt. That was all. But to Winter it was clearly suggestive of a curtsey, a gesture so ladylike and anachronistic that it seemed to strike clean through him like a saber thrust. When she returned to her table to gather her overcoat and her purse, he felt as if she had left a jagged hole of loneliness at the center of him, front to back.

He turned back to his laptop. He did not want to watch her leave. He did not want to admire her in motion. He forced himself to read more about Gerald Byrne instead.

"When I returned from the Amazon, I not only knew that I had to change my life, I also knew how," Byrne told one interviewer. "It wasn't a reasoned process. The knowledge was just suddenly there inside me. Eternity had planted it in me through the medium of ayahuasca. I needed to go home to Minnesota. I needed to take up the child life that was still there within me, to take it up where it had abruptly left off, that night my mother killed herself. I needed to go to the church where my father had preached and pray to God there with the faith of the child I'd been and still somehow was. Because I understood now: God was not my father. He was not just something outside me. He was the Eternity within me as well.

"I bought a small house not far from my old neighborhood," he went on. "I upgraded the internet there so I could work remotely without making too many real-life trips back to California. I went to church every Sunday.

"Every step of the way, I had this powerful sense that Eternity was guiding me. That's why it was a delight but not altogether a surprise when I looked up from my prayers in church one day and I saw Molly Shea for the first time."

14

Winter's phone buzzed in the middle of the night. It woke him from a deep sleep.

He fumbled for it on the bedside table. He answered: "Yes?"

Silence. Someone was there, but whoever it was he said nothing. There was not even a breath. Just silence.

Winter cut the connection. He glanced at the clock. Three a.m. precisely. It was sometimes called the devil's hour because it was directly opposite the holy hour, three p.m., when Christ died on the cross. "In a real dark night of the soul, it is always three o'clock in the morning, day after day," as F. Scott Fitzgerald said.

Winter lay back in bed, wide awake now, eyes open. He gazed up through the darkness at the ceiling. That was not Fitzgerald calling, he thought. That was Gerald Byrne—or one of his minions—maybe Nelson, the bodyguard. Byrne, the preacher's kid, would have known about the devil's hour. Byrne, who had spoken in an interview about Hamlet and Persephone, might even have known the Fitzgerald quote. He might have thought that was a nice touch, Winter being a literary man. The call had been designed for Winter especially. Byrne had been sending him a warning.

Winter had been expecting this, or something like it. He had come to realize that this had been his plan all along. He had told himself he didn't have a plan, but he had come to realize that he did have one, and this was it. This was why he had confronted Byrne on the Marin headland. This was why he had openly accused him of engineering the death of Adam Kemp. This was why he had boldly gone to his mother-in-law's house to question her. He knew word of his visit would get back to Byrne. He knew it would make Byrne angry.

And that was what he wanted. That was the plan. To make Byrne angry. To make Byrne angry at him the way he'd been angry at Adam. Angry the way he must have been angry at Charles Merriman when Merriman had tried to blackmail his bride. He wanted Byrne so angry he made a move against him. A man that rich, that powerful, that connected—there was no other way to expose him. He had to get him to show himself.

Winter reached behind him. He had hooked a holster to the back panel of the bed frame. He touched the pebbled handle of the 9mm Beretta there. Then he rolled onto his side and went back to sleep.

When he went out the next day he rigged the apartment door. It was a simple trick. He spit-pasted one of his own brown-blond hairs to the crack beneath the hinge. He walked to campus through the cold and cloudy weather. He attended a faculty meeting. He held office hours in his cubicle in the Gothic, and several students came to see him. He gave a lecture on Wordsworth's sense of the past, the lost connection with nature that foretold the coming of modernity. Sure enough, when he returned to his apartment, he found the hair was gone from beneath the hinge. That meant the door had been opened while he was out. Someone had broken in.

It had to have been Nelson. The break-in was too clean, too seamless. There was not a trace of it left behind. Nelson—a man with Nelson's training—would have even spotted the hair. He would have expected to find it. He would have been able to remove it when he came in and then replace it when he left. But he hadn't replaced it. Because he wanted Winter to know he'd been there. Again, it was a warning.

The camera confirmed this—the camera Winter had hidden in his television set. It was a sophisticated device, motion activated. It was supposed to send a notice to an app on his phone if anyone set it off. There had been no notice. But when he checked the app he found five seconds of run time had elapsed and yet there was no video. In other words, someone had activated the camera without setting off the notification. Then that someone had stopped the camera, erased the video, and reset the camera by hand.

This was serious spy stuff. The sort of stuff Winter himself had been trained to do. So Nelson was sending him a clear message. Or Byrne was sending him a message through Nelson. The message was this: anything Winter could do, Byrne could do, and nothing Winter could do could stop him.

But Winter didn't need to hear this message. Winter had already guessed as much. He had seen the way Nelson moved on the headland trail. He had suspected the truth when Mrs. Shea had told him her story. He had confirmed his suspicions with research after he'd gotten home.

He had researched the fate of Lou Walsh. Walsh was Mrs. Shea's tyrannical boss, her late husband's partner, the guy who had propositioned her then bullied her when she refused him, underpaid her and overworked her, and ruined her reputation to keep her from fleeing to his competitors. According to a Twin Cities news site, the ignominious end of Walsh's career had come about soon after Byrne and Molly had become engaged. A client accused Walsh of cheating her out of part of the settlement from a lawsuit.

The accusation aroused suspicions in Walsh's other clients. When they investigated, some of them found he had cheated them too. Then two of Walsh's mistresses came forward to add to the scandal. Walsh had been disbarred. His wife had left him. The prosecutor had threatened to bring charges. It was unclear why he hadn't. Walsh had slinked out of town and disappeared.

That was exactly how Winter would have orchestrated such a scandal. That was exactly how he had been trained to do it.

And he'd been trained how to rig a car crash too.

When the police had looked at the remains of Charles Merriman's Toyota Yaris, they could find nothing wrong with it. It was an inexpensive car and several years old, but a solid make with a high reliability rating. The tracks in the snow indicated that Charles had not turned the steering wheel when he hit the curve. A hiking witness confirmed this. He had just gone straight over the cliff. There was no question of suicide. Charles had been unusually cheerful in the days before the crash. He had no drugs or alcohol in his system. The police concluded he must have fallen asleep at the wheel.

Winter did not think Charles had fallen asleep at the wheel. Winter thought Nelson had had the same sort of training he had had. How to cause a scandal. How to cause a car crash. How to come and go without a trace.

That was it. Winter was sure of it—almost sure. His main uncertainty centered on himself and his own motives. Was he spinning a wild tale about Byrne because he envied him? Because Byrne had moved beyond his past. Because Byrne had found Molly. Byrne had found love. Why else did he have such a passion for this? Why could he not let it go? Even if he was right about Adam, about Walsh, about Charles Merriman, why should it matter? Who were they? A brute, a bully, a blackmailer. They got what was coming to them. Good riddance. Why this passion?

But no—no, he told himself. There were more. He was sure of it. He was almost sure. There had to be more. Byrne had traveled to the Amazon. He had traveled into Eternity. He had seen the face of the Savior. He had discovered the Savior was himself. He had saved Mrs. Shea from Lou Walsh. He had saved Molly from Charles Merriman. He had saved Evelyn from Adam Kemp. There had to be more. How could there not be? After all, Byrne had started the Good World Project, hadn't he? He was trying to save the whole world, wasn't he? *Let there be light.* There had to be more.

Winter was sure of it. He was almost sure. But it was going to be difficult to uncover the truth. Even more difficult to prove it. Impossible to prove it. With Nelson trained as well as he was. With Byrne so wealthy, so powerful, so well connected. Impossible—unless he could catch them in the act.

Which meant he had to make Byrne angry. Angry at him. Really angry. Angry enough to play the Savior.

Which meant Winter knew exactly what he had to do next.

15

The fund-raising gala for the Fairy Tale Fund was what the journalists liked to call "a star-studded event." It was held in a luxurious hotel off Wilshire Boulevard in Los Angeles. A number of famous Hollywood entertainers were in attendance. They were the stars in "star-studded."

Their stardom meant precisely nothing to Winter. By and large, he thought modern American culture was trash. Having grown up an isolated rich kid, he had developed an early taste for classical music and high literature. The stuff his students watched on their devices and especially the music they listened to seemed to him less like art than like a rank odor rising from a pit of bubbling green slime. As a result, he didn't recognize most of the celebrities at the gala and he could not have cared about them less.

In the area outside the ballroom, glamorous ladies and their artfully disheveled escorts posed for photographers on a red carpet. Winter watched them as if he were an anthropologist observing the rituals of some primitive tribe—except that he probably would have had some respect for the rituals of a primitive tribe.

He did get a small thrill when he spotted a starlet who had been in a German crime series he had enjoyed during a free trial of some streaming service. He remembered a novel he had read many years ago, *The Moviegoer* by Walker Percy. Percy wrote of the aura of "resplendent reality" that seemed to surround film stars and such people. Looking at the German starlet, he could see what Percy meant. He wondered if she—the starlet—experienced it too, if she felt she was more real than other people. He wondered if Gerald Byrne felt he was more real than Adam Kemp and Charles Merriman.

It was an interesting question, but he couldn't think about it now. He couldn't let his literary mind distract him from his main purpose. His main purpose was to hide himself in the gathering crowd and keep a sharp eye out for Byrne's security men.

Byrne himself, Winter knew, would not be at the gala. He was in Washington to testify before Congress on Byrne's latest "anti-hate speech" policy. Several congressmen and political commentators had recently been banned from the social media platform after they'd expressed opinions of which Byrne did not approve. One of the congressmen had condemned Byrne for "effectively gutting the principle of free speech." He had summoned the tech mogul to D.C. to explain himself.

So Byrne wasn't there in Los Angeles. But Molly was. Mrs. Byrne was the chairwoman of the Fairy Tale Fund. She was the night's keynote speaker. That meant Byrne's security people would be there too. It was possible they would even be on the lookout for Winter. So he was on the lookout for them.

When all the photographs that could be taken were taken, the glittering celebrities left the red carpet. They rejoined the throng of wealthy donors. They all streamed together into the grand ballroom. Winter hid himself in the crowd, one more tuxedo among the many.

He was glad to find the ballroom was dimly lit. The place had been decorated to seem enchanted. The walls and ceiling were hung with purple crepe. The crepe was studded with fairy lights. The overhead lights were turned low. Against that background, the diners looked as if they were floating in starry space. A fairy tale night—that was the idea. Winter was glad of it. It was murky. It made it difficult to make out faces from a distance. It gave him a sense of safety and anonymity.

He had made a large donation to the fund under a cover name—Edgar Black. He had arranged to be seated at table five, close enough to the stage to do what he had come to do.

He sat down. He introduced himself to the other donors at his table. The make-believe Edgar Black worked in the field of renewable energy. Winter figured that would strike his fellow diners as both admirable and stultifying. They would smile and nod and pretend to listen to him, but they wouldn't remember a word he said. So it went. Meanwhile, he scanned the room until he found what he was looking for: Molly.

She was seated just two tables away. As his eye picked her out, he noted that she too, like the German starlet, possessed the strange hyperreality of fame. The other diners at her table—table one—were clearly the wealthiest of the wealthy. Some of them may well have been famous themselves. One of them—judging from his good looks, poor hygiene, and near-complete self-absorption—was likely one of the Hollywood stars Winter didn't recognize. Still it was Molly who held his gaze, who held everyone's gaze. It was as if she were a colorful three-dimensional figure rising out of a black-and-white photograph.

At the same time, she seemed to him—as she had seemed when he watched her on video—charmingly unpretentious. She was dressed in a gray chiffon gown with a lacy bodice. She wore only a small gold cross around her neck for jewelry—that and her marriage rings. It was an elegant outfit, but it didn't hide—it wasn't meant to hide—her squat, full figure. She was not built along the sleek lines of the Angeleno ladies around her. She hadn't had her face surgically altered as they had. Except for the hairdo and the splashy duds, she still looked like what she was. An ordinary American woman.

But, again, charming. She spoke to those around her with girlish enthusiasm, bouncing in her seat. Her cheeks were flushed. Her eyes were sparkling. Her hands were moving around in the air. She threw herself back and giggled with her fingers pressed to her lips. Sweetness, silliness, liveliness, affection, and devotion—they all seemed to bubble out of her as if she were champagne in human form. Winter smiled, watching her.

Then he stopped smiling.

Because there was Nelson. Well, of course. He would have to be there. Byrne was going to guard his wife with his best man.

The bodyguard stood by a side door like a statue of a bodyguard. Legs akimbo, hands clasped just beneath his waist. Only his eyes were moving. Dressed in a black suit with a black tie on a white shirt, he was as inconspicuous as he could be, except for the fact that he was as handsome as any actor in the room. He was scanning the area around Molly's table. It was a professional scan. He widened its scope by slow degrees. It hadn't reached Winter yet but it would soon.

Winter did his best to turn away from him. He didn't like having his back to the man, but it was the only way he could keep from being recognized. If Nelson did recognize him, it could mean serious trouble. The bodyguard could call the police. He could tell them about the confrontation on the headlands, about his intrusion into the life of Molly's mother. He might convince the police to haul him off, even to toss him in jail. As Adam Kemp had learned, a night in jail could be very unpleasant when you were on the wrong side of Gerald Byrne. Winter was relieved when the dim lights dimmed even further, the room went dark, and the night's presentation began.

An apparently famous singer came onstage and began to sing one of her apparently famous songs. The audience listened, rapt. Winter listened and wept inwardly over the death of Western civilization. How could anyone bear this stuff?

As the song went on, he managed to steal a couple of glances Nelson's way. The bodyguard had apparently satisfied himself that the area around his charge was clear. He was watching the doors now. Winter felt he was relatively safe for the moment.

After the singer, there was a film about the work of the Fairy Tale Fund. The ballroom got even darker. That was good. There were two large screens hung above the stage. As a narrator spoke about the poor children who were fed by the fund and the sick children who were healed, the children's faces appeared on the screens, smiling poignantly. Winter was moved by their stories. He knuckled a manly tear from the corner of one eye. He kept the other eye on Nelson.

Next, the head of a film studio was honored for his hefty contributions to the fund. Winter tapped his fingers on the table during the accolades. He wished he could put the whole event into fast motion, to get it over with before Nelson spotted him.

The lights came up again for dinner. He considered leaving but didn't want to draw attention to himself. Instead, he kept his back toward the bodyguard. He chewed his salmon without tasting it. He went easy on the Chardonnay. He willed himself not to glance over his shoulder. He thought he had been mad to come.

Finally, the lights dimmed again. The time for the keynote speech had arrived. A man who was someone or other stood up to make the introduction. Winter thought the man must have passed away earlier in the evening: no one this boring could still be alive. But even the dead have to stop speaking eventually. The corpse uttered his final words: "It's my honor to introduce the chairwoman of the Fairy Tale Fund, Molly Byrne."

Up Molly strode. The audience stood and applauded. Some whistled. Some cheered. It was explosive. Startling. Because it was real, Winter thought. They really loved her. They probably loved her for the work she did, feeding poor children and healing the sick and so on. But Winter suspected there was more to it than that. They loved her for who she was, he thought. Unpretentious. Joyful in her good fortune. The Cinderella Girl.

When the applause died down, she said in her funny pipsqueak voice, "All right, well, I must be the luckiest girl in the world. I get cheered for spending my husband's money."

Winter listened to her speech with his head leaning on his hand. It was his way of hiding his profile from Nelson.

"I look at my own three children," Molly said. "Gerald's children and mine. I look at how much they have. How fortunate they are. And then I see these children, the Fairy Tale children, who light up with happiness when they receive even a single toy at Christmas, or a chance at a good education, or even just a hot meal . . ."

As she spoke, more pictures of happy children flashed on the screens above her head to right and left. Once again, Winter was moved. Once again, doubts rose up inside him. Why was he here? What was he doing? What did it matter if a woman-beating drug dealer threw himself off a roof? If a crooked lawyer was exposed? If a blackmailer drove off a cliff? Look at all these happy children getting toys for Christmas and a hot meal! Maybe he should forget what he, after all, only suspected. Maybe he should just go home.

But no. There had to be more. He was sure of it. He was almost sure.

He did not go home. He waited through the speech. The audience laughed at Molly's jokes. They sniffled into handkerchiefs as she told stories about the children whose lives had been saved and changed. Winter also laughed at her jokes. He also sniffled. He was glad he had donated to the fund. What good work they were doing!

Molly finished. The audience rose to its feet again, applauding. Winter rose to his feet, safely obscured from Nelson's view by the standing crowd. He watched as Molly came down off the stage. She waved sweetly at her admirers. She moved to her table. Her fellow diners congratulated her. They gathered around her. One kissed her cheek. Two others shook her hand.

That was Winter's moment. He stepped into the small cluster that surrounded her. He extended his hand to her.

"Congratulations, Molly," he said.

She shook his hand without thinking. He pressed his business card into her palm. He saw the slight dullness of confusion in her eyes. He saw her glance down at the card.

Her smile went off like a switch had been thrown. Then she looked up at him. Their eyes met.

Winter was shocked. He nearly gasped aloud.

He had written only five words on the card he'd given her: *I know about your husband.* He had expected her to be puzzled. He expected her to be mildly concerned. He expected she would show the card to her husband. "Have you heard of this man Cameron Winter?" she would ask.

Byrne would be furious. He would feel that Winter had crossed onto forbidden ground. Molly was his wife, and she was more than his wife. After his trip to the Amazon, Byrne had traveled back to his father's church—back into his childhood. He had found a woman there with a secret sorrow, a sorrow like his mother had had. His mother had died, but Byrne had given this woman life.

145

Not just life, a perfect life. Just as in his Amazonian vision, he was the Savior. He was her Savior. He was his mother's Savior. He was the Savior of his own past. He would destroy anyone who threatened that salvation. When Winter handed Molly that card he was making that threat. If anything would coax Byrne into the open, he thought, this would do it.

That was what Winter expected anyway. That was what he was prepared for. He was not prepared—he was not prepared at all—for what in fact he saw in Molly's eyes when she looked up at him. All her joy was gone. All the sparkle—gone. Like that, like magic, hey *presto*. She read the card and looked at him and all he could see on her face was shock and horror.

My God, Winter thought. *She knows!*

But now she was turning away from him. She was turning toward the door where Nelson had been standing.

Winter followed her gaze. With another shock, he saw that Nelson was not standing at the door anymore. He had already spotted Winter. He was already stepping quickly toward him, trying to maneuver between the standing people and the tables and the chairs.

Winter took off, heading for the exit as fast as he could.

Nelson came after him.

16

What followed was a slow-motion chase through the ballroom. The standing people and their tables and chairs formed a sort of maze between the stage and the exits. Winter had to weave through them with Nelson weaving his way behind. The walls and ceilings decked out as the night sky with purple crepe and fairy lights seemed to render the pursuit celestial, as if the two men were constellations come to life, weaving through the stars.

Neither man ran. Neither wanted their confrontation to become public or disrupt the event. Winter dodged the obstacles with urgent purpose, a man on a mission. Nelson moved faster, more nimbly. By the time Winter reached one of the doors, the bodyguard had halved the distance between them. A few yards separated them, no more than that.

Winter pushed through the door and was quickly gone. The door swung shut behind him. Three seconds later Nelson burst out of the ballroom and went charging after him. He charged forward a few steps—then he halted in his tracks.

Winter was behind him. The moment the door had swung shut he had stopped short, tacked back, and planted himself in a spot by the wall where the door would hide him when it opened again.

Nelson had rushed right past him. He halted when he realized how he'd been tricked.

The bodyguard hung his head, shook his head in aggravation, self-disgust. His shoulders sagged. Winter could see an old, jagged scar on the back of his neck. Someone had knifed him once.

"Technically," Winter said, "you're dead now."

Nelson slowly turned around. He faced Winter. He grinned, that grinless grin showing a lot of teeth. Winter, leaning against the wall, tugged his black tie loose with one hand until it hung open on his white shirt. He unbuttoned his collar.

"A schoolboy prank, Winter," Nelson said, still grinning–not grinning.

"Yes. But you fell for it," said Winter. "And if I'd followed through, this conversation could have included considerably more bloodshed."

They were standing in the expansive area where the red carpet was. The wall behind the carpet was hung with a Fairy Tale Fund banner. The other walls were covered in flocked gold wallpaper. The whole scene was lit by two grand chandeliers.

"We could have that conversation now," Nelson suggested.

But before he could make a move, two men in suits came onto the scene. They walked side by side through the area, talking business. Clearly, this was no place to kill a man. It was much too public.

One corner of Winter's mouth lifted. He pushed off the wall, letting his hands slip into his trouser pockets.

"Tell you what," he said. "Why don't you walk me to my car instead?"

He had parked his rented Corvette on the street several blocks away. He had wanted to be able to avoid the crowd at the valet stand in the event he needed to make a quick escape.

"Hard to believe it's February," Winter remarked as the two men strolled shoulder to shoulder along the sidewalk of the broad boulevard outside the hotel. The Southern California air was balmy. It smelled of spring.

"I hate this city," said Nelson. "It's ugly and there's no weather. Like a big parking lot where nothing ever changes."

"It's a welcome break from the cold, though."

"I never mind the cold."

"Neither do I actually. I like it."

"Well, that covers the weather," Nelson said. "Good talk. How'd it be if I ripped you to pieces."

"Oh now, now," said Winter.

"What the hell do you think you're doing, Winter? What the hell is this all about? Your friend Adam Kemp was a piece of garbage."

"You're half right. He wasn't my friend."

"He killed himself because he got caught stealing from a gangster."

"Mm. So you keep telling me," said Winter.

"And what difference does it make anyway?"

"I'm not sure, to be honest. I'm still working that out."

"The point is, you don't know what you're dealing with."

"Don't I?"

"No," Nelson said. "You don't. What do you think, Mr. Byrne is just some guy? He's a powerful man, an influential man. Wealthy? He has more money than most countries have. He knows everyone everywhere, everyone who's important anyway. They all listen to what he says. They meet in Switzerland. They meet all over, places I've never even heard of. People I've never even heard of. They don't need anyone to hear about them. That's how important they are."

"All right," said Winter.

"It's not all right. That's what I'm trying to tell you." Nelson's handsome face was set hard. Fury had turned his features to stone. "What do you think you would do if you knew something about him? Tell someone?" He snorted. "Tell who? No one you told would tell anyone else. Not even the news media, them least of all. If he says someone can't say something, they can't say it, not so anyone'll hear. Doesn't matter if it's the president or what. You want to tangle with a man like that? Is Adam Kemp worth that? Is Adam Kemp worth anything?"

"It's an interesting question," Winter said.

Nelson stopped on the pavement. Winter stopped and faced him. Sparse evening traffic sailed past them, headlights reflected in the wide windows of the boulevard's clothing boutiques and antique stores.

"Byrne could make it so you lose your job," Nelson said. "He could make it so you'd never find another job again. He could ruin your life, Winter."

"He could do considerably more than that, though, couldn't he?" said Winter.

Once again, Nelson grinned that grin that was not a grin in any meaningful sense of the word. Once again, he shook his head in aggravation, glaring past Winter into the night.

"Let me tell you something, okay?" he said, and he spoke with surprising sincerity now. He stopped all the grinning. He punctuated his words by tapping the surface of the empty air with his fist. "Mrs. Byrne is the finest woman I've ever known. I can't even describe her to you. I watch her sometimes with her children. The way she is. I think about my own mother. I choke up. My own mother was not like that. I choke up thinking about it. About what a good person Mrs. Byrne is. I'm not even kidding."

He met Winter's eye. "A man like Byrne, he could have any woman he wanted. He used to. He used to do all that. He still could. He could have women all the time. It's what a lot of men in his position do. Married or not. I've worked for them. I know." He opened his fist and held his hand up. "But not him. Not Byrne. Not anymore. I would know if he did. He doesn't. He stopped. You know why? Because of her, because of what she's like. Mrs. Byrne. That's how fine a woman she is. And that's the kind of man he is. He really loves her."

"Sounds like he's not the only one," Winter said mildly.

The bodyguard's eyes flashed fire. "Don't get funny with me. Not with me. Not about her. I'm not a subtle guy. I'll tear you to pieces right here and now. Police? The news? I don't care. Right here and now, Winter."

Winter didn't react. He stood with his hands in the pockets of his tuxedo pants, his disassembled bow tie hanging loose around his open shirt. He was aware of a slight elevation in his heart rate. He was ready for a fight, but he did not really expect one, not out in the open like this.

For a few more seconds Nelson seethed, his fine features out of whack, contorted, flushed. But Winter was right. He would not attack. Not here.

"These are good people," he said. "Just . . ." He seemed to seek the right word in the Angeleno ether around him. "Stop," he finished finally. "Just stop. She's . . . you don't even know. And Mr. Byrne will do anything to protect her. Really. Anything. I mean, when this gets back to him. Tonight? What happened? I mean it. You may have already gone too far. You understand me?"

Winter answered nothing. He only nodded: he understood.

"You don't know how small you are," Nelson said. "You don't know how big he is. You don't know how quickly you can be over, and no one to say a word. Like that. Just over, Winter. And no one to say anything. Tonight? I'm telling you. You may have already gone too far. Just stop. Just stop."

He was finished then. He drew a breath. He shook his head one last time. Then he turned and walked away, back toward the hotel.

Winter watched him go. When he was gone he looked around him. The cars rushed by on the boulevard. The lights flashed in the storefront windows. The gibbous moon sailed across the meridian above, where the stars were washed away by the LA lights.

He felt himself a small and solitary figure in a vast and sprawling city under a vast and sprawling sky.

PART THREE

THE PRINCE
OF SHADOWS

So in our last session we were talking about assassins, right? About me and Roy being trained to be assassins. But maybe putting it like that gives the wrong impression, or at least a distorted one.

Assassins are not at all what you might think they are. In the movies, they always seem to be men with guns—or pretty women with guns. I don't actually go to the movies much. I find them incredibly insipid. But I see the posters, the ads, and there's always a picture of a man with a gun or a pretty girl with a low-cut dress and a gun.

But at the level we were working on in the Division, the government level, we don't really need guns. We have drones. A geek in Kansas whose training mostly involved playing video games until his mother told him it was time for bed can guide a device into a terrorist's ear canal and blow his head off without ever leaving Topeka. Sending some seductress to lure a bad guy into a bedroom at the Burj Al Arab so she can garrote him with his own belt in the underwater room is very cinematic, but what's the point if you can send him and his entire entourage to Kingdom Come by pressing a button seven thousand miles away?

The whole point of an assassination, in the sense I mean, is to destroy a man without anyone knowing you've done it. The whole point is for men—it's almost always men—to be neutralized as if by accident or by natural causes instead of by someone else's hand.

You see, Tolstoy was wrong about this. Individuals do matter. They really do. History is a force, it's true, but it's a force with faces. It's individuals who make it do what it does or at least they have a hand in it. And if a specific individual is taking history in a direction that is against the interests of our country, against the direction in which the leaders of our country feel it's right or good that it should go, then the question becomes how can that individual be made to exit the historical scene without our leaders having to explain their role in his departure.

This is what Roy and I trained for. This is what we learned how to do.

It wasn't about killing per se. Most of the time, nine times out of ten, you don't have to kill a man to neutralize him. Killing is a last resort.

Intelligence is key. Information. Information can be far more dangerous than a gun. You can see a gun coming. You might protect yourself against a gun. But information . . . it can come at you out of nowhere. That's what they taught us at our classes in the woods. With the Recruiter walking between our desks, looking over our shoulders, goading us. Poetry Boy. Half, half, half. *Those were the lessons we learned. How to find out what mattered to a target, where his weaknesses were. What might be used to put him out of commission or ruin him or bring him down. What might drive him to suicide. What might cause one of his enemies to take him out. That was what we studied. There were computer tricks—booby traps and backdoors that would let you into a diplomat's files or download child porn onto his computer. But that was not our department. We had a geek squad for that. Gathering intelligence and putting it to use—that was almost all of what we learned how to do.*

There were, I have to admit, a few things, one or two things, that had a cinematic feeling to them. Gadgets and gizmos that we were trained to use, even to build, some of them. There was one device, for instance. You could make it in your basement with materials you got at the hardware store. An almost invisible device that you could place in the workings of a car. You could track the car with it and then, at just the right moment, set it off. It would freeze the brakes and the steering. At just the right moment, you could send a man driving over a cliff or into oncoming traffic. And best of all you could destroy the device remotely after it was used so there was no trace of it. Just an unfortunate accident. The man must have fallen asleep at the wheel. It was not something you wanted to use often. But if once or twice, every few years, a movement leader, say, or a generalissimo or some obscure but influential party member made a bad turn on an icy mountain road, well, it might not even make the news.

We had a drug that could cause temporary symptoms of insanity. Used properly, it could destroy a man's reputation or career and be out of his bloodstream before anyone thought to check. That was one we did use the women for. To get close enough to dose the target. There is not one recorded incident that I'm aware of where a man turned down an invitation from an attractive female operative. They just don't do it. She beckons. He goes. It's a law of nature.

We had a gas that could cause a heart attack. That was a little trickier. It could be detected if a smart coroner knew what to look for, and if it wasn't administered right it could cause multiple deaths, which would blow the whole game. Then of course there were faked suicides and other violent scenarios that could be staged in certain circumstances without drawing attention to the United States. If there was a protest near an embassy, for instance, one or two of us might be on hand to make sure a riot broke out—and that the right attaché was tragically killed in the melee.

But for the most part all that stuff—devices, drugs, faked scenarios—these were not strategies we wanted to use if we didn't have to. It's much harder than you would think to pull this stuff off without getting caught, and not getting caught was the whole point. Getting caught could be a diplomatic and political disaster. Avoiding those disasters was the central brief of the Division.

No, it was mostly information we used. Intelligence, manipulation. To destroy people, to destroy their influence, to cause someone else to do the work of killing them. That was the business we were in.

I think that's why it didn't trouble me, at first, all psychological considerations aside. The people we targeted were very bad people, first of all. Truly evil. And it's not like we put a gun to their heads and pulled the trigger, or not often anyway. What we did do—well, there was something organic about it. If we exposed the fact that some Nazi was sleeping with a Jew or some white supremacist was having it on with a black girl or some Islamist cleric was homosexual—well, we didn't make the man a hypocrite. He did that himself. We just arranged for it to become known so as to destroy his credibility within his own bigoted circle. If some politician or thought leader made indefensible remarks in private and we caught it on audio it wasn't we who said what he said. We just brought it to light, that's all. And if we informed one drug dealer that another drug dealer was snitching to law enforcement, or if we told one warlord that a weapons merchant was selling him faulty matériel at the behest of another warlord, it wasn't us who killed the bad guy. In effect, they brought it on themselves.

Later, after a few years in the business, after I did some things, and some things happened, and consequences ensued and so forth—and after I grew to emotional manhood too, because remember, I went into the killing business very young—it was then that my conscience started to go dark on me. But at first it was almost like playing a kind of game. And as I say, our targets were some of the worst people on earth. Some of them, most of them, I'm still not sorry to have arranged for their destruction.

But it was different for Roy. Working for the Division troubled Roy from the beginning. It shifted a fault line in his character that I hadn't realized was there. Maybe I looked up to him so much I hadn't wanted to see what was happening to him. Or maybe I didn't want to ask myself the questions that he was asking. What are we doing? Who are we fighting? Who are we fighting for? What are we letting them turn us into?

Anyway, after our brawl in the hotel room, I won't say we drifted apart. That's not quite right. It's more that Roy drifted away from me. After that, when we got leave, he'd go off on his own a lot of times. I'd be left to drink alone. Chase women alone. A lot of times, I had no idea where he was. And when I'd ask him where he'd been I'd get no answer.

Once, though, I saw him. It was pure coincidence. Pure chance. We were in a city on the East Coast. We had reached a point in our training where we traveled to different places to learn different skills. So we were in this East Coast city learning how to trail a target in an urban environment. And we got a couple of days off. So I went to the boho district to find a good bar with willing women. And I found my way to this after-hours club. It was the sort of place you had to hear about from the locals. You had to flash a billfold at the peephole like in the old speakeasies from the twenties. And in I went. It was noisy. Crowded. Packed, really. And I just got a few steps through the door and I saw him. Roy.

He was seated at a table by the window. He was alone with a girl. I don't know what it was about her or about them that made me stop in my tracks. I just stood there staring with the dancers shoving me from every side, the music pounding in my head. The woman looked Middle Eastern but it wasn't just that. Roy and I dated all kinds of women. But the way she and Roy were leaning toward one another, the way they were talking. It wasn't romantic. It wasn't boy-girl, night-on-the-town stuff. It was more like we used to talk, he and I. Intense. Serious. Caught up on the wave of our ideas. It made me suspicious somehow.

All I know for sure is that when I saw him something in my stomach turned over, something toxic and ugly, like a creature rising up out of mud and then sinking back down again. I felt ill. I felt suddenly sorrowful. And I turned on my heels and walked out of the club then and there, before he could see me. I wandered around the city for an hour or so. Then I went back to my hotel and pillaged the minibar until I could sleep.

So that happened and then, a week after that, maybe two weeks, when we were back in the woods—back at Cathedral Station—the Recruiter summoned me to his office.

My relationship with the Recruiter had changed a lot by then. It was sort of like you said. As Roy had drifted away from me, I had adopted the Recruiter as my new mentor. It was the Recruiter who had made me into a secret soldier, who had given me a purpose and a cause. And more than that he had taught me—I don't know what you'd call it exactly—he'd taught me a way to be in the world. When I was in a room with him, I watched him like a boy watches his father. I imitated him subconsciously. His gestures, his way of speaking, his deadpan irony that was not irony but also was. Half the time I didn't even realize I was doing it.

Anyway, he summoned me to his office. A little barracks cubicle, barely big enough for a desk and two chairs. He was sitting at the desk when I came in. He gestured me into the chair across from him. I sat. He leaned forward. His face was not much more than a foot away from mine. With his hands clasped on the desktop, he regarded me intensely. It went on a long time. Silence. Staring. It made me squirm in my seat.

"Do you believe in God, Poetry Boy?" he asked me suddenly.

I was taken aback. "I . . . I don't know, sir," I said.

"You don't know."

"No, sir."

"You can't decide whether the universe was fashioned in the Mind of Eternal Wisdom or whether it was farted randomly out of the Asshole of Nothingness. You're not willing to take a position on that question. Do I understand you correctly?"

"More or less, sir, yes."

"More or less. That is more or less your piss-poor absurdly ridiculous response to the most important philosophical question of any man's life. That is what you're telling me," said the Recruiter.

I nodded, trying not to look as idiotic as I felt.

"The United States government has been training you now for nearly half a year. We have spent a great deal of time and effort not to mention the pillaged tax dollars of your hardworking fellow citizens teaching you how to kill or otherwise destroy the enemies of our nation. Does that bother you?"

"No, sir."

"Why not? Are you a psychopath? Are you a madman who is willing to kill on demand without remorse?"

"I don't think I'm a psychopath, sir."

"Are you aware that that's exactly what a psychopath would say?"

I almost laughed but caught myself. "Yes, sir."

"And you're aware that the mind of Eternal Wisdom has delivered a commandment saying thou shalt not kill, as it is written in his Holy Word, which is the Bible?"

"Uh . . . yes. Yes, sir. I've heard of that."

"You've heard of that, have you? You've heard of God's Holy Word the Bible?"

"I have, sir."

"But you, Cameron Winter, are not constrained by God's Holy Word the Bible because you take no position on whether God exists or is merely an illusion created by inhaling the toxic effusions of the Universal Rectum. Is that a fair restatement of your deeply considered philosophical outlook?"

"I think so, sir."

"You think so. All right, then. We've established that you are a godless psychopath who will kill on demand without the remorse or even the philosophical hesitations that would raise him above the intellectual level of a rabid beast. I think we can safely say you are ready for your first government assignment."

At this, I felt excitement begin to course through me. The preliminaries were over. This was the business at hand: I was being dispatched on my first real-life mission for the Division.

"Sir," I managed to say.

The Recruiter had not moved so much as an inch since I'd entered. He was still leaning forward on his desk, his hands clasped on the desktop, the expression on his dark brown face utterly unreadable. "Alright, then," he said in the same brusque monotone. "Here are your orders. You are to transport a laptop computer from one certain city to another certain city and deliver it into the hands of workers in that second city. Would you like me to tell you why?"

"It's not necessary, sir."

"Of course it's not necessary to you. We've established that you're a godless psychopath and can therefore have no basis for forming a judgment as to the moral worth of this assignment. But I am not a godless psychopath. I am a God-fearing, Jesus-loving patriotic American and therefore feel compelled to explain to you that I am, in fact, sending you on a mission of high moral worth. This laptop computer contains the specs for a new armed drone that, when built, will be about the size of a mosquito. With this new drone, we will be able to deliver death to our nation's enemies in a manner both target specific and completely undetectable. The specs for this addition to the arsenal of democracy are too important to be trusted to the internet where they might be stolen by some thirteen-year-old bucktoothed Chinese geek and used against us by his Communist overlords. Do I make myself understood?"

"I believe it's the Japanese who are traditionally depicted as buck-toothed, sir."

"Are you trying to tell me that you cannot distinguish between the beauteous and complex creation of Eternal Wisdom and a random Cosmic Fart, but you presume to instruct me on the proper use of derogatory racial stereotypes?"

"I withdraw the comment, sir."

"You will be ready tomorrow at zero-five-thirty. You will not carry a phone or any other device that can be tracked or connected to the internet. You will be driven to the airport where you will fly to the first of your two cities. In the airport, you will stop at a Steak N Brew restaurant and order a cup of coffee. While you are drinking the coffee, an operative will approach you and speak the following words: 'Excuse me, but didn't

we meet at the conference in Seattle?' To which you will respond: 'Yes, of course. I remember.' You will then chat briefly and when the operative walks away, the laptop will have been placed near at hand. You will take the laptop and pick up an ice blue Dodge Charger that has been left for you in lot two, space forty-seven-F. The Charger will have no GPS or internet connections. You will drive to a certain motel, where you will stay overnight. And in the morning, you will continue on to the next city where you will stop at the Steak N Brew restaurant in the North Pine Mall. There, you will see this man."

He moved for the first time since I'd entered the room. Drew a phone from his jacket pocket. Showed the photograph on the phone's screen to me for about a second, then withdrew it. "You will approach this man and you will say, 'Excuse me, but didn't we meet at the conference in Seattle?' to which he will reply, 'Yes, of course, I remember.' You will then chat briefly and walk away, leaving the laptop where he can pick it up inconspicuously. You will then drive to the airport and fly home, where you will be collected by our operatives. Do you copy that, Poetry Boy?"

Now, of course, these instructions had been so complicated that it was everything I could do just to listen and commit them to memory. I barely had time to ask myself the questions that would occur to me later, and I'm not sure I would have dared to ask the Recruiter even if they had occurred to me then. The only thought in my mind or desire in my heart was to fulfill my duty with efficiency and excellence. So my answer was simply, "I copy that, sir," and nothing else.

The Recruiter moved again—he nodded once. "You are dismissed. You may return to your nihilistic and morally confused existence."

"Thank you, sir."

I got up out of my chair.

"And you'll be taking Spahn with you," said the Recruiter, as if it were an afterthought.

I stopped. I was not sure why my heart misgave me, but it did. "Roy?" I said.

"That's right. He's already been briefed."

For a moment, I stood staring at him, trying to locate the source of my misgivings.

"What's the matter?" the Recruiter asked me. "You don't want to work with Spahn?"

"No, I—"

"Are you some sort of racist, Winter? Do you have some objection to working with a mulatto American?"

"No, sir!"

"Good. Then that will be all."

As I walked back to my barracks I was in a divided state. My mind was so occupied with memorizing the details of my instructions that I hardly had time to notice that my heart was in turmoil. But it was. So many questions were nagging at me—and nagging at me urgently because of the suspicion, just beneath the surface of my consciousness, that the answers hinted at something ominous. It almost seemed as if the complexity of the briefing was itself a sort of distraction, a strategic ruse designed to keep me from seeing the truth.

Why was I being used as a courier? That's not what I had trained for. Could they really not trust this material to the internet? Were our systems really that insecure? Why a laptop and not a drive? Why did they need two of us to do the job? And since there were two of us, wouldn't it have been safer to drive overnight and avoid staying at a motel? And all that talk about morality and God came back to me too. Was the Recruiter just trolling me? Or was he trying to tell me something? Was that part of the riddle or part of the distraction?

It wasn't until later that night, early, really, the next morning, as I lay in my bunk staring at the ceiling, that these questions and my misgivings all resolved themselves into a single conjecture, one awful idea. That strange habit of mind came over me. I stopped trying to work the riddle out and simply let its components play through my mind like puzzle pieces tumbling in space. No opinions. No theories. Just objects, tumbling.

Then, with a sharp breath, I sat up in the dark. My heart thundered as I peered into the shadows. Everything was suddenly clear to me. My mission was not the laptop at all, not some transfer of supersecret technology at all.

My mission was Roy. Of course it was. It couldn't have been me. I was all in. The Division was home to me now. The Recruiter would know that.

No, it was Roy. I had trained to become an assassin and I was being sent out on my first hit. And my best friend was the target.

17

In nearly forty years as a therapist Margaret Whitaker had rarely felt afraid while doing her job. Once, shortly after she'd begun her practice, an angry male client had flown into a rage, and that had been unsettling. He was a tall, burly man. He had leapt out of his seat. He had stood screaming down at her, shaking his fist. But she had stayed calm. She had struck an imperious pose in her chair. She had commanded him to sit down right that minute—and he had. It was a bad moment, but the rest of the session—and the rest of the man's therapy—had passed without incident.

Then there was the time—even worse, in its way—when another male client had formed a romantic attachment to her. He had laced their conversations with sexual innuendo. He had described his fantasies about her in elaborate detail under the guise of doing therapeutic work. After she terminated his therapy, he had phoned and emailed her obsessively. That had raised her anxiety level for a while. But finally her husband answered one of the man's phone calls and gave him a talking-to. After that he moved on.

Most of her clients were what therapists called the Wounded Well. They were decent, high-functioning people just trying to get past some childhood trauma or to fix their marriage or to become more effective at work. There wasn't a lot of danger involved in dealing with them.

But as Winter's long narrative came to an end, Margaret became aware that she was afraid. In fact, she suddenly realized she had been living under a cloud of fear for the past several days.

Ever since she had noticed the wooden dog.

Margaret was—or thought of herself as—an old cat lady now, but when her husband, Mark, had been alive, they had had a dog. Victoria was a golden retriever. They had gotten her for their son, but as their son grew into a troubled adolescent and went astray, Victoria had become theirs—hers and Mark's. She was a beautiful, enthusiastic, and affectionate creature, and they had come to love her with a passion. She was a consolation, Margaret suspected, for their failure as parents.

When Victoria died at the ripe old age of fifteen, Margaret was grief-stricken. In a sentimental moment, she bought a little wooden carving of a retriever as a remembrance. She had put the wooden dog on the living room mantelpiece, facing out at the room. She would look at it from time to time and smile, remembering Victoria.

Years went by. Her husband passed. She sold their house and moved into her apartment. She brought the little wooden dog with her. She put it on a shelf in the dining nook. But this time she positioned the retriever facing toward the window, toward the east.

She did not like to admit this to herself, but placing the wooden dog just so was a symbolic and superstitious gesture. Margaret had been raised a Lutheran. Mark had been an atheist. During their marriage she had stopped going to church.

Apparently, though, some of her early training had stuck with her because, in her widowhood, she started going to church again.

She told herself this was more for practical reasons than religious. Church gave her a society. Church work gave her a feeling of purpose. Other than that, she wasn't very clear or specific with herself about what she believed.

But deep down, without thinking about it much, she did harbor some vague hope of an ongoing existence after death. Reunions. Reconciliations. Relationships redeemed and restored. And she hoped Victoria would be there, good loving girl that she had been. Margaret had pointed the wooden dog to the east because that's where the sun rises again at the beginning of a new day. It was a silent prayer that there would be a resurrection.

So now she was afraid. Because the dog was always on the shelf and always facing directly east. And someone or something had moved the dog.

She could not be absolutely sure of this. She might have bumped the shelf herself walking past. The cat might very well have climbed on it and turned the wooden dog with her tail. There was no specific reason for her to believe anything dark or threatening was going on. Margaret scolded herself for being a nervous old biddy. She told herself she had let Winter make her jittery with all his talk of assassinations and secret government skulduggery. She spent too much time daydreaming herself into his past, imagining a younger Margaret in a dangerous affair with the dashing spy. She could call it countertransference all she liked, but that was just a fancy-pants term for infatuation. She had developed a crush on her tweedy and lethal client, and now her fantasies had metastasized into a sense of menace.

She told herself all this. The problem was: it didn't quite explain away the menace. After all, it was Winter himself who had warned her to be careful, who had told her not to keep detailed notes of what he said to her. He had been serious about this. He must also have thought there was at least a chance that something ugly might happen.

Which made sense. Winter trusted her enough now to open up to her about the violence in his past. He needed to confess it to her. He needed her maternal absolution. Which was good for his therapy. But there was no getting around the fact that it meant he was sharing secrets with her. Important secrets she was not supposed to know. He could blur the details. He could refer to "a certain city," or to "gadgets and gizmos," and avoid getting too specific. Still, the fact remained. He was telling her about a classified, deadly, and probably illegal government operation: the Division. It didn't require her overactive imagination to see there might be some danger involved in her knowing about that.

So it had been a shock when, shortly after their last session, she noticed the dog. She had been sitting in her easy chair. She had been sipping her morning tea and stroking the cat in her lap. She had glanced up and noticed the wooden retriever on the shelf just above eye-level to her right. She had seen it was no longer facing east. It was facing northeast. Not as it would be if the cat had brushed it. Not as it might be if she herself had jostled the shelf. No matter how many times she talked herself out of this, she knew it was positioned exactly as it would be if someone had picked it up and set it down again—carefully, but not quite carefully enough, not quite understanding how specific the symbolism was, not quite realizing that she would notice the difference of even a quarter of an inch.

She had become afraid. She had become convinced that someone had been in her apartment. She had tried to deny and suppress the fear. She had tried not to notice it was there. But today, with Winter seated in the client chair right in front of her, with him telling her his sinister tales again, the fear had blossomed inside her like a black flower. Her throat was dry. Her hands were unsteady. For a long moment she didn't know what to say.

"Why are you telling me this, Cam?" she asked finally.

He came out of a fugue state. He blinked up at her through his wire-rimmed glasses. "Why?" He seemed to give the question serious thought. When he responded, he spoke slowly, as if feeling his way toward the truth. "I'm almost forty, Margaret, and all alone. Crushingly alone. Spiritually alone. Without even memories of real intimacy. Barely with dreams of it. The regrets you have about yourself, the chances you missed, the roads you never took—you learn to live with those after a while. You reconcile yourself to the life you have and the lives you never had and never will. But the sins you've committed against others, the hurt you've caused, the lives you've damaged, ended—how can you forget those? How can you forgive yourself for them? And where can you go to reconcile with the dead?"

He offered a wan smile, a *wintry* smile, she thought. He said: "I'm not looking for much at this point anymore. Really just a woman to ask me how things went at the end of the day, to care how things went and be cared for in return. But that's the very thing, the one thing, I can't seem to allow myself." He gestured with one hand in the air. "I need to tell you these things, Margaret. I need to tell you how it came to this. I need you to hear the worst of it, and then in honesty—in honesty, only if you can—I need you, you specifically, to pronounce me worthy to be loved."

Margaret gazed at him calmly, trying to hide the flaming anxiety inside her. "Some people go to God for that," she said.

That smile again. "Some people do, I guess. I came to you."

She almost answered him with her whole heart. She almost said: *No. No. It's too much, my darling. It's too much to ask of me. I'm an old woman, Cameron. I live alone. I'm afraid. I'm not up to it. Violence is familiar to you. Not to me. I just want to live in peace and die and see my sweet retriever running to greet me out of the rising sun. Don't tell me these things anymore.*

It was right on her lips to say all that. But she didn't say any of it. She didn't even tell him about the little wooden dog. Because she understood that Winter was right. He needed this. He needed to tell her. He needed to show her the blood on his hands and cry out: *Look! Look what I've done!* and have her draw him to her breast and murmur, *There, there. There, there.*

She wanted that also. She wanted it too much, and not entirely in the right way, not entirely in the professional, therapeutic, make-believe maternal way that was required of her. But all the same, she wanted very much to give him what he needed, wanted it so much that she couldn't bring herself to tell him about her fear. She could not bring herself to tell him that they—whoever *they* were—had come into her home and moved her wooden dog and that she was terrified they would come back and hurt her.

"Well," was all she said finally, "our time is up for today."

18

Winter left the therapy session deeply troubled. What, he kept asking himself, had Margaret been about to tell him? What had she stopped herself from saying out loud?

He could not imagine what it might be. She had become so important to him, such a powerful influence in his life, that he could not fully cope with the idea that she also might have a complex inner life, a life complete with flaws, sins and failures, regrets and fears. He was so immersed in the good work she was doing in him, he could not spare a thought for what he might be doing to her.

And he didn't have time to spare that thought now. Now, he had to hurry to meet Stan-Stan Stankowski.

Stan "Stan-Stan" Stankowski was an undercover federal agent and, not coincidentally, a lunatic. He looked on his assignments as if they were episodes in a television show that was constantly playing itself out inside his mind. He approached each new undercover placement as if he were a method actor approaching a role. He immersed himself in his cover so completely that his own personality vanished. Which was just as well. It was not the sort of personality one wanted running around loose on the streets of a civilized city.

The last time Winter had seen Stan-Stan, he had been infiltrating a biker gang. His five-foot-seven frame had been thick with muscle and his acne-scarred face was barely visible between the bottom of his black watch cap and the top of his bushy white beard. Today, apparently, he was infiltrating . . . an accountancy firm? . . . the IRS? . . . the cast of a summer stock production of *How to Succeed in Business*? Winter couldn't be sure. But in any case the leather jacket and bushy beard had been traded in for a gray suit and a close shave. Somehow, he seemed less muscular than he'd been. Somehow, his acne scars were gone. Somehow he had utterly transformed himself into a prim, slim, bespectacled, and thoroughly boring man of business.

He was sitting in a booth near the dimly lit rear of the Nomad Tavern. He was drinking coffee and reading a paper edition of the *Wall Street Journal*.

Winter slipped into the booth behind him. "A newspaper?" he murmured. "What are you, Stanley, undercover in the 1950s?"

"Try not to be a pain in the ass when you're being a pain in the ass, would you, Winter," Stan-Stan muttered in response. Even his voice was different than it had been when he was a biker. Then it was a threatening rumble. Now it was a narrow whine.

The two men were seated back-to-back, separated only by the backs of their benches. The tavern was furnished with other such booths, plus tables and a bar, all made of dark wood. Colorful state flags billowed above, tacked up over the pressed tin ceiling. The place was about a block from the capitol building, so it was a local lunch spot for government underlings. They were still seated here and there, lingering over the last crumbs of their lunch. Stan-Stan fit right in.

A waitress approached. Winter ordered a couple of eggs and toast. As the waitress retreated Stan-Stan said, "Oh good. I wouldn't want you to go hungry while you're blowing my cover." He had put an earbud in his ear so people would think he was talking on the phone.

"I need to know about a guy named Nelson," Winter said.

"The British admiral or the country singer?"

"A bodyguard for a billionaire named Gerald Byrne." Winter put an earbud in his ear too. He smiled at the waitress as she returned to pour him coffee—smiled distantly, as if he were listening to a voice on the bud. He waited for her to leave before he said, "I think he's ex-Division."

"You're an English professor now, right? Poetry? Roses are red, violets are blue, that sort of thing? What do you care what he is?"

"I think he's running wet ops for Byrne."

There was an uncharacteristic silence from Stan-Stan. A government-trained assassin pulling hits for a private citizen was no small matter. Winter seized the pause to press on.

"There's only one guy who would know for sure," he said. "Only one guy who would know and also might talk to me."

More silence. Then Stan-Stan gave a deep chuckle, a loud chuckle, as if the person he was pretending to talk to on the phone had just made a hilarious joke about commodities trading or some such thing. "Nobody sees the Recruiter, Winter. He's kind of like God that way. He's also like God because he can give you cancer just by thinking about it. You don't want to bother him."

"He'll see me."

"Why? Because you're a highbrow fop with a face like a kewpie doll?"

"Don't hate me because I'm beautiful, Stan-Stan."

Winter heard Stan-Stan sigh out of a sip of coffee—"Ah!"—heard his cup clatter against its saucer. Then again came the uncannily transformed sound of his voice. "The next time you look over your shoulder, Winter, not only will I not be here, I will never have been here. This aggravating sense I have that I've been gulled into risking my life to trade spy versus spy fantasies with a fatuous amateur whose main business is inflecting verbs will have gone away because this conversation will not have occurred. I won't even have to teach myself to stop thinking about you because it will be as if you don't exist. I believe I've conveyed my response to your request without stooping to the use of a four-letter obscenity but, believe me, the obscenity is implied."

"Thanks, Stan-Stan. I'll wait to hear from you."

The waitress brought Winter his plate of eggs and toast. He began to eat. And just as predicted, when he next looked over his shoulder, Stan-Stan was not even a memory.

19

When Winter taught his Wordsworth class that afternoon, he found himself going on an unplanned riff about Wordsworth's autobiographical poem *The Prelude*. He started thinking out loud about how the poet's developing views on politics and faith changed the way he wanted to tell the story of his life and gave new shades and meanings to incidents in his past. This raised several questions in Winter's mind. Was Wordsworth rewriting his life to fit his new wisdom? Or was he uncovering new meaning in his life as his wisdom deepened? Does the truth about our biographies reveal itself as we go on, or does the truth actually change as we change?

These questions so fascinated Winter in the moment that even he could hear he had become passionate and eloquent. When he ended the lecture he felt as if he were coming out of a trance of inspiration. The students apparently felt it too. They actually applauded him. Then they gathered around him, chattering with enthusiasm. It was a gratifying moment.

He had planned to head for his office in the Gothic next. There was a new trail he wanted to follow in his ongoing research into Gerald Byrne. Instead, though, buoyed up by his successful lecture, he found himself heading for the Independent coffee shop.

He'd been avoiding the coffee shop these past few days. He did not want to see Hannah Greer again. That is, he did want to see her, but he thought it wouldn't be a good idea. His therapy had made him hypersensitive to his solitude, and the pang of longing Hannah had caused in him was deep and real. He especially didn't want to go to the shop hoping he would see her there—and that was the only way he could go since he did hope so, and so he hadn't gone at all.

Even now, as he crossed the campus heading toward the Independent, he was aware that his upbeat mood was betraying him. Feeling vital and vibrant, he was allowing his yearning to draw him toward Hannah like an invisible cord. He kept willing himself to change the direction of his steps but he couldn't seem to do it. He could only go on, wondering at the power women had. To do this to men with just their looks, their manner, a word or two, not even that. It was a power sometimes more dangerous to themselves than to others, and yet such a power. What must it be like to be one of them in the beauty of her prime?

He reached the Independent. Hannah was not there. He was both relieved and sorry at the same time. But he pretended to put her out of his mind. Supplied with his usual afternoon coffee and croissant, he set up his laptop and went to work. He called up videos of Henry Woolsey.

Woolsey was—or had once been—a podcaster who was—or used to be—very popular on the political right. A rotund, cuddly-looking little man who favored grandfatherly cardigans and circular specs, he had an emotional delivery that had had a wide appeal. He mixed his charm with deep research into what he considered looming crises and dark conspiracies on the national and international scene. He unfurled this research to his video audience through elaborate charts that he energetically scribbled on blackboards, and he had a flair for explaining his ideas in such a way that they came to seem urgent and personal to the audience. Before the crisis that had destroyed his career, that audience had risen into the millions.

Winter himself had no politics anymore, not since the Division. Since his experiences undercover, he felt only the warm assurance that the nastiest possible people were making the worst imaginable decisions at all times. Other than that, he was done with the political aspect of the human enterprise.

Because of this, he had never experienced the talents of Henry Woolsey. Watching Woolsey's videos now on his laptop, he found the commentator engaging, even occasionally mesmerizing. How much of what he said was actually true he had no way of judging. Maybe he was crazy. Maybe he was exactly right. Winter had taught himself not to care about such things.

All he wanted to know was this: what had Woolsey said about Gerald Byrne in the weeks before he destroyed his own career?

That turned out to be a difficult question to answer. Woolsey's rants against Byrne were remarkably hard to find. It was as if—it was almost exactly as if—they had been purposely scrubbed from the internet. That was why it had taken Winter so long just to find out they even existed. He had stumbled on the fact of them only while surfing some obscure and dark-minded conspiracy forum for information on Byrne.

Now, at his table in the Independent, he followed the outlaw pathways into even deeper and darker corners of cyberspace. At last, he began to unearth what looked like videos of the original Woolsey videos. Shaky images, hollow sound. But he could make out the sense of them well enough.

"While Gerald Byrne conspires with his fellow billionaires to channel the whole world's taxes toward his pet projects, to ration our energy use, and to silence all opposition, he himself pays no taxes at all, he himself flies anywhere he wants in fuel-guzzling private jets, and his opinions shape the algorithms of what we can and can't find online. He's a prince of shadows, out to control the world."

There was more like this, a lot more. So much that, after a while, Winter began to feel overwhelmed by it. It was like being underwater, as if Woolsey's ideas were a suffocating element in which he was submerged. To break the spell, he turned away from the monitor—and who to his wandering eyes should appear, seated in the farthest corner of the coffee shop, but his old nemesis Lori Lesser.

When he first saw her, she was leaning over a notepad, but she raised her eyes to his so quickly he felt sure she must have been watching him this whole time.

Their eyes met. She smiled thinly. If he had harbored any hopes that she might have forgiven him for his rebuff of her advances, those hopes would have died then and there—but he had not harbored any, so no harm done.

She nodded a cold, cold greeting at him. For the life of him, he could not think of a single response that would improve his standing with her. A friendly smile and she would think he was insensitive to her hurt feelings. A nod as cold as hers and she would feel he was hostile. What other choices did he have?

He finally allowed a vague expression of some sort to flicker over his face in answer. He could read in Lori's eyes that she took this as an insult. She sniffed and went back to scribbling whatever she was scribbling on her pad.

Ah well. He returned his attention to Woolsey.

He next located a video with a far more solemn tone, even an ominous tone. Leaving the crowded blackboards behind, Woolsey sat on a step on his set and addressed the audience directly. He spoke as if amazed by what had happened to him.

"I was visited by an ambassador from Gerald Byrne yesterday. I won't give you his name. It doesn't matter. He called my producer to make an appointment. We met in a local restaurant for lunch. As I began eating, he leaned over the table toward me and these were his exact words. He said, 'You are interfering with Mr. Byrne's plans, Mr. Woolsey. Do you understand what I'm telling you. You are interfering with Mr. Byrne's plans.'"

The final video before Woolsey's career-destroying disaster was almost impossible to find. It had not only apparently been scrubbed from the sunlit boulevards of the internet, it seemed to have vanished even from its hellish, criminal, and pornographic casbahs. Another thirty minutes of searching and all Winter could come up with was one two-minute clip embedded in someone else's mocking satire. The clip showed Woolsey running from blackboard to blackboard again, babbling excitedly about a French businessman and politician named Arnaud Baptiste.

"Baptiste was mobilizing—mobilizing—resistance to Byrne's plans. He had made visits here—here—and here . . ." he cried wildly, smacking the edge of his chalk against the board with every *here*.

When Winter saw this his eyes widened. He straightened in his chair. Suddenly, his blood was up. A hunter's rush reddened his cheeks. All this time, since he had first formed his suspicions about the suicide of Adam Kemp, he had thought—he had been almost sure—he would find something more. Something more than a woman beater hounded to his death. Something more than a blackmailer sent flying off the road into fiery perdition or a bullying businessman exposed for his misdemeanors. He knew the ways of these secret assassinations. He had himself carried them out. Once you began to weed the garden of the world, it was hard to stop short of blood-drenched perfection. He had felt sure—almost sure—there would be more and now . . .

Now there was Arnaud Baptiste.

"Don't you see? Don't you see?" Henry Woolsey was crying out from the laptop, smacking the edge of his chalk against the board in helpless, hopeless urgency. "Arnaud Baptiste was standing up against the Good World Project. For you. For us. For liberty! Just like me, he, too, was interfering with Gerald Byrne's plans!"

The video ended. Winter slumped in his seat. He gazed at the dark monitor. His hands moved across the keyboard.

A single search brought up the information he already vaguely remembered. Arnaud Baptiste had been killed in a riot in Paris two years before Woolsey's videos were made. He had been dragged from his car and beaten to death by a mob. His was only one of several deaths over the days of unrest. The city had been in chaos. The perpetrators were never found.

"Professor Winter."

Startled out of his grim conjectures, Winter looked up quickly. His lips parted in surprise.

Hannah Greer.

Once again, she was standing suddenly beside him, standing like a schoolgirl this time, with her books held to the graceful curve of her breasts. Her golden hair was wound around her head in a corona braid—just the way Charlotte used to wear her hair, like a German fraulein from days of yore. Once again, she was dressed with antiquated ladylike charm. A long orange skirt. A white blouse with orange embroidery. A lapis necklace blue as her eyes. Her eyes were gleaming with enthusiasm.

Winter plucked the earpods from his ears so he could hear her.

"I'm really sorry to bother you again, but I had to tell you," she said. "I audited your class today. I heard your lecture on the *Prelude*. It was . . ." Like all students, she seemed to search for just the right adjective before settling on exactly the same adjective every other student used. "Amazing!"

"Oh, well, thank you," Winter said with cool modesty. But his brain was a house afire. A quick sidelong glance told him that Lori Lesser was still in the shop, still watching him—glaring at him now with frank hostility and suspicion. And meanwhile his heart—well, it wasn't breaking. It was already broken, long broken. And something about this young woman in front of him seemed to bring warmth into that cold and broken place.

He almost laughed at himself aloud. He had wanted her to turn up. He had come to the coffee shop hoping she would. It was a secret he had only half kept from himself. Now to have her appear beside him while Lori was there, right there glaring at him and no doubt plotting his professional demise—well, it was a fine irony. Because it was what he deserved, wasn't it? If he was going to lust after a student not even half his age because his lonesome soul was frozen in the past, then to be hounded by a snake-haired fury like Lori was only rough justice.

Even now, of course, he might have turned Hannah away. But, of course, he didn't. Some rebellious contrarian impulse in his masculine nature had already resolved to invite her to sit with him. It amused him to stoke the fire of vengeance in Lori's heart. Oh, what a piece of work is a man!

"I know you're busy," Hannah said. "And I don't want to bother you, but if I could just sit for a second . . ."

"Please do," Winter answered smoothly.

Well, she asked, he told himself. And it wasn't his fault she had happened to be auditing his class during one of his most brilliant lectures. He hadn't even known she was in the hall at the time. This accidental meeting in a much-trafficked coffee shop was a wholly innocent, completely blameless, spotlessly innocuous . . .

But he forgot what he was lying to himself about when she sat across from him and he felt the force of her sweet anachronistic presence so very, very close.

Now she was talking to him with enthusiasm—with passion, really. *Let's call it what it is,* he thought. Her eyes were bright. Her elegant white hands were in motion. She repeated his lecture back to him in a girlish celebration of its originality and brilliance.

The heat that flooded his mind was pathetic even to himself. It was not the heat of a man for a woman. Not even the cheap ego heat he might have felt while being flattered by a pretty teen. It was a warmth remembered, the warmth of long ago. As a little boy, he had lain in bed one Christmas Eve, in a strange bed in his nanny's house, awake and afraid of phantoms. Charlotte had come in to sit with him, just a child herself, but an earnest little mother spirit in the dark. She had patted his hand until he was comforted and could sleep. How hungry for that simple, feminine tenderness he had been back then. How hungry he was for it now, this very minute. And there it was in Hannah's bright, passionate eyes.

Still in the grip of his perverse masculine sense of humor and rebellion, he shifted his glance from Hannah to Lori. Again, he almost laughed aloud. Rage had turned her face to ice and her eyes to fire. It was what she would have looked like had she been a satire of herself, a cruel portrait scrawled on a wall by her enemies. To Winter, the situation felt as hilarious as it was dangerous.

"Well," Hannah said finally. "I've taken up too much of your time."

"Not at all," said Winter. "I always have time for flattery."

"Oh, but it's not flattery. It really isn't. I was afraid you would think it was. But it's not."

"No, no, I understand. You're very kind. I appreciate it, Hannah. Really."

"Well . . ." said Hannah—and she should have risen to go, but instead he saw her search his eyes for something more.

"I'm sure we'll speak again soon," he said. That was all he said, but it was all that was needed. He felt the unmistakable *click* of understanding and connection between them. It was right there in her bright gaze, imperceptible and unmistakable: she was willing, willing for them to meet again. Soon.

As she walked away he glanced back at Lori. He nearly pitied her. Because what could she do? A student had sat with him to discuss a lecture. Nothing more. And though doubtless she could see as well as he could the invisible and yet utterly visible play of attraction between them, she could never make her case against him, not even in the feverish sexual star chamber of a university like this one. Nothing had happened, only everything. The way of a man with a maid.

Suppressing a small smile of nasty satisfaction, Winter popped the earpods back in his head and returned to his laptop, back to Henry Woolsey.

This last video—the video in which Woolsey destroyed himself—this was the only one of the relevant videos that was easy to find. Suspiciously easy. It hadn't been scrubbed from a single site online. It was not only available everywhere but available in various forms as well. It came complete. It came edited into supercut compilations of its highlights. It came with music and with Woolsey's voice autotuned for added comedic effect. If Woolsey's conspiracy theories against Gerald Byrne had disappeared into wherever things disappear when powerful men decree they must, then this video was sprinkled like apple seeds across the fertile soil of the internet's hostile imagination.

Winter sat watching. Unconsciously, he pursed his lips, wrinkled his nose. It was the expression of a man who had caught the stench of something rotten.

It was rotten, all right. On the laptop screen, Woolsey was ranting at his blackboards again. But this time, instead of heavily researched speculations, he was off on a tirade of the ugliest racial hatred imaginable. It was bizarre. Despite the usual accusations of his enemies, Woolsey had never before said a word that Winter found in any way bigoted. Yet here he was, spitting—literally spitting out—half-baked slurs against blacks and Jews. Frenetically, he scratched connections onto his chalkboard, connections this time not between one fact and another but between one low prejudice and another. It actually made Winter flinch at times with moral disgust. The ugliness seemed to be gouting out of Woolsey's mind like arterial blood.

And what made it even more painful to watch? Winter knew that such a moment of madness could be easily induced through the expert use of drugs. He himself knew how to do it. He himself had done it once upon a time, destroying the career of a would-be dictator who had been gaining too large a following in a foreign land. He had no doubt that Nelson the bodyguard knew how to do it too.

You are interfering with Mr. Byrne's plans, the messenger from Byrne had told Woolsey. *Do you understand what I'm telling you?*

Winter wondered if that messenger had looked anything like the handsome Eurasian bodyguard who had told Winter much the same thing outside the hotel in Los Angeles: *You don't know how small you are. You don't know how big he is. You don't know how quickly you can be over, and no one to say a word. You understand me?*

So it had been for Woolsey: he was over. After this truly disgusting tirade, he had been banned from the main social media sites, including

Gerald Byrne's Byrner. He had lost all his sponsors and most of his supporters. The supporters who remained were despicable racists. His tearful apologies profited him nothing. His attempts to demonstrate that he had reformed were embarrassing and pitiful. The deed was done. As far as the internet was concerned, he had exposed his twisted, hate-filled soul and there could be no hiding it ever again.

The video ended. Winter sighed. He removed the earbuds. It was only then that he noticed his phone was buzzing where it lay on the table next to his plate of croissant crumbs. The identity of the caller was blocked. He answered.

"Professor Winter," said a woman's voice.

"Speaking."

"My name is Brenda Wallace."

"I'm sorry, I don't know . . ." But then he remembered. Brenda Wallace had been Brenda Shea, sister to Evelyn Shea, who had been beaten by Adam Kemp, and to Molly Shea, who was now Molly Byrne. Brenda was the Serious One, the eldest of the Shea sisters. She had married Jack Wallace and helped him turn his furniture store into a multistate chain.

"Oh yes," said Winter. "Yes, of course. What can I do for you, Mrs. Wallace?"

"There's someone who'd like to meet with you," she said.

Winter's heart sped up. He was stunned into silence. *Molly?* he thought. But who else could it be? She must have been responding to the card he had slipped into her hand at the fundraiser. *I know about your husband.*

Winter was still trying to formulate some sort of reply when Brenda said, "I'll pick you up outside your apartment building tomorrow morning at eight a.m."

"I'll—I'll be there," Winter stammered.

But Brenda was already gone.

20

Winter waited for her in the lobby of his building. Outside, the day was bright and clear but very cold. Even where he stood, the bitter air reached him through the front doors. He kept his ivy cap on and buried his hands in the pockets of his shearling coat as if he were already out in the weather.

His mind was racing. Full of questions. Had Brenda called him from a secure phone? Was his own phone secure? Would she take care that she wasn't followed here? How closely was Byrne watching him?

That he was being watched, of this Winter was certain. Nelson had been in his apartment and had, at the very least, taken a good look around. Winter had scanned the place for spy tools afterward, but he couldn't be certain it was clean. And while Byrne might not be able to access his hard drive directly, he could surely break through his encryption programs to follow him online. He knew now that Winter was on to him.

Which was what Winter had wanted. To haunt him. To get on his nerves. To make him angry. To smoke him out. But he didn't want to endanger Molly in the process.

Through the glass doors, he saw Brenda's car pull to the curb outside. It was a sleek silver Cadillac—a perfect vehicle, he thought, for a proudly successful midwestern businesswoman. Winter didn't hesitate. He hurried through the glass doors. Glanced about himself only briefly as he took the two steps across the sidewalk. Quickly opened the Caddy's door and smoothly slipped into the passenger seat. A second later, Brenda hit the gas and they were on their way, as if escaping.

Brenda Wallace drove the city streets in silence. Winter stole glances at her to take her measure. She was, in his estimation, the least attractive of the three Shea sisters. Evelyn was the beauty of the bunch. Molly had a homey and vivacious charm. Brenda—the Serious One—was not only plain, there was something dry and forbidding about her. That was Winter's judgment anyway.

She looked like her mother minus the cheerful simplicity. She had the same pie-plate face but her skin was pasty, and her expression was absent any show of cheer. Her hair, dyed straw yellow, was cut short and kept curly like her mother's but in her, at her age, this struck Winter as almost aggressively sexless. Likewise, her body—in a flowered wool blouse and white slacks beneath her open overcoat—was full at breast and hip yet somehow managed to convey no more softness than a bag of cement. Winter felt this was intentional at some level, a statement of identity in contrast to her sisters.

He judged it best to keep quiet as they drove. He sensed she was brimming with the urge to talk to him. He thought if he questioned her she would resist him. But, if he only waited, she would come around.

This, it turned out, was the right strategy.

After she had guided the Cadillac onto the interstate, after they were heading away from the city, Brenda Wallace finally looked over at him from behind the wheel.

"Well, you've sure caused a lot of trouble, haven't you?" she said. Her voice had the high flat tones of the north country.

"Have I?" said Winter quietly.

"Oh yeah. Oh yeah." The blocky city skyline with its central dome fell away behind them. Snowy farmland surrounded them, bright under bright blue skies. "Even famous people have a right to their privacy, you know. Pup, he's real protective of that. Especially with Molly. With all of us, but especially with her. There's always some reporter nosing around into other people's business, you know."

Winter directed his best mild-mannered smile to her stolid profile. "I'm just an English professor," he said.

"Well, whatever you are, it's the same idea."

There was another silence after that, a grim one. Again, going on instinct, Winter waited it out. Whatever she was going to tell him, she would tell him in her own time, he thought. She was angry, but not at him, or not only at him. She was just angry in general. An angry woman. Her anger would push the words to the surface like the bubbles in boiling water.

Sure enough, she went on unbidden. "Mind you, I was suspicious of him too at the start."

"Of Pup, you mean?" he asked, as if surprised. "Why suspicious?"

"Oh, just, you know, a man like that, all rich and so forth, lighting on an everyday girl like Molly. Not that she's not a sweetheart. Everyone knows how sweet Molly is. She always was, even as a baby. But a man like Pup, all rich and so forth. Well, it had my antennas twitching, I'll admit."

Winter remembered what Mrs. Shea had told him about her eldest daughter. Brenda had a tendency to suspicion. She prided herself on seeing into people, on ferreting out their hidden motives. Wasn't it she who had first spread the warning about Molly's first boyfriend, Charles Merriman?

Winter played to that pride. "I suppose a businesswoman like yourself has to have good judgment about people."

The flattery worked. She nodded as she drove. Her face remained expressionless but her pleasure at the compliment shone through. "It helps, that's for sure. It helps to know who you're dealing with. A lot of phonies out there. A lot of dishonest people."

"Yes, I can imagine."

"And there she was, Molly, all brokenhearted like she was. All her happy plans ruined by that—that Charles. And she's just a church secretary in the middle of nowhere. And one day she looks up from her cookie table and there's a billionaire standing in front of her, telling her how *appealing* she is? You just have to ask yourself, don't you: where'd that come from, what's that about?"

Winter could imagine Brenda as a younger woman, growing up, the oldest of three girls. Not so pretty and vulnerable and artistic as the youngest sister, Evelyn. Men flocked to Evelyn. Like flames to a moth, he thought wryly. Nor was Brenda so cheerful and domestic and *appealing* as the middle sister, Molly. There'd always be some fellow willing to take care of a girl like Molly. Which was all Molly wanted, after all.

But Brenda. Brenda was plain. Serious, aggressive, smart. In a world of fortune and men's eyes, a girl like that has to have her wits about her. Brenda did. She had built herself the life she wanted. Found herself a good husband. Turned his furniture store into a profitable chain. Gave her mother a couple of grandchildren to fuss over. It may have taken some planning and effort but she got it done: marriage and work, children and security. She could dust her hands off and look around at her accomplishments, well gratified.

And it would only be human to feel just a twinge of competitive satisfaction at the fact that her sisters had done nowhere near as well as she. Evelyn, pretty as she was, how the men had used and abused her. Molly, lovable as she was, fooled and abandoned by the deceptive Charles. Dowdy Brenda had outdone them both, romantically and professionally. She loved her sisters. She buried her feelings of triumph over them. But those feelings were there. That was only human.

Then, suddenly, along came Gerald Byrne. A billionaire. Suddenly standing in front of Molly's cookie table at the church.

And just like that, he asked me out, Molly had told the TV interviewer. *He said he found me very appealing.*

Just like that, Brenda's success among her sisters had become second best—second best by a country mile. All the bitterness and envy and competitive pride that had been buried by her victory in the secret sister wars, all of it flared up again. That too: only human.

That was the way Winter imagined it, in any case.

"You only had to go on the internet to see that Pup had cut a pretty wide swath through those starlets out there in Hollywood," Brenda went on. The morning sun glinted harshly off the snow all around them. Her pale eyes glinted too as they peered, adamant, out the windshield. "Well, even Molly thought twice about that. I'm her older sister, you know. She's always told me everything. She was calling me on the computer just about every night. Asking me for advice. And I was saying to her, 'Well, what's his game? What's he after?' And you know Molly. She's so innocent. She believes anything you tell her. She says to me, 'Well, he's tired of all those glamour girls. I think he just wants someone to settle down with.' And I didn't say anything, but inside, I was thinking, 'Oh, right!' Because a man never gets tired of some things, let's face it."

Byrne had worked hard to overcome Molly's defenses, she went on. Their very first date, he took her out to dinner at a steakhouse in the city. It was the sort of sumptuous venue Molly had never seen before, not even at her graduation dinner. And here were the maître d' and the waiters all fluttering around Gerald Byrne like he was king of the world and they were his subjects. And meanwhile he was telling Molly the sad story of his life. His father's corruption. His mother's suicide. His attempt to lose himself in luxury and beautiful women. The depression and disillusionment that followed. How could Molly feel anything but tenderness for a poor little rich boy, so hurt, so vulnerable? A man who said he was weary of the emptiness of his success and was searching for the sort of love and meaning that could only be found with a woman exactly like her.

"He tells her he's been watching her at the Sunday school, you know," Brenda went on. Winter did not think he was imagining the bitterness dripping from her voice. Her tone suggested there was some dark ulterior motive hidden behind Byrne's actions. "He'd been sneaking out during the sermon sometimes and going into the meeting hall, just to peek in at her where she was with the children. Children, they always loved Molly, you know. Even my own kids when they were little. She would come over and they'd go running to the door, 'Aunt Molly! Aunt Molly!' They loved her."

Winter could imagine Brenda's jealousy in those moments. How she would tell herself, well, they were still her children, her family, her life. And look at Molly, all alone and brokenhearted as she was.

"So Pup would see that, you know. He would sneak out of the sermon and go watch her, the way she was with the little ones. That's what he found so appealing about her, he told her. The way she was with children. And oh, that was meat and drink to Molly, believe you me."

On their second date, Byrne and Molly walked by the Mississippi together, shoulder to shoulder at first, then hand in hand. Molly did then what she had not yet done outside her family. She told Byrne the whole humiliating story of her love affair with

Charles Merriman. She held nothing back. Her devotion to him. Her gullibility. Her po-faced naivete from their purity pledge to her discovery of Charles and Brian in bed together.

"I'm sorry that happened to you," said Byrne. This was the moment when he took her hand. The bikers whizzed past them on the path. The fine clouds sailed behind the skyline. The stone arch bridge stretched picturesque across the mighty river. "I'm sorry that happened to you, but in a selfish way, I'm glad too. Because it means you're still available."

"Well, Molly just fell for that hook, line, and sinker," Brenda said. "Remember, this was a billionaire talking to her."

True enough, thought Winter. A billionaire talking to a "nobody from nowhere." But that didn't mean he wasn't sincere. Winter had seen Molly with his own eyes. And she *was* appealing. A woman of quality and charm. Why shouldn't a man want her? Why shouldn't Byrne want her? Fresh from his depression, fresh from his experience of enlightenment in the Amazon. Why should he not realize her value? And why shouldn't she welcome his attention?

"How was a girl going to resist all *that*?" Brenda said, nodding at him knowingly from behind the Caddy's wheel.

Molly did not resist it, not for long. There were a few more dates. He escorted her to the state fair—the get-together, as the locals called it. She and her high school chum Maddie had submitted a quilt in the competition there. They went on a double date, Maddie and her husband, Molly and Byrne. Their quilt didn't win the blue ribbon but they got an honorable mention. And Byrne was charming all day long. Easy and natural with Molly's friends. Rooting for the ladies' quilt with real enthusiasm. Cursing the judges for blind women when the quilt didn't win.

It was all delight. Love and delight, coming for Molly on the heels of betrayal, humiliation, and heartache. And maybe too,

Winter thought, even Molly, sweet as she was, felt a small bit of triumph as she reported every moment of it to her older sister. Even if Brenda had lorded her successes over her only unconsciously, wouldn't the younger sister enjoy a bit of unconscious payback? Sister stuff. Winter could only imagine it. And he did.

On it went. Between Brenda's chatty telling of these tales, and Winter's strategy of waiting through her fuming silences, they slanted north across the state line into forest and lake country. The sun, which had been a pale fire in the expanse above the open farmland, now played hide-and-seek among the winter trees.

"I kept warning her what was coming," Brenda said, out of one of those silences. "A man like Pup is not going to be making any purity pledges, that's for sure. But I knew all along there was no stopping it. I told my husband: this is a done deal right here."

Literary man that he was, Winter could not help recalling some of the so-called carpe diem poems of sexual seduction as he listened to the story of how Molly had finally, even gratefully, surrendered her "long-preserved virginity."

Byrne's urgings were gentle and patient.

Had we but world enough and time,/This coyness, lady, were no crime.

And maybe his suit was helped along by the size of his mansion and a couple of fortifying glasses of red wine, which Molly was not used to.

That's the way Molly told it anyway. Because all this, too, she had shared with her older sister, talking face to face over their laptops the next evening. It was a comical story, the way she narrated it. There were plenty of silly moments. Startled innocence, slapstick incompetence. Still, though, she must have known how it would sound to her sister—her sister, who had "warned her and warned her" against taking this next dangerous step with a man with such a romantic history. What was his game?

"Look, she's a grown woman," Brenda told Winter. "And that purity pledge hadn't helped her out much, now had it? All I'm saying is, Pup knew what he was about. That's all. He was an expert at this sort of thing. A leopard doesn't change his spots. That's all. Enough said."

Afterward, awaking in Byrne's bed in the middle of the night, Molly had a moment of panic. She remembered Brenda's warnings. She became anxious. She suffered regret. She lay curled on her side with her naked back to her first true lover. He sprawled next to her, fast asleep, softly snoring, generating body heat in a way that both charmed and disturbed her. Suddenly he seemed a stranger. Suddenly she remembered her religion. Suddenly she had fears of pregnancy and disease, though he had taken every precaution. She felt the weight of lost time and the foolishness of her long mistake with Charles. She began to cry into the darkness, struggling to stifle the sound so she wouldn't wake Byrne.

But he did wake. He rolled over toward her, throwing his arm around her, a heavy weight yet somehow comforting in the way it claimed possession of her. She longed to be possessed.

He murmured out of half sleep. "Are you crying?"

"I'm sorry," she said.

"Don't be sorry. Why are you crying?"

She snuffled into the shadows. "It's all right. Go back to sleep."

"No, really. What's wrong?"

"Well . . ." she said, the word squeaking through her tears. "It'll probably sound stupid to you. But tonight mattered to me. A lot. And I could understand how maybe it's just another night to you. All the girls you've been with. But it really mattered to me."

Byrne stirred himself. Rubbed his eyes. Tried to bring himself awake enough to rise to the occasion.

"Is that why you're crying?" he asked, confused.

"Well . . . yes," she said tearfully.

"Because you think this was a one-night stand?"

"Uh-huh."

"I was looking for a one-night stand so I figured a virgin Sunday school teacher was my best bet?"

She gave a forlorn little laugh. "Yes."

"Well, you can stop crying," he told her.

"What do you mean? Why?"

"Because I'm crazy about you."

"You are?"

"Yes, of course. I wouldn't be here if I weren't. That doesn't even make sense."

There was a long silence as her sniffles subsided. "Why?" she said then.

"Because it would be cruel and unnecessary. That's not me."

"No. I mean, why are you crazy about me?"

"Oh, now you're just fishing for compliments."

"Well, I'm a girl," said Molly. "I'm allowed to fish for compliments."

"At three o'clock in the morning?"

"Yes. It's a rule. You can check the book."

Byrne laughed. He pulled her close to him and kissed her hair. "That's why I'm crazy about you. Because you're a girl."

"Well, that's not very specific."

"No, but I mean all girl, a girly girl. You're in for the whole girl ride. I love that. You put flowers in rooms. You straighten things when they're crooked. You treat children like they matter. You take care of people. You give yourself away. Everywhere you go, you make everything better, Molly."

Did he know what this meant to her? What a balm it was to her insecurities?

"Charles used to make fun of me," she said. Her tears were finished now. "He always used to say, 'You're such a girly girl, Molly!'"

"Well, maybe Charles liked manly girls," said Byrne. "I like em all pink and fluffy. Like you. Now go to sleep."

But she didn't. She lay awake, smiling into the dark, listening as he started to snore again.

Brenda told this story in a critical tone. She told it as if her sister had been caught up in a con, a scam, a cheap seduction.

"He knew just the right things to say to her, all right," she told Winter with a knowing nod.

The silence that filled the Cadillac then seemed to Winter rank with her suspicions, sour with her sourness. He looked out his window. He watched the woods pass by. He saw the sun vanish behind branches, then pierce through in lancing bursts of light. All the scenery seemed sour to him.

And it occurred to him: maybe it wasn't really Brenda's sourness all around him. Maybe it was his. Because, he realized, he was sour too. He felt envious too, just as Brenda did. She was envious of Molly, who had come from behind in the sister sweepstakes to win not just love but wealth untold and even a measure of fame and power. And he—Winter—was envious of Byrne because Byrne had found the love Winter so desperately wanted while he, Winter, was lost and wandering in the twilight country of the past.

Winter looked out glumly at the harsh February sun stabbing through the trees. Brenda was bitter and envious. He was bitter and envious. But from Molly's point of view, what was wrong with any of it? The whole thing had been a fairy tale for her. She was the Cinderella Girl.

And who was he—Winter? Who was he in this tale? He was the evil stepsister. The dragon. The villain of the piece.

"Don't get me wrong," said Brenda suddenly, as if her mind had been traveling along a similar track. "Pup's been good to her. I won't deny it. I've come to have real respect for him over time. And I love Molly more than anything. Everybody loves Molly. I would never do anything to hurt her."

It was a moment before Winter could turn from the view, turn from his own thoughts, and look at her, at her plain and unhappy profile.

"No," he said quietly then. "No. Of course not. Why would anyone want to hurt her?"

21

Brenda and her husband had a house by the lake. A gray and white house on a snow-covered hill. Molly must have seen them coming up the long driveway. Cold as it was, she was waiting for them just outside the front door as the Cadillac rolled to a stop. She had put no coat on. She was dressed only in jeans and a long-sleeved red blouse, plus the small gold cross she seemed to always wear around her neck. She was hugging herself against the bitter wind that came off the water.

Winter stepped out of the car, carrying all his self-doubts with him. But Molly Byrne was bold and unhesitating. She walked down the little slate path and offered him her small hand. He shook it. They looked at one another solemnly, she with her head tilted up to his greater height. Close like this, he found her eyes remarkable. He wasn't sure at first what he saw in them, but then he was: a certain wholeness of integrity, a sturdy country honesty. Well, of course. Why would she have summoned him here if she was not that woman?

"I'll come back in an hour," Brenda called to them through the Caddy's window. Then she buzzed the window shut, put the car in gear, and reversed out of the drive.

"Come in out of the cold, Professor Winter," Molly said.

Inside, the house was blonde wood and big windows. The windows looked out on the water, gorgeous with ice and snow. The sun was blinding on the snow's white surfaces, but out toward the lake's center the water still ran black. It was a dramatic scene, the colors vivid and stark: blue sky, yellow sun, white snow, black water. Winter stood with his hands in his coat pockets and gazed out at it, lost in his sorry thoughts.

"Would you like a cup of coffee?" Molly said.

It was a moment before he could pull himself from the view to turn to her. "No. Nothing, thank you."

She put out her hand. "Can I take your coat then?"

He watched the scenery some more as she hung his coat in the front closet. *Why here?* he asked himself. *Why did she want to meet me here?*

"Well," she said behind him, and he turned from the window to face her. "I guess there's not much point in small talk, is there?"

"No," he said.

"Would you like to sit down?"

He only gestured in reply and remained where he was. For some reason, he didn't want to sit. She seemed to understand. She lifted her hands from her sides, then let them fall. "The ball is in your court, isn't it? The card you gave me? What you wrote on it. What is it you think you know about my husband? And what do you want?"

He allowed himself a smile. "Do you think I'm a blackmailer?"

"I don't know what to think. I'm asking you."

"Oh . . ." He shook his head. "I think you do know what to think, Mrs. Byrne. I saw it in your eyes at the fundraiser. And then you call me here." He waved a hand at the house. "Why here? Because your husband doesn't watch you here. Isn't that it? He thinks you're visiting your sister, so he doesn't make you take a bodyguard. You don't want him to know we're meeting. You're afraid of him."

Her face went tight and formidable at that, her expression turned dark. She crossed her arms beneath her breasts. "My husband would never hurt me."

"Not you, no. Me. You were afraid for me. Weren't you?"

That must have been the truth. It broke through her resistance. A look fell across her features like death's shadow. It seemed to speak of all the fears that kept her up at night while her husband slept beside her, while her children slept, while the life she loved lay silent in the darkness. She had been waiting for Winter a long time, for someone like Winter. The dragon of her fairy tale. She had been dreading his arrival. Now here he was. She probably would have preferred a blackmailer. Even a reporter might have been better than this. Someone with a self-interested motive. Because here—as she must have realized—here was a man who, whatever his inner complexities, wanted nothing from her but the disastrous truth.

All this struck Winter to the heart. Looking at her just then, all he wished was not to be himself. Not to be doing what he was doing. But how could he stop? He went on relentlessly, cruelly. "You were afraid I would drive off a mountain like Charles Merriman. Weren't you? Or throw myself off a roof like Adam Kemp. Or have my sins exposed like Lou Walsh, your mother's boss. Or go mad and ruin myself like Henry Woolsey . . ." Again, the sound that escaped her struck him like a blow. "You wanted to meet in secret to keep me safe."

Her eyes filled. Her lips trembled. She turned her back on him to hide it. "What are you suggesting?"

"Molly," was all he said.

She wiped her eyes with her hand quickly, spun fiercely to confront him. "Don't you call me that. Don't come here with your insinuations and speak to me like you know me. Who are you?"

"I'm an English professor."

"The hell you are. What do you want?"

Winter sighed. Did he even know what he wanted? "I guess . . . I just want it to stop," he said. "It has to stop, Mrs. Byrne. It has to. Now that I've seen it, I can't unsee it. And neither can you. It has to stop."

"I don't . . . I don't know what you're talking about," she said without conviction.

He ignored this. "I might have let Adam Kemp's suicide go. I really might have. He chose it. I had no sympathy for him. If I hadn't felt guilty about the whole thing, I might never have even seen it for what it was. But I did feel guilty. I felt guilty I hadn't stopped Adam or helped him or done something to keep him from becoming what he became. But once I knew that your husband had destroyed him it was too late. I recognized the techniques. I suspected all the rest."

"What?" said Molly. "Suspected what?" He could hear her torment. She did not want to know what he knew, but she could not turn away from it any more than he could. "Come out and say it."

"Your old boyfriend Charles Merriman," he said. He saw her fight down a sob. "Life put him in a tough spot. To find out you're gay in a community that doesn't accept you, it's a tough spot. It was like he was two people inside and they couldn't live with one another. And look, he handled it badly. Obviously. He lied to himself. He lied to you. He got lost. He went wrong. He tried to blackmail you. I understand."

Her eyes were red with unfallen tears. She bared her teeth at him. "Why did you do this? Why did you pry into my life?"

"I don't know. I had to. I couldn't stop. I couldn't unsee it." He stepped toward her, forcing himself to look at her pain, the pain that he was causing. His voice was as strained as hers. "Because here's what I'm getting at. Wrong as Charles was to do what he did, what was the worst that could have come of it? What would have happened if your husband had just let it go, Molly? What if he'd told Charles to publish and be damned. There'd have been a few embarrassing pictures of you on the internet. A bad month or two in the media. So what? You could have lived with that. And maybe Charles would have come to himself. Maybe he wouldn't even have gone through with it."

"Charles . . . had an accident," she said. "He fell asleep at the wheel. He drove off a cliff."

"His wheels and steering locked in place. There's no other explanation."

"Well, what does that have to do with Gerald?"

"The car was rigged."

"You can't know that."

"I do know it. I know how it's done. God help me, I've done it. I was trained by the same people who trained Nelson."

He heard her breath catch. She stared at him. "An English professor . . ." she said, her mouth twisting. She swallowed hard. "Well, maybe it was Nelson then. Maybe Nelson took it upon himself . . ."

"No, Molly. Nelson loves you, but he loves your husband too. You're mother and father to him. He acts on orders."

She turned away and so did he. The two stood with their shoulders toward each other, their eyes averted. Beyond them, out the window, the desolate lake shimmered in the wind: blue sky, yellow sun, white snow, black water.

"Even after I found out about Charles, I might have tried to forget it," Winter went on, speaking down at the shag rug. "Not for Byrne's sake. For yours. I see what you are, Molly. Mrs. Byrne. I see who you are. Your husband was right about you. Wherever you go, you make life better. You deserve every good thing that's come your way. Even the things he killed to get for you."

She covered her face with her hands. "Stop!"

"So even after I found out about Charles, I might have let it go. But I knew there was more," he said.

Now, Winter felt something within himself give way. He suddenly found he could not go on standing. He moved to the white sofa and sank into it wearily. She moved to a white armchair across from him, lowered herself stiffly onto the cushion. She sat erect, her hands folded in her lap. She gazed at him so stonily he could not tell whether she was looking at him or past him, out the window, at the lake.

"Do you know the name Arnaud Baptiste?" he asked.

She began to shake her head no, then gestured vaguely. "I've heard it."

"He was a businessman, like your husband. Wealthy like your husband. The sort of man who showed up at all the same meetings your husband did. But he had a different point of view, a different philosophy."

Winter took his phone out of his pocket. He found the video he'd saved. He started it playing. He held it out to her so she could see.

Baptiste was a small, broad-shouldered man with a classically handsome face that seemed chiseled onto the square block of his head. On the video, he was standing at the center of a circle of microphones. He was speaking English in a flowing French accent that made him sound to American ears like a seductive lover.

"I do not think a small number of billionaire technocrats should decide the fate of the nations. That they should sit upon their mountains of gold, and wave their hands like foppish princes, declaring who can speak and who must be silent, whose tax dollars are to be spent where and on what. The nations belong to the people who live in them. Let them decide these things for themselves."

"He opposed your husband's Good World Project," Winter told her. "He may have been wrong, he may have been right. I don't do politics. I can't judge. But he wasn't an extremist. He wasn't hateful in any way that I can make out. He had a wife and two young children. He supported charities. He did good works. And he had his opinions like your husband has his. He made his arguments at the same places your husband did. He had influence. He was winning followers. He was a thorn in your husband's side. An obstacle to the realization of your husband's vision."

Molly continued to sit rigidly in her chair. She seemed to stare past the video. Winter could not tell if she was watching it or not.

He drew the phone back to himself. He called up another video. He set it playing. He held the phone out to her again.

"Baptiste was stabbed to death in this riot in Paris. Dragged from his car by masked men who were protesting whatever they protest in France these days. It's always something, as far as I can tell."

He continued to hold the phone out to her. She continued to look past it at the window, at the frozen lake.

"Look, Mrs. Byrne," Winter said.

Her eyes flickered down to the screen, then flickered away.

"What do you want me to see?" she asked him.

"The masked men," said Winter. "The mob. Dressed in black. Black balaclavas covering their faces. They dragged Baptiste from his limousine. Look. They surrounded him. And when they dispersed, he was on the pavement, bleeding to death."

Molly was silent. She shook her head, almost imperceptibly. All her denial was in that movement.

"There's one man in the mob—right there," said Winter, pointing a finger at the screen. "You can't see his face under the balaclava, but you can see the back of his neck clearly enough, for a few seconds at least. There's a scar on the back of his neck. From an old knife wound, I think. Nelson has a scar just like it. Exactly like it."

Winter heard the air come out of Molly as if he'd punched her. For a long moment, the silence between them continued. Molly went on staring out the window at the bleak colors of the February world.

"Why did you do this?" she whispered. "Why?"

"Because once I understood how Adam Kemp died I guessed all the rest. And Molly, believe me, if I keep looking, I'll find more like this. This is what your husband does. This is who he is."

He was finished. He stopped the video. He slipped the phone back into his pocket. He sat leaning forward, his elbows on his thighs, his hands clasped between his knees. He watched her as she sat erect, staring out at the frozen water, at the pitiless sun in the pitiless sky.

In her silence, Winter's eyes flicked to the gold cross gleaming on her blouse. He began to compose a speech in his head. In the speech, he told Molly Byrne that her husband had had a vision, a drugged vision in the jungles of Brazil. He had seen a god who was both the mind of the universe and somehow his own mind at the same time. In his speech, Winter confessed to her that he did not know anything about God. He did not even know whether or not God existed. But he knew this: if God did exist, he might be many things, but he was not Gerald Byrne. And Gerald Byrne was not God.

He did not make the speech out loud. He didn't have the nerve. He felt it would be cheap somehow, coming from him, a nonbeliever. And he did not want to appear cheap in front of Molly. There was something about her that made him feel he had to live up to her, had to be worthy of her, even in this, even as the dragon in her fairy tale, breathing destruction on everything she had.

"When I first married Gerald, he had bad dreams," Molly said then. She spoke quietly, distantly, still gazing out through the window at the blue sky and the black water. She spoke, Winter thought, like a child in a medieval ghost story he remembered, a murdered child who sang though he was dead. She spoke, Winter thought, as if he had destroyed her, as if she were dead inside and all that was left was her voice.

"He didn't have them before we were married. Before we were married, he was fine. But afterward, after the wedding, the nightmares started. Terrible nightmares. Night terrors, they call them. I would wake up in the middle of the night, and I'd be alone in bed. He'd be gone. Then sometime, usually just before dawn, he'd come back and lie down next to me until it was time to get up and begin the day."

She swallowed. She went on. The same voice, a dead woman's voice. "Finally, one night, when I woke up and found myself alone, I got out of bed and went to find him. I felt like the heroine in an old gothic novel or a fairy tale. The bride walking down an empty hall to discover the dark secret of her new husband. But there he was in his study. Just sitting alone at his desk, staring out the window, his back to the door. The window was open but I could smell the dope, the marijuana. I could see the ashes in the ashtray. He'd been smoking to calm himself."

She stopped here to draw a breath, an unsteady breath. A smile played at the corner of her mouth as she remembered. "At first, he told me to go back to bed, but I wouldn't. I sat across from him. I told him: All the time we were dating, he gave me things. Jewelry. Clothes. A whole new wardrobe. I had no money of my own. He gave me a credit card so I could buy myself whatever I wanted. I objected, even at the time. I told him I didn't want any of it. But he pleaded with me. He said, 'A boy likes to give things to his girl.'

It was such a sweet thing to say, I couldn't bring myself to make him stop. But now . . . Now that we were married, I told him the truth. I said I didn't care if he gave me clothes. I didn't care how big our house was—our houses were. I really didn't. I never did. It was him . . . it was him I wanted. And if he gave me the world and kept himself from me, I told him, then he would have given me nothing."

Now, finally, she shifted her eyes—just her eyes, the rest of her motionless. She shifted her gaze to Winter's face and he could not remember any feeling quite like the power of it. He had to grudgingly admire Byrne for finding this woman, this "nobody from nowhere," and bringing her to light. He wondered how many more there were like her, obscure and magnificent as she had been, hidden in the shadows thrown by the garbage fire of the greater world.

"So he told me," she went on. "He told me about the dreams, the night terrors, how bad they were. He said he had always had bad dreams whenever a woman got too close to him. That that's why he couldn't stay with any of them. It wasn't just the sex, he said, and the glamour of going one to another. It was also the fact that, whenever he stayed with a woman more than a few days, whenever he got too close, he started to have these horrible dreams about his mother. He would see her at the rectory window. He would see her throw herself out the window into the storm. He relived it as if he were right there, right then, as if it were happening again. He had never told anyone this before. It wasn't in any of his interviews. He told me, and he began to cry. Sitting in his chair across the desk from me. His face just . . . crumpled up. And he sobbed like a child. He had hoped the dreams had gone away. After he came back from the ayahuasca trip, he believed he had gotten past them. Then when he married me they all came back, same as ever. It was being married that did it. The intimacy of that."

Winter had to work to keep his eyes on hers. The steady certainty of her gaze unnerved him. It seemed to come from far away inside her, some fine and private place.

"I made him come back to bed with me," she said. "I made him wake me up after that, wake me up and tell me every time the bad dreams came. I would tell him that his mother could see that he was with me now, that he was all right and I would take care of him. After a few months the dreams were gone. I made them stop. I stopped them." She lifted her chin, the slightest gesture of pride. "You know about the ayahuasca. His trip to the Amazon. You know the story he tells. But it wasn't him who slew that monster in the doorway of the universe, Professor Winter. It was me."

Now she removed her gaze from him and he felt that too. He felt the loss of it. What a woman she was.

"Do you know why I call him Pup?" she said, asking but not really asking him. Looking out the window again, speaking, it seemed, to herself. "I mean, I know it's ridiculous obviously. A man like him. A pet name like that. It's silly. But I did it for my sisters, actually. My mother too. I wanted them to know him. So they could become his family. He needed that. It's part of what he was looking for in me, I think. A family to be part of. I couldn't tell them about the bad dreams. That was too private. But I wanted them to understand him at some level. So they wouldn't be afraid of him or overawed. Rich as he was, powerful as he was, dominating as he can be. I wanted them to realize at some level that he was also just a motherless boy and he needed us."

Now she drew breath. She rose from her chair, rose majestically.

"He's my husband and the father of my children," she said down at him. "Do you understand that?"

"Yes, of course. Of course."

"I don't blame you for what you've done. I can see you too, Professor, like you see me. I can see what you are and that you're a good man and how lost you are and I'm sorry for you. But he's my husband and the father of my children."

Winter ran through his speech again, about the cross she wore and how Gerald Byrne wasn't God. But he could no more have spoken it aloud than he could find the nerve to meet her gaze. He only nodded, looking at the floor.

"Brenda should be back for you soon," she said then. And she walked out of the room.

22

Brenda had one more story to tell as she drove him home. She saved it for the end of their journey. She drove in silence until then.

Winter was silent too. Gazing out the passenger window at the snowy fields, seeing none of them, nothing. His mind was all inner images and sensations. His sensations were all sorrow. He felt hollowed out with a black, black hollowness. He was sick of himself. He wished he was with Margaret Whitaker right then, spilling out his guilty secrets. There were already too damn many of them before he'd gone to see Molly. He had already been filled up with them. Choking on them. Now there was one more.

Then, when the white dome and the white stone and the redbrick faces of the city skyline appeared ahead of them, when they could see the skyline reflected, wavering, on the surface of the winter water, Brenda began suddenly to speak.

"Molly's always been a very religious girl, you know," she said. She spoke as if she had already been speaking in her mind, as if she was just now letting Winter join the conversation. "And when I say very, I mean very-very. My mother always called me the Serious One. Evelyn, she was the Pretty One. Molly was the Domestic

One. But really, when it came to religion, it was Molly who was serious. I mean, I go to church. Obviously. We all do. I believe in God, obviously. But Molly, even when she was little, she always took it to a whole other level."

She glanced from the windshield to Winter, as if to make sure that he was listening. He was, though he wished he wasn't. He was sick of Brenda too.

"That night, that first night she spent with Pup—for her, that was her wedding night, you see. Oh, I knew it was going to be like that. Sure I did. Why do you think I was so worried about it? I'm not some old prig, no matter what you think. I had a fling or two before me and Jack got together. I know my way around. But not Molly. I knew for Molly there'd be no going back. That was it for her. You understand what I'm telling you here?"

Winter nodded—vaguely, because he wasn't really sure he did understand or that he wanted to understand or if he cared whether he understood or not. He only knew that Brenda's jealousy offended him now. He was disgusted by it. It reminded him too much of himself.

"Still, I sat her down, you know, to have a talk. I thought that was my sisterly duty."

Winter turned away, back to the window, so she wouldn't see his sneer of disdain.

But Brenda may have guessed his feelings, because she added with some emphasis: "I'm her older sister, that's all I'm saying. I felt I had a duty to her."

Winter managed to nod at the window, but he still couldn't look at her.

"So I sat her down. I sat her down. I said to her, I said, 'Molly. I don't want to stick my big nose into your business. That's not the sort of thing I do. And God knows I don't want to ruin your fun.

But I'm your big sister,' I said. I said, 'And I just don't want you to get hurt again, the way you did with Charles.' Well, of course, that made her laugh. And her face turned all red. And she said, 'I don't think that's going to be a problem.' You know, meaning that Gerald wasn't a gay man. But I said, 'Well, there are all kinds of ways a man can hurt you.' And God knows that's true. It's like men have some kind of laboratory somewhere where they invent them. Like their scientists are working around the clock!" she added with a bitter little snort.

"So I said to her, I said, 'You know, you have to understand, a man like Gerald Byrne, with all his money and all, he can have any woman he wants to any time he wants to.' And I said, 'I know you two are all stars and violins right now, but marriage—marriage is a day-to-day thing, one day after another. And it goes on a long, long time, and I'm just concerned for you, is all.' I said to her, 'I'm just concerned, at some point, Gerald's going to find he's tempted to return to his old ways. 'Cause when he does, believe me, there's always going to be some hottie around, you know, to make it easy for him. And men aren't angels.' That's what I told her. I said, 'Men aren't angels, you know what I'm talking about.'"

Winter glanced over at her with a thin smile, then looked out the window again, thinking, in his sour mood, what a meddlesome, jealous old biddy she was. With her older sister wisdom and her grim suspicions. What a meddlesome old biddy! But he knew it was really himself he was sick of, not her.

"And Molly," she went on. "Molly, she gave me that angel look of hers. That sweet angel innocent look, you know, like butter wouldn't melt in her sweet mouth. She gave me that look and you know what she said? This is after one night, remember. One night with him." Brenda held up one finger. "But I knew this would happen. I knew it. That's why I sat her down in the first place. She turned to me and said, she said, 'It doesn't matter anymore, Brenda. It doesn't matter what happens.' She said, 'I'm his now. I belong to him. I'm his forever.'" Brenda shook her head. Threw her left hand up and let it land on the steering wheel so that her wedding ring smacked against it. "That's what she said. My hand to God. I would not make that up. 'I'm his forever.' After one night. That's Molly."

Winter felt the black hollowness in his belly roll over, as if to reveal the blacker side of blackness on its underside. He nearly groaned aloud. What the hell was he doing? What the hell had he done?

"I'm just telling you," added Brenda.

He turned to her again. He wanted to strangle her. Later, looking back on it, he thought he might have said something then, something cruel he would have regretted later. But just at that moment he heard his phone double buzz. A text.

"Excuse me," he muttered.

He fished the phone out of his pocket. The text was from an unknown source—but he knew it was from Stan-Stan Stankowski.

It said: *The Recruiter will see you.*

Winter turned away from Brenda silently and stared out the window.

PART FOUR

THE YIN OF
THE PLEROMA

So anyway, this is how I killed my friend. This is how I assassinated Roy.

By the time we set out on our first mission together I had it pretty well figured out in my mind what was going to happen. By the time the sun rose I already had my suspicions. Then, each stage of the journey, it became clearer to me. By afternoon I knew.

Roy and I were waiting outside our barracks in the woods at zero-dark-thirty. An SUV came to pick us up. It was driven by a silent stranger, someone I'd never seen before. A spook—a spy—of some sort, I guess. He drove us out of Cathedral Station to the airport. We did what the Recruiter had told us to do. We flew to a certain city, like he said. We stopped at the Steak N Brew in the airport there. We ordered breakfast. I had steak and eggs. We chatted but I hardly knew what we were chatting about because the whole time, I was thinking, What the hell?, *you know. Because none of it made any sense. Except it did. It did make sense. And I was beginning to understand.*

After a while, sure enough, this woman came up to our table. Attractive woman. White, forty, very professional looking. A businesswoman type. She was carrying one of those enormous purse-slash-briefcases women have. She acted as if she'd just been passing by and happened to recognize Roy.

She gave Roy this big smile and she said, "Excuse me, but didn't we meet at the conference in Seattle?" Just like the Recruiter told us she would. Like in some stupid spy movie. Then she stood beside our table and she and Roy chatted awhile. Roy asked her how business was. I remember she said something like "Oh, you know, I haven't been home in six weeks, but other than that it's all good." Something very natural like that, very real. Roy introduced her to me. We shook hands. He invited her to sit down. She said she couldn't, she had a plane to catch. Yadda yadda yadda. And so on.

And by that time I was thinking, Of course, of course. *The coin had finally dropped. The whole thing had become obvious to me. In fact, it was so obvious, I kept thinking to myself that Roy must see it too. But he didn't. I could see it in his eyes. He had no idea what was happening.*

So finally the woman walked away. And I glanced down and, lo and behold, there was a laptop case on the floor, right by Roy's feet. As if it belonged to him, as if it had been there the whole time. It was that smooth. Even I didn't see her put it there and I was this close to her. Anyone watching casually would have assumed the laptop had been there all along.

So on it went. Roy and I finished our meal. We got up to go. Roy picked up the laptop as if it belonged to him. Casual as that. And out we went to the parking lot. Lot two, space forty-seven-F. Just like the Recruiter said. I still remember the number all these years later. There was the ice blue Dodge Charger, stripped of its GPS and satellite radio. No connection to the internet. Not that it really mattered. None of it mattered. The spycraft. None of it. It was all a distraction. Just a setup to catch Roy.

I got behind the wheel. Roy got in the passenger seat. We started driving. It was about a six-hour drive to get to our motel.

And here was the funny thing . . . a painful thing, really. It's painful to me now, I mean, when I look back on it. But even then it had a wistful quality about it, a sunset quality, like it was the end of something, which I guess it was. But here was the thing: we talked the whole way. Roy and I. Through the whole drive, six hours, we talked and talked together, just like in the old days, just like when I was in school and he was my sensei, teaching me karate, and we would go out to bars after class and lean over our beers and talk about what a man could do in the world that would be worthy of a man, that would mean something.

All the grim distance that had grown up between us was suddenly gone. The whole cloud that had hung over us since that night he beat the crap out of me in the motel. The doubts. The moral misgivings. Suddenly, we were just brothers again, him the older, me the younger. Like the old days.

I don't even remember all the things we talked about. Whether the world could get better, whether it ever got better, or whether there was just an illusion of progress created by technology and medicine. Sure, we lived healthier, and things were easier, but had any of it made us better as human beings or were we still savages, just with better tools? Anyway, it doesn't matter what we talked about exactly, the point is the atmosphere of it, the friendship—the friendship was suddenly back.

It made me think, well, maybe I have this wrong, maybe I've misread what's happening. Or maybe the Division has it wrong. Maybe they set this whole thing up and it was a big mistake. I'm not sure I really believed that but I guess I wanted to believe it. Because it was nice, that drive to the motel. It was nice to be talking with Roy like that again, like the old days.

And it went on once we were situated in the motel. We went out to dinner together, a tavern dinner just like what we used to do. Drinking wine, eating burgers, going on long conversational riffs, first him, then me. Zen and focus and violence and life and the meaning of it all.

We kept at it after we got back to the motel too. We picked up a bottle on the way back from the restaurant and we just kept going, me sitting in the desk chair, Roy lying on the bed, propped up on pillows against the headboard.

But now the illusion was gone. Because now it was clear: the Division was right. There was no mistake. Roy had gone bad.

See, in the movies? Or on TV? When a guy gets drugged—your hero, your detective, or your spy or whatever—when he gets drugged there's always this moment when he realizes what's happening to him.

Right? The room goes foggy. The girl who seduced him—or the villain he thought was his friend—starts to go in and out of focus. And there's this moment, there's always this moment, when the hero tries to do something, to smack the girl or bring the villain down, or run out of the room, whatever. But it's too late, the drug has done its work and he collapses dramatically to the floor.

But in the Division, see, that wasn't the way we did it at all. We were much more precise than that. We were trained to dose a man so he never saw it coming. You know, he just got sleepy after a while, the way you do when you're up late, drinking. No foggy room, no villain going in and out of focus. Even when you woke up in the morning, there'd be no blackout or anything. You'd remember it, like, oh yeah, I got sleepy after a while and dozed off. If you weren't suspicious to begin with, you might never even realize you'd been knocked out.

But of course I was suspicious. I'd been suspicious since the night before. Since that crazy briefing with the Recruiter. The laptop. The drive. The stopover. It had made no sense then, and now I knew that it was all a setup. It was all there to create this moment, this opportunity for Roy to act. So I was waiting for it. I was expecting it. The minute I felt the sleepiness coming over me, I knew. I thought, Of course. Of course. *All that good feeling between us in the car and in the tavern, that feeling like we were friends again, brothers again, now it was clear: that was Roy's part of the game. He had just played that role—that role of being my friend again—so I would let down my guard and he could drug me.*

I remember a kind of grief came over me, grief for this man who was the first mentor I'd ever had, the first real friend, the best friend, still the best. I even thought of warning him then. At the last minute. I thought it was so obvious, all it would take was a word to wake him out of his trance. I would say, "Don't you see? Don't you see, Roy, what I'm doing here? How can you miss this, man? This is exactly what we trained for.

This is what we were taught to do. It's an assassination! You're not drugging me! I'm killing you! I'm assassinating you just like we trained for."

Somehow, though—somehow the very fact that he didn't get it, that it was so obvious and he was blind to it, that very fact condemned him in my mind. It meant he had gone over, gone rogue, gone bad, completely. That glitch in his head, that glitch the Recruiter had played on, just like he played on all our glitches, had sent him off the rails. He was gone.

So I didn't say anything. I just said to him, "I'm gonna lie down here for a sec. I just want to close my eyes here, just for a second." Like I didn't know I'd been drugged.

And as I crawled from the chair onto my bed Roy reached out to me from his bed. He reached out and grabbed my elbow. Shook it. Said, "I love you, man." Then swatted me upside the head. Like the old days, when we were friends.

I laughed. But I was thinking, Don't you see? How can you not see?

I lay down and we went on talking for a while, then I drifted off. Smoothly, naturally. It was perfect. I was dead to the world for the rest of the night. No chance of my waking up and catching him at his work. He had set the dose exactly right. Just like we were taught to do.

And just like we were taught to do I had trapped him.

In the morning we got up. We got back in the Charger. We drove to the next city. To the mall. To the Steak N Brew. We ate breakfast together. The man came in—the man in the picture the Recruiter had shown me on his phone. He came in and sat down. He had a tote bag with him, a carryall. He set it by his feet. I remember it had a folded newspaper sticking out of it. I don't know why that has stayed with me but it has.

Roy and I paid our check. We got up to go. I pretended to spot the man, as if I hadn't seen him before. I went up to his table. I said, "Didn't we meet at the conference in Seattle?" And when I walked away a few minutes later the laptop was in his bag and no one could have seen me put it there.

So the mission was done.

We went back to Cathedral Station. About a week after that we were all relocated to D.C. All of us who had made it through the training, I mean. We were set up in apartments at various places in the area. I was placed in Alexandria, Virginia. Roy was in Georgetown.

There was an interval. A waiting period. It must've been about two weeks. I'm not sure—I don't remember now—what was in my mind during that time. I think I more or less buried the whole thing somehow, tried to pretend it never happened or that it would have no consequences. But I remember feeling a sort of subliminal tension, a sort of electric buzz of anticipation. I knew, more or less, what was coming. I just didn't want to think about it.

Then, one day, there it was. In the news, of all places. We didn't even get a briefing on it. I literally read about it online before anyone in the Division said a word.

The country—the country Roy was working for, one of America's enemies—its entire network suddenly collapsed. All its programs were poisoned. The work it had been doing, trying to develop nuclear weapons, was completely destroyed. Reactors failed. One was said to have exploded. A couple of technicians were killed. Records were erased. Their entire wicked enterprise was set back—oh, years, maybe a decade. More. I don't know. It was a catastrophic strike on their computer systems, a thoroughgoing hack, top to bottom.

It was pretty easy for me to guess what had happened. The Division geeks had built a trapdoor into the laptop Roy and I were transporting. The so-called blueprints for some superminiature drone or whatever were supposed to be in there, but that was all just cover stuff, a made-up story, a ruse. The whole point of the exercise had been to give Roy the chance to betray his country, to do his dirty work for the bad guys. To drug me. To rip off the laptop while I slept. To meet his geeks in the parking lot outside and let them steal the blueprints. They took the blueprints back to their evil empire. Opened them up to study them. And when they opened them up, they installed the trapdoor that let us into their network. Our tech guys went to work and boom, we just destroyed them. A universal hit. It was a very successful operation.

The intelligence community had been desperate for a success at that point, so they leaked the results to the media. We—the supersecret Division that had actually pulled the thing off—we didn't hear a word about it until it was right there in the news: "Nuke Plans Scuttled by U.S. Intelligence, Sources Say."

The minute I read it I knew what I had to do. I went tearing out of my apartment. It was maybe seven o'clock in the morning. I got on the Metro. I figured it was faster than a car at that hour in D.C. traffic.

I ran all the way to Roy's apartment building. This huge brick complex near the university. I phoned him the whole way over. Got no answer. Stood at the door buzzing his apartment. Stabbing the buzzer, holding it down. Got no answer.

Finally, I don't why, it occurred to me to go to his garage. It was around the side of the building, down this driveway, this ramp. I ran the whole way. There was a barred iron gate at the entrance. I took hold of the bars and peered through. I don't know if it was just chance, or if we were so connected, I somehow read his mind. But the moment I looked in, that was the exact moment when Roy came hurrying downstairs with his suitcase. I could see him through the bars. I was holding on to the bars like I was in prison, except in reverse, because I was on the outside and he was locked in. I was shouting at him through the bars, "Roy!"

He just ignored me. Went to his car, an old Chevy pickup he'd bought himself. I saw him through the bars, tossing his bag in the cab. I kept shouting, "Roy! Roy!" And he never even looked at me. I think he would have driven right out of there without ever saying a word. I think he would have run me over if he'd had to. Except just then, someone else from the building was driving in, coming home from a late night, I guess. And I guess whoever it was, he must have pressed his remote as he was coming down the street, because the bars started moving in my hand. The gate rattled open as if by magic. And I ran into the garage, shouting, "Roy! Roy!"

He was just about to climb into the cab when I got to him. I was reaching for him and—I don't know why, I guess I just knew him so well—but a second before I put my hand on him I realized he was going to deck me, he was going to just turn and lay me out and drive off. And that's what he would have done, no question. He whipped around just as I reached him, whipped around with a sweeping arm block, followed by a backfist that was meant to break my nose. Only I was ready for it—I don't know why—and I dodged it and barreled into him, knocking him against the side of the truck.

He threw me off, just pushed me off by main strength. I stumbled back and for a second I thought we were going to square off and go at it, another one of our old karate fights, but for real this time, maybe even life and death.

But what was the point? I could never beat Roy. Even with all our Division training, he was still the sensei. And he wasn't really going to kill me, not even then. So what was the point?

We just stood there instead. I don't know, about six feet apart. We stood there, him with his hand on the open door of the pickup, ready to climb inside, and me—I don't know what I'd been thinking, why I'd come, what I was expecting to accomplish.

The guy—the guy who'd been driving home, who opened the garage door with his remote—he drove into the garage just then. So we waited. Waited for him to park. To go inside. The two of us just standing there. Looking in each other's eyes. That whole long time.

Then the guy was gone. The heavy entrance door into the building slammed behind him. The sound echoed through the garage.

I said to Roy, "Where are you going? Where do you think you're going to go?"

"I'm not going to prison, I'll tell you that," he said. "I'm not going to be just another black man dragged into the system."

"Why the hell not? Where else is there? You going to go over to your pals, to your chums, to your allies, your fellow 'people of color' or whatever?"

I was being sarcastic but he was dead serious. He was absolutely grim. He said, "That's right. That's where I'm going. To my fellow people of color."

I said, "Roy! Roy, what are you talking about? Those bastards'll kill you. What you did. They'll think you knew, man. They'll think you purposely destroyed their network. They'll never believe you were set up. I mean, the whole thing, it was so obvious. The Division played it perfectly. They knew you wouldn't see it before it happened and now no one will believe you didn't see it because it was so obvious the whole time."

"They'll believe me," he said—in that same grim tone, except his eyes shifted side to side so I knew he knew it wasn't so. "They won't hurt me." But he knew they would. I could tell.

And I just kept saying, "Roy. Roy. This was the whole play. This was the whole setup. It was a hit. Don't you see? It was a hit on you, man. 'Cause they knew. The Division knew just what you'd do. That's what they're good at."

"Yeah," he said, staring me down. And then, with the emphasis heavy on the first word, he said: "They knew."

Well, I stammered at that. How could I explain it to him? Could I tell him I hadn't known? It was true. I hadn't known. But I also had. They hadn't told me, I mean, but I wasn't going to lie to him. I had known.

"It was so obvious, Roy," I finally said.

"Yeah. I guess it was. I guess I just missed it, that's all."

There was no point in defending myself. I pleaded with him instead. "Don't do this. Don't walk into their trap like this. Stay. Do the time. What can happen? It's America. You'll watch TV for ten, fifteen years, then they'll let you go. It's the federal system. It won't be some state hell house. You'll do push-ups. You'll find Jesus. Get tattoos. Then you'll be out. You'll write a book and get famous. Go on TV. Start a business. 'Prison Strategies for CEOs' or whatever. You'll be rich. It's America. You'll die with a fortune, an old man. Them—the bad guys—they will kill you, Roy. They won't even think twice. They're not your brothers. They'll kill you just like that."

The way he looked at me then—the disdain, the little snort he gave, the way he shook his head—I can see it in front of me now, like he's still standing here now.

He said, "If you could hear yourself . . ."

I sagged. I nodded. I said, "I hear myself."

"The bad guys. Like it's that simple. Like it's all about nothing."

"All right. All right. I'm just desperate, that's all. I'm your friend. I don't want you to die."

"Maybe you shouldn't have killed me then. Friend," he said.

I lost it. I don't know. Maybe it was the guilt. But I was furious with him. I started shouting, "Oh, for God's sake, I didn't make you do it. Take some responsibility!"

"You don't get it."

"I don't get it! I'm the enemy now. I'm the bad guy."

"There's no escape from history."

"Oh yeah, yeah, yeah! History," I said. "History! You're a victim of history now! What a crock. You get born with a soul of your own, Roy. Screw history. You get a soul of your own. You make your own choices. Take some damn responsibility."

He snorted. "Yeah. Right. Enjoy your trust fund, Cam," he said. "Makes those choices a whole lot easier."

He started to get into the pickup. I rushed him. He just turned, just stuck out his hand, flat, hit me in the chest with it, just stiff-armed me, stopped me in my tracks. We stood there like that. Just stood there looking in each other's eyes.

"Roy," I said to him. "Please."

"Congratulations," he said. "You killed me good, Cam. They trained you well. You killed me good."

He got in the truck. Started it up. Drove out of the garage. I was standing there, shouting after him.

"You don't have to do this! It's your choice! You don't have to go!"

He didn't even brake. His taillights never even came on. He went through the barred gate as it was still rumbling open. The roof of the pickup barely cleared the bottom bar. A second earlier and he'd have smashed right through it.

Then he was gone.

About a month later we got the video. The Recruiter called us all in to watch it. He wanted us to see it before it started turning up online so they . . .

I'm sorry. I'm sorry to be emotional, Margaret. It's raw. It's still raw, all these years later. Just give me a second here.

You want to know the funny thing? The weird thing? The person I was angry at? Was him! Roy. I'm still angry at him. Right this second. He's dead and gone and I'm still furious at the guy. I can't blame the ones who killed him. That was their nature. That was who they were. They were just living out their philosophy, age old, time out of mind. I can't blame the Recruiter or the Division. They'd found a traitor in their midst and they did what they do. They used him. They blew up the bad guys' nuclear program. Hurrah for us, right. They used him, just like we pay them to do. They did their jobs.

But Roy, he lied to himself. He made up some noble fantasy about what, after all, was simple treason. This was his country. His own, his native land. It called on him, a native son, to serve in its defense. He didn't have to go. They didn't force him. They called on him and he said yes. Without reservation. Without irony. And then—then he plotted his betrayal.

And for what? This is what gets me, what makes me so angry at him. For who? For what? His buddies? His great good pals? His fellow travelers through history?

They made him kneel in the sand at gunpoint. On the video. They made him recite some doctrine of theirs for the cameras. Then they decapitated him. They sawed his head off with a knife.

I'm sorry. I'm sorry for being so emotional. I blame him. I blame him. He was my friend. I had to watch them do that to him. He was like a brother to me. I blame him.

I wonder if in the end it occurred to him he might have made a mistake.

Or maybe . . . what do I know? Maybe he thought he was right to the very last. Really, what do I know? Because it was true about me. What he said. I was born with everything. Money. Caste, if there is such a thing. Whatever there is to be born with, I was born with it.

So maybe—I'm sorry—maybe he died blaming me. I don't know. But I wonder. I still wonder to this day.

I wonder if he realized he had made a mistake or if he died blaming me.

23

It was a difficult moment for Margaret Whitaker. Winter's story had horrified her, yet she had to disguise her horror. It had terrified her, yet she had to suppress her fear. She had to allow Winter time to express his emotions. She had to respond to him without judgment. She had to allow him to expel his toxic self-disgust, and then prepare to marshal all her skill in order to mother his pain away. And at the same time, she had to figure out whether she was going to tell him about the little wooden dog on her shelf or just chalk up the whole episode to paranoia and try to let it go.

For the moment, she knew simply to sit in silence. She'd been in the therapy business a long time and she realized Winter needed to be left alone. Women didn't mind a bit of crying if there was crying to be done. There was no shame in it for them, generally speaking. But men—men like Winter—men couldn't stand it. A virile dampening of the eyes for some great cause or loss might be okay. But otherwise? Crying was like bleeding to them. It was something they did if they had to, but they wanted to stanch the flow as quickly as possible and get back into the battle of life. Men didn't want her sympathy. They didn't want her Kleenex. They didn't want anything but for the bleeding to stop. Anything she offered Winter right now would only serve to annoy and alienate him.

She watched him quietly. He wouldn't even let the tears fully fall. He swiped each one away angrily with his palm as it emerged from the corner of his eye. When he felt he was finished—when he felt sure that his wound had scabbed over—he snatched a tissue from the box on her coffee table as if he were ripping a man's face off. He blew his nose with a noise like he was shouting curses at a driver who had cut him off in traffic.

"So anyway, that's how I killed the best friend I ever had," he muttered with a show of bitter nonchalance.

She smiled gently. The horror of Roy Spahn's decapitation was stuck in her throat as if she'd swallowed a tennis ball, but there was only sweet sympathy in her eyes.

"Brace yourself for more of this, Margaret," Winter went on miserably. "We're just getting started. By the time I'm done, you'll have a whole mound of severed heads in your office, each with my name on it."

"All right, Cam, all right," she murmured.

"Too much? Am I pitying myself?"

"A little."

"Well . . . it's . . . unpleasant, carrying this stuff around. It's like . . . a stain on you. A bloodstain you think everyone can see. Or should see, if they don't. If they admire you. If they love you. You can't help thinking: 'Oh, you don't know. You don't see the stain.'"

"I see you, Cam. It's all right."

"It was treason," he burst out angrily. "I was doing my job. I don't even know why I should feel bad about it."

"He was your friend."

"He was my friend," he echoed back to her, his lip trembling. "He was my friend."

Again, they were silent. Again, Margaret struggled with what to do. She knew how he needed her now, how badly. Her skill, her love, her healing authority over him. But the terror of his tale, the deadly stakes, made it seem even more urgent that she let him know about the wooden dog.

Over the next minute or so an idea began to form in her mind. In what she would later consider one of her better professional moments, she began to think of a way to perform her two tasks almost simultaneously. To both comfort him and lead him to what she needed him to know.

She shifted slightly in her chair to draw his attention. When he glanced at her, she said, "It seems to trouble you that Roy might have gone to his death hating you. Blaming you in his last moments, without taking responsibility for his actions."

He sighed wearily. Nodded wearily. He was running out of energy now. His emotions had exhausted him. "Yes," he said. "Sometimes I get so frustrated with him, I lie awake and curse at the ceiling as if he were floating up there, looking down on me."

"Had the positions been reversed, would you have blamed him?"

She watched as he blinked, as he tried to think it through. "No," he told her finally. "I'm sure I wouldn't have. I would have figured: I bought the ticket, I had to take the ride."

"So why do you think he might have reacted differently?"

Winter's whole body moved as he tried to bring the insight out of himself. "Because Roy . . . you know, when it came down to it, he was a pretty messed up guy, really."

"That's right," said Margaret. "You have a more integrated personality than he had. For whatever reason, you're more solidly built."

"Yeah. Well. He had to deal with issues that I didn't have."

"Maybe so. But the point is, when the Recruiter played on your fault lines, your personality held together. His ruptured."

"Yes. I guess that's true."

"The Recruiter sounds like he was a very good psychologist."

Winter smiled with fondness and admiration. "The best I ever saw. Present company excepted, of course. He was uncanny, the way he saw into people."

She continued to lead him to comfort, away from the brother figure he'd lost and toward the father figure he'd found. "And with Roy gone, the Recruiter became your mentor."

Winter nodded, still smiling faintly. "He was tough on me, but in a good way. He made me stronger."

"And yet he was the one who sent you on the mission with Roy. He was the one who sent you on all the missions that trouble you now."

Winter defended him, as she had known he would. "That was his job. And he did it incredibly well. He had this wonderful certainty about him. About good and evil, right and wrong. It was so straightforward and yet ironic at the same time. I don't really know how to describe it."

"But it was helpful to you."

"Yes. He helped me to become myself. He turned me into a warrior."

His smile, and the fond, faraway light in his eyes, made her smile too. She was taking his horror onto herself, uncovering the strength beneath it. She was showing him the almost holy logic by which he had passed through anguish into the fullness of his identity. She was doing her job.

"Is that who you are now?" she asked. "A warrior?"

He shrugged. "I'm an English professor."

"Cam," she said.

He gave an embarrassed laugh. "All right. Yes. In my own way. It was always there, but the Recruiter brought it out in me."

"And it's still there, isn't it? You're still a warrior."

"In my way. Yes."

"Your strange habit of mind."

"That's right."

"It leads you to uncover 'acts of evil.' That's what you told me in one of our first sessions. It allows you to see crimes and solutions to crimes that other people can't see."

"Sometimes, yes."

Looking at him, studying him, she saw how the strength had returned to his features, and even a new strength, the strength of beginning to know himself as an act of becoming, a traveler in time, a human being, imperfect and forgivable. This was her work in him.

She decided the moment had come for her to do what she was certain now she needed to do.

"Are you at war with an evil now, Cam?" she asked him.

He was quick. He caught the change of direction at once. His eyes cleared. They hardened. His gaze met hers directly.

"Yes," he said. "I think I am. I'm at war with something. Something that shouldn't be. I think it is evil actually. Yes."

"An evil that only you can see because of how you think, because of who you are. Because of who the Recruiter helped you become."

"Yes."

"And it's difficult."

"It's complicated. Yes."

"Yes," she said. "Complicated. Painful. But it has to be done."

"It has to," he said. "It has to be stopped."

Their gazes were locked on one another now. She could see him thinking, trying to get ahead of her. He was so sharp. He must have realized she had wanted to say something to him during their previous session. He must have known she had stopped herself. He was alert, waiting for her to deliver.

"Is must be dangerous, then," she said. "There must be people who want to stop you."

"Yes. They're going to try. I want them to. I've been trying to draw them out."

"Just like the Recruiter taught you."

"Yes. Why are you asking me these things, Margaret?"

She slowly drew in a long, steadying breath through her nose. She didn't have time to appreciate it then, but later she would tell herself it was well done, a good job. She had brought him back from his heartache to his strength with a new understanding. He was ready now to hear what she had to say.

"There is a little wooden statue of a dog on a shelf in my apartment," she told him.

She saw his posture change. He became tense and ready. A weapon, expertly made. She found it frightening—and thrilling.

"I bought it as a memorial to my late dog Victoria," she went on. "I always set it on the shelf facing east—toward where the sun rises—because I hope I'll see her again in the life to come. It's silly I suppose. But it's always set like that, just so."

He understood. "Did someone move it?"

"I don't know. I'm not sure," said Margaret. Her voice trembled a little. "But I think so, yes. It seems to have moved anyway. Maybe it's nothing. Maybe I bumped into the shelf. Or my cat . . ."

He shook his head. "No," he said. His gaze turned inward as he worked it through.

"Is someone going to hurt me, Cam?" she asked him.

"Oh, no," he said at once. "No. No one. It's not like that at all."

"Are you sure?"

"Yes. You have my word. Don't worry."

"But someone did come into my apartment."

"Yes, I'm afraid so."

"For my computer? Is that it? Were they looking for my notes about you?"

"Yes."

"I'm so sorry," she said. She was aware that her hand was at her throat, her wrinkled, trembling hand worrying at the yellow topazes of the necklace on her tan sweater. Like an anxious old lady, she thought. How she wished she were younger. "You did warn me. I'm so sorry, Cam."

"No, no," he said kindly. "It's my fault. I'm sorry it happened."

"But the notes . . ."

"It's all right, Margaret, really. It doesn't matter now. But you should probably be careful in the future."

"I'll destroy them."

"It doesn't matter. But in the future."

"Of course. But I'm safe, you think. Personally."

"I promise. Completely. It's nothing like that. I would never let anyone hurt you."

"Thank you. That makes me feel so much better. I guess I'm becoming a nervous old lady."

"Not at all. You had every right to be concerned."

She straightened, a show of confidence. A show for him. "Well," she said, making her voice more hearty now. "I'm very glad you became a warrior. I know you will protect me."

He smiled suddenly, the first smile like it she had ever seen from him. It was radiant—radiant with strength and pleasure.

It was, as she would tell herself later, a job well done.

24

It had been a long time since Winter was in the Arizona desert. He had forgotten how extraordinary the landscape was, especially near dawn. Glancing up from the screen of the GPS on the dashboard of his rented Jeep, he suddenly found his senses overwhelmed. Rock formations of exotic strangeness and beauty stretched beneath a sky of uncanny colors that blended as the day's light spread. Stark buttes brooded against rose ridges of clouds. Weird red mesas loomed majestically out of a pellucid blue background. All of them together, all around him, looked like an ancient ruin petrified, the remnant of a once thriving city that had fallen from the stars.

How apt a metaphor that seemed to him, as he went where he was going: to be traveling through a territory that looked as alien to him, and yet as present to him, as his own past.

The house, when he finally arrived there, seemed to fit right in—to fit with both the landscape and the literary trope. It was a red box of a building designed to nestle seamlessly in a shelf of the surrounding formations. Winter wouldn't have even seen it there if it hadn't blipped on the GPS: "You have arrived."

As his Jeep coasted to a stop in the nearly invisible driveway, his tires rattling the red rocks, the Recruiter emerged through sliding glass doors to greet him.

Winter grinned at him through the windshield as he killed the engine. But he imagined—he always imagined—the Recruiter could see past any polite facade. The Recruiter could peer straight into his heart, and his heart was startled at how old the man had grown. They had not been separated as much as a decade, and yet the Recruiter seemed to have put on eons. His cropped hair was gray. His face was harshly lined as if grooved with the sharp edge of a stone. Winter supposed it could have simply been the effect of the years. There was a moment people reached when age just caught up with them and showed itself. But he suspected it was more than that, the mark of trouble. The government's secret and sudden dismantling of the Division had taken its toll on the man.

The two of them shook hands with real feeling. The Recruiter slapped Winter's shoulder and said, "Well. Poetry Boy."

Inside, the little house was sparsely furnished and entirely masculine. Winter doubted the Recruiter had even had a woman in to clean. He had always wondered about that aspect of the Recruiter's character. There was a rumor he'd been married once, but Winter had never seen a human female get anything like intimate with him. Now this house. He found the strictly masculine solitude of it depressing, lonesome.

There was a living room and a kitchen. A bedroom he never got to see. There was comfortable, serviceable, ragged furniture Winter forgot as soon as his eyes went over it. Everything was swept and orderly in military fashion, but there were no gentle touches, no flowers, no art. Only the windows everywhere. They were large on every wall. They enclosed the house within the big sky and the weird desert, where the deeper reds were now going out of the rocks as the sun rose higher.

"Sit your butt down, Poetry Boy," said the Recruiter. His voice was thin and tremulous, as if he were old enough to be Winter's grandfather. "Juice or coffee."

"Coffee please."

"Black or black with sugar. I haven't got any milk."

"Black is fine."

"Good." He went into the kitchen as Winter settled on a color-less, overly soft sofa. "I was afraid university life might have weakened your moral character, such as it is," the Recruiter called back to him as cupboards opened and liquid burbled in the kitchen out of sight. "I was afraid you might ask for a half-caf, lemon-scented, strawberry frappe topped with fairy dust or something."

"Hell, no," Winter called back. "In fact, you can put some nails in it for good measure."

He did not know why he imagined the Recruiter chuckling at that. He could not remember the Recruiter ever having chuckled before.

Winter sat looking down at the low coffee table in front of him. It was colorless like the sofa. There was a mug of cold coffee on it, a plate of crumbs, and a Bible open to the Book of Revelation.

"I'll take that away if it bothers you," said the Recruiter, bringing him a steaming mug. He even walked like an old man now, his legs akimbo, his back bent. "I wouldn't want the Word of the Living God to disturb your faculties and render you unfit for academic life."

"It is a danger."

"No, I think I'll leave it there, if you don't mind. I'm sure the devil will protect his own. And meanwhile I'll enjoy hearing the serpent of sin squirming in your soul as we chat."

Winter laughed. "You're looking well, chief," he said. He sipped his coffee as the Recruiter hobbled to his easy chair on the far side of the coffee table.

"I don't have to respond to that, do I?" The Recruiter settled into his seat with a sigh. "You're a literary man. You can string together a set of elaborate obscenities as well as I can. I can trust you to imagine my reply and make it one that will cause you to feel the sort of crippling and abject shame appropriate to someone who has uttered a womanish lie unfit for men who have killed America's enemies together."

Winter lifted one corner of his mouth in a sad smile. "All right. You look about a hundred years old. They really seem to have done a job on you."

"That they have," said the Recruiter. "'Henceforth, let no man trouble me, for I bear on my body the marks of the Lord Jesus.'"

"That bad, was it?"

"The United States government has infinite resources and went out of its way to bring them down upon my dusky head. They were shocked, I tell you, shocked to find such goings on in their innocent midst."

"I'll just bet they were," said Winter. He sipped his coffee again, then set his mug down. Leaned forward with his elbows on his thighs, his hands twisting together. He looked into the worn face of his old mentor and remembered as if all at once how much he had come to love him in the days gone by. "Are you bitter?" he asked, with genuine curiosity. "Did they manage to make you bitter?"

"No," the Recruiter said at once. Then: "Was I too quick with that? Still—no." And with that telepathic mind of his, he added, "Ah, but you're thinking about your old friend, aren't you?"

Winter knew he shouldn't have been surprised that his mind was transparent to the man, but how could he help it? "How could you know that? That is who I was thinking about."

"Half-Roy Half-Spahn."

"Ach. You were always a hard man, chief."

"I was. I am. I harvest where I have not sown. But you don't have to worry that I'll go wrong like our treasonous and therefore departed friend. The service was never transactional for me, the way it was for him. I mean, I didn't do what I did because our leaders deserved it, any more than Jesus saved my soul because I was worthy of salvation. I did what the Lord informed me would befit a man—a man and an American. So did you, by the way, Poetry Boy. You're not to trouble yourself any longer over Roy's sorry end. A man works that hard for something, he ought to get what he deserves."

Winter retrieved his coffee mug and lifted it to his mouth, vainly hoping to hide behind the steam. But what was the point? He didn't even know why he'd bothered to put on flesh that morning. The Recruiter always saw right through him like an X-ray, easy as that.

The older man slapped his own thigh. "But you didn't come here to talk about the late Mr. Spahn."

"No."

"You came here to talk about Nelson Chen."

"Did you know him?"

"I knew them all, my son. I know them still. By heart."

"You keep tabs on us." This was not a question. It was a startled realization.

The Recruiter wagged his head. "I'm not the government. Not anymore. My own resources are limited. But I have friends. I hear things. And your man Stankowski brought your concerns to me, as you asked him to."

"Chen works as a bodyguard for a man named Gerald Byrne," said Winter.

"Yes, I read up on Byrne after I spoke with Stan-Stan. What's your intel?"

And while the Recruiter sat as still and strange as the buttes and mesas out the window, as deep as the desert out there and as ruined as the past, Winter told him the story as he himself had uncovered it. He began with Adam Kemp's suicide. Moved on to Charles Merriman's car crash. Touched on the ruination of Lou Walsh and the podcaster Henry Woolsey. Then he went on to the core of the matter.

There was Arnaud Baptiste, first of all, killed in the Paris riots. But he'd found more now too, as he had warned Molly he would. There was also a Swiss banker named Arthur Keller who had gone fishing on the Lake of Thun one spring morning. His motorboat had vanished slowly into the thick mist beneath the Bernese mountains and had never reemerged, never ever. There was a plane crash in Kenya that killed three Christian activists who opposed what they called Byrne's "Secular Colonialism." There was also Richard Mulholland, a former CIA agent who had arranged a meeting with a British reporter, Sam Levine. When Levine arrived at Mulholland's safe house, Mulholland lay dead in a pool of his own blood. He had cut his wrists, the coroner said.

"Levine swore Mulholland was going to expose some sort of conspiracy between former members of the American intelligence community and a cabal of international businessmen led by Byrne. He believed Mulholland was murdered but never came close to proving it."

"I would be disappointed if he had," said the Recruiter. They were the first words he had spoken since Winter began his narrative. "I trained you people better than that."

"Nelson was good, then."

"You were all good," said the Recruiter. "Even you, theologically confused and philosophically deluded though you were. Still, you're right. This has Division fingerprints all over it."

Winter nodded. He wanted to tell the Recruiter about Margaret Whitaker's wooden dog, but he was loath to let the man know he had needed therapy to deal with his guilt and sorrow.

"What aren't you telling me?" the Recruiter asked.

Well, so much for trying to hide anything. "I'm seeing a therapist," he confessed.

"Of course you are. How could you not be laboring under a neurosis when you remain an unbaptized heathen crushed beneath the burden of your sins?"

"I'm pretty sure I was baptized, actually. It was sort of a social thing."

"Those don't count. Your therapist is an elderly female I assume." Winter was too taken aback to gasp out the question: *How did you know?* but the Recruiter answered it anyway. "You always were a mama's boy."

"Jesus, chief."

"Don't take the Lord's name in vain, son. I know you think he isn't who he said he was, but as it happens you're mistaken. Is your mummy substitute any good at her job?"

"She's terrific, actually. If she were younger I'd be her love slave."

"I suppose we may all be thankful for having been spared that nauseating spectacle. And, let me guess, you let her take notes on your sessions. You were too overawed by her maternal presence to play the man's part for once in your life and demand that she refrain."

"I did suggest it."

"Ah. You suggested it. You said, 'Please, Mummy, don't record my deepest secrets on a computer that's password protected by the name of your dog and an exclamation point.'"

Winter laughed ruefully. "Pretty much."

"And now her apartment has been broken into."

"It does look that way."

"So we can assume the enemies of God and man have gathered up the contents of your spilled guts and are currently strategizing your assassination."

"That's my guess. At least I did everything I could think of to push them into it."

Though his face remained a stony and unreadable blank, this remark made the Recruiter's eyes grow brighter. "Ah, did you? So you retained some skills, at least."

"One or two."

"But not enough? And so you've come crawling back to the Magic All-American Negro of Christ to help you bring your counter hit to fruition."

"Something like that. I thought of handling it myself."

"But they have eyes on you."

"I'm sure they do, though I also made sure there was no way for them to track me here."

"Mm. And they're not watching me. I would have known if they were. They'd be dead in the desert by now."

"Exactly."

"All right. So what is it you want from me?"

"Well, I assume you only have to pierce the night sky with some sort of spotlight signal and a merry band of former government assassins currently wreaking secret havoc in war-torn hellholes around the globe would reassemble to assist you."

The Recruiter lifted his chin. "A romantic notion but not completely implausible. And you want these Invisibles to work a counter op while you pretend to fall into Nelson's clutches."

"Nelson is waiting for me to do it myself. He'd spot it a mile off and counter my counter."

"But he'll never see me coming."

Winter nodded. He never would.

"You realize that under those circumstances we couldn't even contact you," the Recruiter said. "You'd never even know for sure we were there. Or what we were doing. You'd have to remember your playbook and hope for the best like the cheerful, optimistic, faith-enlivened person you have never had either the courage or the decency to be."

"I could fake it."

The two men sat in silence for a second or two after that. The desert scenery all around them now seemed oddly one-dimensional in the full light of later morning: a painting of an alien ruin rather than the real thing. The Recruiter rubbed his lifted chin with one hand and Winter was struck again—struck with some sadness—by how old he looked, how weary. But no, not bitter. Just as he said: not bitter; in fact, at peace.

"What else is worrying you?" the Recruiter asked then. "There's no point in troubling your mind over what has to be done."

Winter let out a breath. He hadn't even been aware he was holding it. "It does have to be done, doesn't it?"

"Certainly it does. What's the problem?"

"Oh, the usual, I guess. Collateral damage. Byrne has a wife and children."

"He should have thought of that before he became evil."

Winter chewed the inside of his cheek. "It is evil, right, chief? It isn't just me. I'm not just seeing it that way because I envy him."

"Oh, by all that's holy! Of course it's evil! He's conspiring with the powerful to suppress the freedom of the common man and destroying everyone who gets in his way. What on earth made him believe that he was God?"

"A drug he took in the Amazon."

The Recruiter made a noise of disgust. "It's the original sin, Poetry Boy. The sin of Eden reenacted like a childhood trauma.

It's the old mental illness of princes and kings. His fellow princes won't stop him. They share his delusion. So the Lord has appointed a judge from among the people, and behold, in the winter of our republic, Winter is his name."

"Yikes."

"Indeed."

"It's just that she . . . his wife, I mean . . ."

"Ah. His wife, his wife. Another mummy figure for you. With all these mummies, it's beginning to look like ancient Egypt around here, appropriately enough."

Winter shut his eyes. Pinched the bridge of his nose. He had not forgotten what a hard man the Recruiter was, but he was even harder than he had remembered. "She's . . ."

"Well?"

"She's a good woman, chief."

"I'm heartened to hear it. Good women are important. And rare. Like good men. They make manifest the feminine aspect of God, who made us in his image, male and female. Oh, I'm sorry, I forgot I was speaking into the echo chamber of a hollow soul, emptied of that spirit only faith can animate."

"She's not, though. A hollow soul. She's like you, a true believer."

"Of course she is. No truly good woman could be anything else. A faithless man might go about his simple chores of architecture and demolition, but only a godly woman can do what good women do. I assume you've explained the situation to her."

"Yes."

"But of course she already sensed it in her secret heart."

Winter only snorted. What was the point of wasting words on the man? He already knew everything.

"And now you're worried that destroying her evil husband will ruin her life and bring her to grief."

"Well, it's pretty sure to do that. She loves him. More than that, she's devoted to him."

"I would hope she would be. He's her husband."

Not for the first time in his life, Winter threw back his head and groaned aloud at the Recruiter's certainties.

"Oh! You drive me crazy. Everything's so simple for you! It's not simple. I'm not stupid to worry about this, chief."

"Not stupid," said the Recruiter. He leaned forward in his chair. His lined black face seemed a carved and thunderous idol. "Weak."

"Weak? I'm weak? I'm weak to care what happens to this wonderful person?"

"Care all you want. Who cares if you care? Are we not men and therefore put on earth to do what must be done? If you want to feel sorry for someone, feel sorry for Gerald Byrne. What? You think I have no feeling for him? You think I had no feeling for half-Roy? No. I mean this sincerely. Mr. Byrne is a poor creature. His father corrupt, his mother guilty of self-murder. The people assigned to manifest God in our lives fail us and we think that God has failed. We are broken, and the devil gets into us through our broken places. It's not fair but so it has been decreed. Now Byrne is lost. The soul God gave him is shriveled to an ineffectual worm. He's Satan's glove puppet. He has to be stopped. But as for his good and godly wife. Well, she'll mourn his destruction and then find meaning in it and through suffering bring herself and her children closer to the throne of heaven. Pity him rather than her, Poetry Boy. Eternity is a long time to burn."

Winter—who notwithstanding his respect and affection for the Recruiter had never been able to share his certainties—was only able to respond with a miserable laugh. "What about my role in it?" he asked the Recruiter. He pointed at the Bible on the coffee table. "The things I'm going to have to do are ugly. Doesn't it say somewhere in there that we should answer evil with good?"

The normally deadpanned Recruiter allowed himself a judicious frown. "It does," he said. "And I'm gratified by even your merely academic and therefore functionally useless knowledge of the Word of God. But I wouldn't worry about it if I were you. It's not doing your duty that will condemn you to the flames of hell, Poetry Boy. It's your idiot unbelief. A little bit of killing here and there won't make a bit of difference."

25

Three days later, damned though he might have been, Winter sat in the Independent coffee shop, snacking on his afternoon croissant. To an observer, he might have seemed placid, even dreamy. An academic on a break, at gaze. But inside he was tense; vigilant, but not only vigilant. Excited too. A warrior again, and full of warrior anticipation. He knew he had goaded Byrne into action. The fight was finally on.

He stole a glance around the shop. He saw a gentle snowfall at the window. He saw students at the tables on either side of him. But no Invisibles—none of the Recruiter's agents, not as far as he could tell. Maybe there were none to find. Maybe his old chief had failed him and he was on his own here. *O, ye of little faith,* he thought. He faced forward and resolved to believe.

On the small table in front of him were his coffee in its paper cup, the remaining half of his croissant on a plate, and his laptop. On the laptop there was a video of an Englishman named Simon White.

White was a Tory Member of Parliament and a former European MP. In the video, he was standing on the floor of the House of Commons, inveighing against a global tax plan that he felt would strip the United Kingdom of its national sovereignty. The plan was a central part of Byrne's Good World Project. Winter huffed softly to himself. Strange, he thought, that White's reputation, maybe even his life, might depend on what happened next in this obscure midwestern coffee shop.

So he was telling himself anyway, when Hannah Greer walked in.

Her beret was flecked with snowflakes. Her cheeks were pink with cold. She unbuttoned her winter coat as she entered. She was dressed, underneath, in that antiquated way of hers. A narrow gray skirt below the knee. A black cardigan with red ties at the throat and flowering vines knitted down the sides, wonderfully suggestive of the Tyrolean. It was funny, Winter thought—funny in the sense of odd—that even now her resemblance to Charlotte affected him. Even now that he knew what she was, she stirred his deepest longings.

He had to admire that. As a construct, as a work of spycraft. He could see how Nelson had given her not a physical but only, as it were, a spiritual resemblance to Charlotte. That was why she had sailed so smoothly under Winter's suspicions. If she had actually looked like his first love, he might have balked at the coincidence. But that she represented only what he felt about Charlotte—that was a brilliant touch. It had made him feel that he was discovering something about her that no one else could have possibly seen. It had made him a collaborator in his own deception. Nelson had studied the notes he had stolen from Margaret Whitaker's computer and had constructed Hannah Greer with care so that her carriage, her dress, even her gestures led him, Winter, to make the connection to Charlotte as if on his own. He had been tricked into tricking himself.

It was nice handiwork. The Recruiter really had trained them well.

Hannah seemed to notice him. That was realistic enough. It was a small coffee shop. She'd be sure to notice him. She brightened as only a young woman can and gave him a silly windshield wiper wave. It was amazing. Even knowing what he knew, his heart was drawn into her performance of youth and innocence. Using database access on loan from the Recruiter he had traced her identity. She was not nineteen. She was twenty-six. A skilled freelance agent, possibly the same agent who had seduced a British intelligence officer in Bangkok the year before and left him dead. Yet just like an actress on the screen she made him believe in the part she was playing. Even now, he could not help himself.

Still, he managed to play his own part in response. He pretended to be a man who was confident he could control his desires. That way, as the performance unfolded, it would seem to her that his desires had crept up on him and led him astray.

He made a casual gesture toward the seat across the table from him, inviting her to sit.

"Let me order a coffee, and I'll join you. Can I?" she said.

"Please do."

When she was seated with him the effect of the illusion was nearly overwhelming. Even knowing what she was he wanted her as if she were really Hannah Greer. The triumph of Desire over Reality.

"I sometimes feel so much of the truth and beauty has gone out of the world, it's almost an act of rebellion to find it in the corners where it still exists," she was saying to him. "Do you know what I mean? Do you think I'm being, I don't know, too young and cynical?"

"You mean, has it ever been thus?" he asked her.

"Yes. Yes, that is what I mean. I mean, sometimes I think, maybe I just haven't lived long enough to realize that culture is always mostly drab and empty like this. Still, there once was a world where Keats and Wordsworth, Coleridge and Blake, Shelley and Byron were all alive at the same time. I mean, this is not that world. I know that much."

He made some equally bland observation, but he was only half listening to himself. His longings distracted him. What could it mean that he was so attracted to her? He knew she was a manufactured lie. How could the trick still work on him so well? It made him wonder: had Charlotte herself been an illusion too? Maybe that elevated, grave, and distant charm she'd had in her youth had been nothing more than a symptom of the insanity that was growing inside her. Or maybe he had imagined that charm, created it himself out of his own longings. Maybe everything he was searching for in a woman was like that: false and deceptive, constructs that women obliged men by putting on like makeup, illusions, like Hannah Greer herself, purposely fashioned to charm men's yearning hearts. Or maybe not. Maybe it was like the Recruiter said, that a good woman was the manifestation of some essential thing. The yin of the pleroma, as the literary Winter put it to himself, the feminine aspect of the totality of God.

He shook himself inwardly. He had to pay attention. This was a dangerous business going on here. A helping of Eros and Thanatos—sex and death—to go with his coffee and croissant.

"I think," he said, "high culture comes and goes. It's cyclical, like everything else. The important thing is what it leaves behind. The works. And even without them, the truth and beauty are always ours to create out of the materials of life. Out of our relationships, for instance. Am I wrong? Doesn't that have to be true?"

"You mean, what happens between people is sort of like art," she said, making an eager, girlish gesture between himself and her. "You mean, we write a kind of poetry with our lives. With our love."

"Well, yes. I mean, even art itself is a transaction between one soul and another, or else it's nothing. And in theory the reverse is true, that every emotional transaction is potentially a work of art. This conversation, for instance."

Hannah Greer raised her eyes heavenward. "I so wish I were in your class this year!" she said. "Every time I even talk to you, it's like, I don't know, like finding flowers in the desert or something."

That was a little much, the critic in him thought, but he managed to chuckle with the sort of humility men pretend to have in the hope it will lure women into their beds. She would notice him doing that, he thought, pretending to be modest in order to seduce her. She would think she had him, fish on a line. Well, good. Let her think it. The play's the thing.

The timing, though—that was the tricky part. If he fell for her too quickly she would cotton on. Too slow, and Byrne might abandon the whole elaborate strategy, might strike him down before he had a chance to strike first. He had to move fast but he had to let the rhythm of seduction play out naturally, so that it was impossible for her to be sure which one of them was doing what.

At last, she said she should be going. She had a class on the hour. He said yes, he had work to do too. He had lost track of time.

"So did I!" she said passionately, a hand to her breast.

Which way was she headed? he asked. He was headed that way as well, he said. They could walk together.

He escorted her to the building the students called the Red Castle. It was a glowering brick fortress with great round turrets on the corners. They lingered at the enormous arching entranceway while other students filed past them. The snow had stopped. The clouds were parting. A rich blue sky with the first hint of evening in it was making its appearance directly overhead.

"Well, I should get inside," she said with a reluctant gesture toward the door.

He eyed the heavens. "It's clearing up. You know, I think I'll play hooky and take a walk. Have a good class."

"Oh!" she cried at once. "Can I come with you? Can I play hooky too?"

"No, no. Absolutely not. Go to your class. I can't be responsible for corrupting you."

"Oh, please, corrupt me. Please. It's all bad prose and theory in there. I get so much more from talking to you."

"Ah. Now you've done it. You've flattered me into submission. How can I say no?"

They walked off together. He thought it had been well done. Five stars for both their performances.

And so to bed.

They walked by the water as the sky grew dark. She began to shiver with the cold. He took her to the Nomad for a glass of wine. It grew late, so they stayed for a pub-style dinner. At some point the tone of the conversation shifted. Even he wasn't sure which one of them had pulled that off. He only knew it was time to make a pro forma show of resistance, one of those displays of fake virtue that is really only one more tool of seduction. It would make her feel, one, that he had enough morals to be a worthwhile conquest and, two, that what was happening between them was edgy and forbidden and romantic. That is, it would have made her feel like that if she were really Hannah Greer—which, he had to keep reminding himself, she was not.

"You know, Hannah," he said. "I think I ought to take you home now."

"Oh, why? We're having such a nice time."

"Because I'm a professor here and you're a student and there are rules about these things and this conversation is becoming something . . . it shouldn't become."

"Oh, I like that. That sounds dangerous."

"You know what I mean."

"I'm not a child, Cam. I'm nineteen, I'm a grown woman. I can make my own decisions. There's nothing wrong with what's happening between us. I want it to happen."

It broke his heart to have her. He was not prepared for the effect of it. She had been so well trained to represent what Charlotte meant to him that to see the blouse beneath her sweater fall in living slow motion to his bedroom floor, to be naked against her nakedness, to have his lips on hers, to be inside her—it broke his heart. He warned himself not to get lost in it. He warned himself it was all pretend. It didn't matter. His body couldn't tell the difference, and, after a moment's hesitation, his soul just took a swan dive into the illusion. What would he have been if this had actually happened? he kept wondering as he watched her beneath him. What would his life have been? Roy and the Division and all that bloodshed—would any of it have come to pass if Charlotte and he had really been lovers?

He lay in the darkness afterward and held her slender body against him and he could have wept with regret. He could have wept because she was not what she was. He could have wept for Roy slaughtered in the wilderness. He could have wept for all the dead he'd left in his wake. He wanted more than anything to close his eyes and pretend that this was real, but the time for that was past. He could have wept that it was past.

"I'm going to have a nightcap," she murmured in his ear, as he knew she would. "Can I pour you something?"

"Sure," he said. "There's a good single malt on the lower shelf of the bar. Do you want me to get it?"

"No. Stay there. I want to bring it to you."

She put on his shirt to go and fetch the drinks. It was a nice touch, that feminine gesture of possession. He watched her move as she left the room, then lay with his hands behind his head. He stared up at the ceiling. The ceiling was where the dead appeared when they returned at night to accuse him. But tonight he thought Roy might have been smiling down at him. Roy—at least the younger Roy, his friend Roy—would have enjoyed this. The utter madness of it. He would have enjoyed Winter's irrational suffering and the pure heartlessness of his strategy. It would have made him laugh knowingly, like the young pseudocynic he had been. Winter could almost hear him.

She brought him a double blast of his best stuff, a glass of wine for her. They drank together and chatted, sleepy and satisfied. He traced patterns with his finger on her naked flesh. He wanted her again, but he didn't know if he would be able to bear it. Anyway, he began to feel the drug take hold now, a subtle effect. This too: well done. Five stars. The pull of sleep felt altogether natural. Nelson had trained her as he had been trained.

He lay back on the pillow. He closed his eyes.

He thought of Charlotte, or Charlotte as she had been, or Charlotte as he once thought she was. Where was she in the wide world? he wondered.

He smiled to himself and lost consciousness.

26

She was wonderful in the morning. Chatty and charming. Fussing around like she owned the place, like she'd moved in, his full-time lover. She brought him coffee in bed. She made him laugh and they made love again in an easy daylight way. It was all such an agonizing delight that Winter found himself wondering if Byrne and Nelson had created her more out of anger than out of necessity. Winter was a man, after all. Any half-attractive woman could have seduced him easily enough. Drugged him. Rifled his computer. Searched his apartment. Had Byrne been so furious at Winter that he'd gone out of his way to rip his heart out like this? Like Hannah was doing right now by being so adorable, everything he desired?

But no, he thought. Byrne was a colder character than that. This wasn't revenge. And it wasn't just seduction. Winter was a watchful man, alert and dangerous. Byrne would have known that. Nelson would have told him. The point had been to fool him utterly. To make certain he would not suspect a thing before the hit was finished. Only in the moment that he fell out the window or drove off the cliff would it occur to him: *Ah, Hannah had been part of it.*

It would have to be that, it would have to be murder. He had gone too deep into Byrne's affairs. He knew too much. It would not be enough to drive him mad or ruin his reputation. Byrne was going to have to kill him.

He walked her home. He kissed her in the doorway. He drew in the clean smell of her skin mingled with the freshness of the winter air. Margaret Whitaker's therapy had lifted him out of the deepest depths of his depression. He had forgotten just how heavy the burden of regret could be. He remembered now.

"Will I see you again?" he asked her. He did not have to act to give the question the pitifully needy tone he was going for.

"Oh, you will," she said with a smile that shattered him.

But he didn't think he would. He thought he would be dead by nightfall or his enemies scattered, one or the other. These operations were delicate and had to be finished briskly. No doubt Hannah had stolen the research from his laptop last night. No doubt she had planted a digital bomb there that would either destroy his hard drive or fill it with damning files, love letters or amateur porn or whatever supported the narrative they were creating. He would have to be exterminated before any of that became apparent to him. The car trick would be best, he thought. It had a nice ambiguity about it. It made it impossible for the authorities to decide whether it had been suicide or an accident. That's what he would have used, the car trick.

Anyway, he told her, "See you soon," and he meant goodbye. He walked to the Nomad Tavern. On the way he found himself stealing glances around again, trying to spot the Invisibles. But again there was no sign of them. Either they were just that good or he was a sitting duck.

At the tavern, he sat moping over a second cup of coffee and the morning's news. Her scent was still on him. It coiled around inside him like a wraith until he felt his heart was a haunted house. He knew he was behaving like an idiot, but he couldn't help it and he didn't care. Those moments he spent inside her, lost in the illusion of her, they had been too real. He would not get over that quickly. He might never get over it.

The ghostly perfume was still with him as he strolled slowly to the Gothic. He climbed the stairs with heavy tread. He was opening the door to his minuscule office—eager to hide inside and nurse his sorrows in private—when Lori Lesser accosted him. There was no other word for it. The dean of student relations was suddenly at his shoulder, her raging face mere inches from his profile.

"We need to talk right now," she said. Her voice was like a hatchet.

That was quick, he thought. He opened the door and gestured her in. "Good morning to you too," he said.

She took the student's chair. He squirmed through the tight space between the edge of his desk and the crowded bookshelf against the wall. He reached his own swivel chair and worked his way into it, never an easy task.

"So," he said in a bland and friendly tone he hoped would infuriate her. "What can I do for you, Lori?"

She was dressed, he thought, like a savage, in clothes she must have scoured from the floor of her closet. Her sweater was ratty, thin, and tight. Her impressive figure threatened to burst through its worn-out places. Her belt was about twenty years out of fashion, so thick she could have slung a sword in it. Her red-gold hair stuck out as if electrified, and her eyes were wild and furious. Being Winter, he thought of Hippolyta, daughter of the queen of the Amazons and the god of war.

"I'm here because I consider us to be friends, Cam," she said, in the same tone he imagined she might have said, *Now I will rip out your heart and feed it to my dogs.* "I know you've never taken what I do seriously."

"Oh, come now, Lori," he managed to murmur.

"But I happen to consider it important that this campus should be a safe space for women. I have a duty, Cam. No matter how much I like you, I can't just sit by while our faculty trivializes sexual abuses of power."

Winter sat silently through the rest of this prologue. His mind drifted to stirring images of Hannah's body and, from there, to thoughts of death. He wondered again how exactly Byrne was going to try to kill him. Had to be the car, he thought again. The same way Byrne had killed Charles Merriman.

Finally, distantly, he noticed Lori had paused.

"Am I being accused of something?" he asked her.

"I know you spent last night with a student. Hannah Greer. She was seen going into your apartment building with you."

"'She was seen.' I like the use of the passive voice. Who saw her?"

"Do you deny it?"

"I don't feel obligated to report my personal life to you, Lori, yea or nay." *And she wasn't a student,* he wanted to add. *It was business. I was sleeping with my assassin.*

Lori flushed. With rage? With triumph? Bloodlust, maybe? "She's nineteen years old, Cam. For God's sake. I mean, I know that's legally over the age of consent but the power dynamic is ridiculous. The university guidelines are very specific on this. When I put your actions last night together with your defense of Adam Kemp—especially knowing what we know about Adam now and his treatment of Evelyn Shea—and add to those the complaints I've received about your curriculum . . ."

"My curriculum?"

"Not everyone is comfortable with your outmoded teaching methods."

"Oh . . ." *For Christ's sake,* he almost said. But he was afraid the Recruiter would swing on a rope and come crashing through the second-story window and smack him in the head for taking the Lord's name in vain. "For goodness sake," he finished lamely.

"It creates a very disturbing profile."

"Nonsense."

"I came here to give you fair warning," she went on relentlessly. "I've already made contact with the student. We're going to meet to discuss this tomorrow."

For a moment, with his heart in tatters, with the threat of death all around him, Winter allowed a little flicker flame of annoyance to flare up inside him. He had the urge to tell Lori to her face what a fool she was, that by tomorrow he might be dead and she might be an unwitting accomplice to his murder. And if the murder didn't come off—if the Invisibles did their work and he survived—she'd be an even a bigger fool than that.

If Winter died today, there would be some sort of manufactured scandal. Damning files would be found on his laptop. Hannah would post tearful posts on social media about how he'd done to her whatever she would say he had done. Lori would issue a statement and shake her head with solemn regret, secretly rejoicing in her triumph. And so she would become a cog in their machine.

But if he lived . . . Ah, that would be different.

If he lived, then by the time Lori took her grievance to Dean Howard Copely, Hannah Greer would have ceased to exist. No records. No files. No friends. No residence. And while Winter did not have tenure and while Dean Copely was a man of almost infinite moral cowardice ready to bend to the whims of the mob of the moment, and while Lori was an expert in the creation of such outraged mobs, even she could not work her will on behalf of a victim who never was. The joke would be on her.

What a joke it would be too. Because if Winter lived, unsupported attacks on his reputation would not be well received by the dean. Winter had been brought to work here five years ago as a temporary fill-in for an ailing professor, but the dean, who was forever having trouble with his wife, had sought him out as a transient and therefore safe male confidant. One day, over too many drinks, Copely had poured out his sorrows to him. He had had a relationship over the internet with an underage girl in Thailand. The relationship may not have been emotionally deep but it did involve a good deal of nudity, and all of those humiliating interchanges had been recorded by the girl's unsavory masters. Copley was being blackmailed.

Within three days of receiving that confession, Winter had made the problem disappear. He had his methods. Soon after that he was hired full-time. Winter would never have used this information to extort the dean in any way. But the dean could never be sure of that, and he was a man who played things safe. So in practice, for Winter, the secret between them was a kind of tenure better than tenure.

If Winter lived until tomorrow, and if Lori flung accusations at him, and if the girl she accused him of sleeping with turned out not to exist, the dean would be only too happy to use the excuse to fire Lori and destroy her career. Unstable fanatic that she was, she was an annoying little stone in his shoe anyway.

In his mood of the moment, Winter felt just nasty enough to let that nifty little plot play out. But then maybe the Recruiter was right about all that God and Satan and heaven and hell stuff. Who could say? He decided he'd better do the moral thing and warn her, just in case.

"Well, thank you for giving me this heads-up, Lori," he said. He would have stood up to signal the end of the meeting but there wasn't enough space between his chair and the wall.

"Cameron, I'm sorry. I really am," she said.

"Not at all."

"This is my job."

"Of course. Let me ask one more favor, though. Whether or not you talk to this young lady tomorrow—"

"Oh, I will. And if you make any move to silence her I'll know about it."

"I wouldn't dream of it. But as I say, whether you speak to her or not, I'd appreciate it if you'd call me before you go to Dean Copely."

"I don't see what good that will do. I've already given you a warning."

He shrugged. "I'd consider it a kindness. There are two sides to every story, after all."

She took a deep breath, looking up at the ceiling. He knew she did not believe there were two sides to anything. "I'll give it some thought," she said.

At that, his phone buzzed. "Excuse me," he said. He reached into his jacket.

Lori gave him a look then that was almost indescribable. There was venom in it but also longing and also regret. For a moment, he had a full understanding of how badly he had hurt her feelings when he'd rebuffed her. In spite of everything, he was sorry for it.

He drew out his phone. Looked at it. No identifier on the readout. He answered.

"Hello."

The office was so small it wasn't possible for Lori to swing her chair around angrily and storm out, but she gave it her best shot. She slammed the door for good measure.

"I need to see you, Professor Winter, right away," said the voice on the phone.

He was startled to realize it was Molly Byrne.

27

He'd been right, then. It would be the car.

There weren't any mountains in this area, but there was high ground about three hours north. That was the place to which she summoned him. Byrne owned a vacation lodge in the hills above the lake. The lodge was closed this late in the season, but Molly said she'd be there by five o'clock, waiting for him. It was a good setup. The light would be failing by the time he reached the winding forest roads above the water. The snow would still be thick on the ground in those regions. When Nelson pressed the button and Winter's brakes and steering failed, it would kill him just as surely as falling off the Jungfrau, especially if his Jeep exploded for good measure, which it almost surely would.

It was a strange feeling, driving toward that moment. This whole episode was strange—like a waking dream. There he'd been last night as if in Charlotte's arms and here he was as if in the Division again. It was as if his life had become some sort of nightmarish Eternal Recurrence of what was never quite the past and never quite the present. He couldn't go back and redeem the way he'd lived and he couldn't get free of it and move forward. Instead, he had the weird, dissociative sense that he was being drawn unstoppably on by his own terminal nostalgia, that there was nothing else he could do but live in the closed circle of his memories, world without end.

But then these assassinations were always fashioned with precision psychology. They were made to be hypnotic, to feel personal, inevitable. He wondered how many of his own victims had felt as helpless in the end as he felt now. He wondered if Roy had felt drawn on to his death this inexorably. He thought he probably had.

So on he drove.

The snow-covered fields gleamed under the sinking sun, then fell away. The forest surrounded him, its naked trees laced with harsh winter light. He was surprised he wasn't more afraid. He hadn't seen the slightest sign of the Recruiter or his Invisibles anywhere. There was always a chance this was going to be one of those epic foul-ups that would make for a good story on some drunken evening when soldiers of fortune gathered in one of their hellhole bars. *Remember Winter? Poor bastard. That one went so wrong.* And yet he loved the Recruiter like the father his father never was. He trusted him. For all his regrets and his loneliness, he drove toward the catastrophe, feeling more or less at peace. His will be done.

The road began to climb and turn. He caught a glimpse of the lodge on top of the hill. It was a vast palace of rustic luxury all rough stone and raw wood. Its many windows were dark, but some caught the sinking sun and flashed amber with it. Then he went around a turn and lost sight of it. The road kept climbing.

He began to wonder idly now where Nelson was. He had to be waiting somewhere near. A GPS can be tracked from anywhere but to set off a device like the one they'd likely put in his car the killer would have to be no more than twenty yards away give or take. Nelson would want to have him in sight when it happened anyway, just to be sure. He would not want to leave the slightest possibility that Winter might walk away from the crash.

The moment for that was coming, Winter could tell. The road was thrashing back and forth before him like a molting snake. The forest ground was thick with snow. There were sharp drops at the edge of the pavement, two thousand feet onto gray sheets of glacial stone.

A perverse impulse made him press down on the gas. *Come and get me.* The SUV gained speed. He scanned the forest out the windows, looking for a man in hiding, but there was no one there.

In the end, Nelson appeared suddenly in his rearview mirror: a sleek black Cadillac sports sedan, coming out of nowhere, curling round the last bend and closing on him quickly. Afterward, Winter thought, he would play the witness. *The man just drove straight off the cliff.*

The road still climbed. The daylight was starting to redden and wane. It was nearing that predusk hour when it's hard to see the subtleties of the pavement. Winter was going close to fifty now. Nelson sped up behind him and narrowed the gap almost to nothing.

Just before the end, Winter rehearsed in his mind the Division playbook for counter ops like this. He understood exactly how it was going to go—if it went well. And it would go well. The Recruiter was a master at the death-by-numbers business. With all respect for Margaret Whitaker he was the psychologist of all psychologists. Everyone who knew him would understand what was about to happen, everyone except his target, everyone except Nelson Chen.

Clearly, Nelson hadn't a clue that it was he, not Winter, who was about to be assassinated. He drove his Cadillac overly close to Winter's rear fender on purpose. He wanted Winter to see his face in the rearview. He wanted Winter to see him smile. To know that he had gotten around behind him, as Winter had gotten behind him back in the hotel in Los Angeles.

As the hairpin turn ahead grew near, as the emptiness beyond it opened onto nothingness and dying light and glimpses of the lake, Winter looked into his rearview mirror and saw Nelson's handsome face break into a grin of triumph. Nelson lifted his cell phone so Winter could see it. He knew that Winter would even know the brand of the phone: it was an assassin's favorite.

Winter moved his eyes quickly from the rearview to the road. He saw the last hairpin turn approaching. He looked in the mirror one more time. He saw Nelson tilt his head as if to say, *Sorry, old friend, but that's how it goes.*

Then Nelson pressed the button.

Winter followed the playbook in faith. He hit the brakes. He wrenched the steering wheel, baring his gritted teeth with the effort. His Jeep spun in a circle, his tires screaming and throwing smoke. Nelson's Cadillac went sailing past him. For a second, the two vehicles were parallel, their windows inches apart. Winter saw the bodyguard's face up close this time. It was frozen now in the realization that a switch had been made, that it was his brakes, his steering he had just destroyed with his own hand.

In the next moment the Cadillac shot off the winding road and into the emptiness of evening.

Winter, fighting to control his vehicle, did not watch it go. He only heard it crash on the rocks, and then the explosion.

28

Winter pulled to the side of the road and brought the Jeep to a gliding stop. He stepped out quickly into the chilly air. He could not see the Cadillac's flames from where he stood, but they must have been high because the air glowed orange. Sparks flew up toward the darkening sky and died.

His breath appearing in puffs of steam, Winter hurried to the edge of the cliff. He looked down. He was startled to see Nelson crawling from the wreckage. The bodyguard rolled weakly back and forth in the snow to douse his flaming clothes. Then he lay still.

Winter phoned for an ambulance. "The man just drove straight off the cliff," he said. The dispatcher told him they were forty minutes out at least. He ended the connection and started down the hill.

It was a hard climb. He had to walk a long way past the rim of the cliff before he could find the footing to descend. Even there the slope was steep. It was hard to keep his balance on the brittle snow. Once, he fell on his backside and slid a few yards down the hill. All in all, it must have taken him twenty minutes to reach what was left of the Cadillac.

The flames had died down by then but he could still feel the heat coming off the metal in waves. He didn't think Nelson could have possibly survived so long, but he was wrong about that. Nelson was a tough guy.

By the time Winter crouched over the fallen bodyguard the daylight was dim and the air was growing colder. Nelson was too weak and broken to move. He lay on his back, his clothes still smoking. His face was laced with running rivulets of blood. His cheeks sparkled with broken glass. One eye was gone. He was panting rapidly, fighting to keep his remaining eye open. He didn't even have the strength to shift its gaze. Winter had to move into his sight line before Nelson was certain he was there.

"I called an ambulance," Winter said.

Nelson gave something that would have been a laugh if he could have managed it. He cursed at Winter.

"No point," he breathed. "I'm dead."

Winter nodded. "Sorry, Chen."

Nelson had to gather his strength to speak again. "Tell me . . . Tell me that wasn't you," he said. "You're not that good."

Winter smiled. "No. That's right."

"The chief?"

"Yes."

"Damn. I thought he was out of the business. You always were his favorite. Poetry Boy. He used to talk about you."

Winter found this absurdly gratifying. He really did love the Recruiter. "Is there anything I can do for you?"

Nelson made a little negative motion with his head. Then: "Stay."

Winter reached down and gently took the other man's hand. He could feel the glass embedded in the flesh at the base of his thumb. The day grew darker.

After a while Nelson said, "Your computer . . . the girl . . ."

"A trapdoor," Winter told him.

"Ah . . . yeah. The chief . . ."

"He always liked trapdoors."

It was true. The counter op on Byrne had been nearly a replay of the counter op on Roy Spahn all those years ago. Like Roy, Hannah Greer had thought she'd rifled his laptop, but in fact the Recruiter had planted a trapdoor on her device. When she handed the drive over to Byrne, it would have allowed the Recruiter into Byrne's systems. Already, his entire network had probably been hacked.

Even as Winter crouched over Nelson's body in the gathering darkness, whatever plans Byrne had ever made, whatever orders he'd given, whatever secret algorithms he'd used to control and purloin information from his powerful site—all of that was in the process of falling into the Recruiter's hands. Doubtless, as it was leaked out to the public over the coming weeks, Byrne's powerful allies would do their best to bury the story. But eventually they'd have to choose between sacrificing Byrne and getting caught themselves. Byrne would have to go. There were just too many bodies to ignore.

And now, there was one body more.

An uncanny silence had come over the forest in the frosty gloaming. In that pervasive quiet, Winter could hear Nelson's breath as if it were the wind. He heard the tempo of it slow. He heard it grow rough and long with a rattling whistle in it. It was difficult to make out the bodyguard's face in the dark, but he saw his remaining eye gleam, then stop gleaming. He pressed Nelson's hand. He heard the man take a sharp breath and whisper something. Winter leaned down closer. He heard Nelson whisper, ". . . love . . . love . . ."

Then came the painfully long death rattle, his last breath, and he was gone.

Winter let go of his hand. He squatted where he was another few seconds. He felt he should make some sort of spiritual gesture: a prayer or the sign of the cross. But it would have been hypocritical, so he refrained. Instead, he merely lifted his eyes to watch the deeper darkness of night falling on the forest and the last light streaking the lake beyond the trees. He sighed again, his breath steaming.

This too, this moment, felt to him like the eternally recurring past. Another death arranged. Another man who might have been his friend destroyed. For all his sensitivities, Winter was a hard character in his way. He felt no guilt about what he had done. It had been kill or be killed. But it was still a sorrow to him, another sorrow added to the burden of the rest. With his literary turn of mind, the darkness falling over the trees seemed symbolic to him. The darkness would soon be everywhere. Hannah had been right. It felt as if truth and beauty were going out of the world.

He pushed to his feet. Looked up the slope. There was still no sign of the ambulance.

He began the long hard climb through the slippery snow back to the top of the cliff, back to the road, back to his car.

29

He continued his drive to the lodge. Only when he'd crested the hill, when he reached the final straightaway and the building loomed before him, only then could he see the lights inside: a few lamps spreading a dim yellow glow behind the enormous picture window on the ground floor, a few more glowing in windows on the floor just above.

The cul-de-sac at the entrance had been shoveled recently but a patina of hard snow still covered the pavement. It crunched beneath his tires as he drew up to the lodge. It crunched beneath his boots as he walked to the front stairs.

The doors were open. He stepped inside. There were no lights on in the reception area. There was no one behind the front desk. The high stone walls were all in shadow. He turned toward the glow. He followed the glow up a flight of three steps. He came into the lobby.

It was a vast space, rough wooden walls, rough wooden beams crisscrossing under a high ceiling. There was an immense stone fireplace but it was long cold, and though it was warmer than the forest in here Winter was glad to be in his heavy shearling and he kept his ivy cap on. There were green leather armchairs and low tables set on rugs with tribal designs. There were a couple of mounted moose heads on the wall and some paintings of bears and mountain lions and one large mural of Chippewas gathered on the plain. A few small lamps were shining here and there, the sources of that glow he'd seen when he was approaching.

Overhead, on three sides, a log balcony ringed the mezzanine. There was a light or two on up there as well but most of it was in shadow. A stairway at the far end of the room rose into that shadow and vanished halfway in gloomy obscurity.

Now, out of that obscurity, there came a soft voice: "Nelson? Is that you? Are you back?"

A figure emerged from the darkness at the top of the stairs. Winter stood in the center of the lobby and watched as Byrne descended. When he reached the bottom of the staircase, Byrne threw a switch on the wall. Three large chandeliers went on above the lobby. A soft blanket of pale light settled over both men.

Byrne stood still, one foot on the lobby floor, one on the step above. He stared at Winter, open-mouthed with surprise. There was something ridiculous about him in that moment, dressed in hipster black with his prophet's beard and his beatnik ponytail and the ayahuasca tattoo on his neck and the ring in his nose—and a look on his face like a six-year-old boy who had just been caught writing on the wall with crayons.

Winter was surprised at how angry he felt, angry enough to enjoy this moment—the moment when a little would-be god discovered he was just a little would-be man. So much death, Winter thought, so much murder to learn such a simple lesson.

"You petty son of a bitch," Winter heard himself say.

By the light of the chandeliers he saw Byrne's face darken with fury. His mouth twisted. He shook his head. "Who the hell do you think you are, Winter?"

"I'm an English professor," Winter said.

But the billionaire wasn't listening. The first shock of seeing his latest victim walk into the lodge alive had worn off. He had now begun to calculate just what this might mean.

"Where's Nelson?" he asked.

"Figure it out, Byrne."

"What? What do you mean? He's dead?"

"I switched the devices, my car to his. He pressed the button and . . ." Winter threw up his hands in a casually callous gesture, just to press the point home. ". . . his brakes failed like you meant mine to fail. He went off the road and crashed the way I was supposed to. He died like I was supposed to die."

As Winter watched, Byrne began to comprehend the full scope of the disaster. His eyes flicked back and forth, to one side then the other. As if he was looking for an exit, Winter thought. But there was no exit. *This is the end of things, you bastard.*

Byrne seemed to hear this thought and to realize the truth of it. All his high cool suddenly deserted him. As if to make an excuse for himself, he spat out the words: "You. You pushed me to it."

"Now you're catching on," Winter said. "That's exactly right. That's exactly what I did. I pushed you to it. It was a hit. From the very beginning. Confronting you on the cliffs in Marin. Bothering your mother-in-law. Bothering your wife. Every move I made was intended to set you off and engineer exactly this. It was a hit, Byrne, like you pulled on Adam and Charles and Arnaud Baptiste and all the others. It was a hit and you were the target."

Byrne's mouth opened and closed but his answer seemed stuck in his throat.

"I'll give you this: you were clever," Winter added with jocular cruelty. "You and Nelson, you were both clever. Hannah was particularly good. You almost got past me with Hannah. Oh, and speaking of Hannah, there was a trapdoor in my laptop too."

The effect of this on Byrne was almost comically delicious. His eyes widened. His body tensed as if he were about to race upstairs to try to stop the invasion of his systems. But he was a tech genius, after all. He understood it was way too late for that. And so he stayed where he was and glared black death at his nemesis. Which his nemesis enjoyed immensely.

Winter wasn't done either. He had one final stake he wanted to drive into the man's heart, into him and his Good World Project. His *good world*!

He took a step toward him. He wanted to be close enough to see his reaction clearly, to drink it in. There was vengeance in his heart. Vengeance for so much death.

"Did Molly know?" he asked. Cool as he was trying to be, he heard his own voice tremble with rage. "That was another nice touch. Having your wife call me. A perfect touch, if you assumed I was acting in the dark. I might have suspected a call from you. But not from Molly. Not from the Cinderella Girl. If I had been acting in the dark, I would have fallen for that, no question. Did she know? Did she know you were using her to lure me to my death? Did you tell her you had made her an accomplice to murder? She was always the best thing about you, Byrne. Did you tell her what you were turning her into?"

The answer came in a gasp from the mezzanine above them: Molly's pale face at the balcony, her horrified expression. Her choked half whisper. "Gerald?"

Byrne whipped around, gaping up at her. His cheeks went so white he seemed a dead man. The flower tattoo on his neck seemed to glow red against his concrete-colored flesh.

Husband and wife gazed at one another, she on the balcony, he on the stairs below. Their hearts were in their eyes, their hearts laid waste.

And with that the anger drained out of Winter. He was done with this. The hit was finished. As he looked up at Molly he was thinking of Nelson. He was thinking of Nelson murmuring ". . . love . . . love . . ." into the gathering dark. Winter had his vengeance now, but there was no joy in it.

He turned and walked out of the lobby. His footsteps sent a hollow echo through the vast and empty spaces of the lodge.

30

The next afternoon, after a long morning of speaking with the police and teaching his Wordsworth class, Winter went to the Independent café for a coffee and croissant. Melancholy in the wake of the events of the night before, he had avoided reading the news all day, and he was avoiding it still. Instead, he sat at his small table and fed his sorrows with some poetry he had called up on his laptop.

> *And when I saw a stranger's face*
> *Where beauty held the claim,*
> *I gave it like a secret grace*
> *The being of thy name.*
> *And all the charms of face or voice*
> *Which I in others see*
> *Are but the recollected choice*
> *Of what I felt for thee.*

Just as he reached the last line he was startled to realize someone was standing beside him. He looked up quickly—and he felt the sort of jolt one feels while watching a suspense movie when the villain jumps out of the dark.

"Lori!" he said. "How nice to see you. Would you care to join me?"

His heart was already slowing after that first shock, but still she was a fright to look upon. Her red winter coat was buttoned up so that the full, soft figure that attracted him was hidden, and there was nothing but her face, full of hellish fury, and that wild, Amazonian hair.

"She's gone," she said abruptly.

Winter almost asked "Who?" just to annoy her but thought better of it. "You mean the young woman you were going to speak to today."

"She never showed. I went to her apartment and she wasn't there. I mean, she wasn't there at all. She'd moved out."

Winter had no response to make to this, so he simply gazed up at her mildly in what he hoped was an irritating way.

Lori Lesser's white cheeks flushed. She had to take a deep breath before she went on. "Her records were gone too."

Winter lifted his coffee cup even though the coffee had gone cold. He tried to sound surprised. "You mean her student records?"

"That's right. They were there yesterday and today there's no trace of them, and no one seems to have ever heard of her. She's not even on the internet anywhere. It's like she never even existed."

"How strange. Someone must have seen her at some point. After all, someone told you they had seen her with me."

Lori only turned redder and more frightening at this but she didn't answer. She couldn't answer, Winter thought, because no one had told her they had seen him with Hannah. It was she who had seen them together herself. In her hurt and fury she had been spying on him.

"Will you still go to Dean Copely?" he asked her, his expression as innocent as a lamb's.

"Oh, please!" she snapped at him. "You know I can't. You know he'd just protect you. He always protects you, doesn't he?"

Winter put his cold coffee down without sipping it. "There's nothing to protect me from, Lori."

She stared at him. She was silent for a longish moment, but it was the silence of a cocked trigger. Finally, she said, "Is this some sort of elaborate little boy trick you two pulled to make a fool of me?"

"Who? Me and Copely? Lori! Of course not. Don't be ridiculous. Look, I don't feel obligated to explain my personal life to you or anyone. But you mistook this situation and—"

"Oh, bullshit!" she said.

She had more room to swing around angrily here than she had had in his tiny office, and she made a good job of it. She started to storm toward the door, but she stopped short and pivoted again. She stormed back to the side of his table.

"I want you to know I'm going to find out, Cam. I'm going to find out what happened. And I'm going to find out what's between you and Copely, too. I'm sick of both of you and your boys' club values. Sick of them." Once again, she began to pivot. Once again, she pivoted back. "I mean, who even are you, Cameron?" she said fiercely. "I'm serious. Who are you?"

"I'm an English professor," Winter said.

It was only after she was gone—after she had left the shop and charged with furious strides out of view from the window—it was only then that Winter felt a deep pang of disappointment. It was only then he realized that all this time, all the time he had been sitting here in the coffee shop, he had been waiting for someone, expecting someone, hoping someone would come in through the door. Not Lori, of course. He had not been waiting for Lori. But now, he realized, Lori was all he was going to get.

It was like she never even existed.

Melancholy settled over him again. He thought of those moments in Hannah's arms. He gazed at his laptop screen.

And when I saw a stranger's face
Where beauty held the claim,
I gave it like a secret grace
The being of thy name.

But it was a line from *Hamlet* that came to him—came to him like a cry from his own heart.

Stay, illusion!

EPILOGUE

31

The aftereffects of Winter's hit on Gerald Byrne were dramatic and brutal but subtle all the same. The average consumer of daily news would never even have realized what had happened.

There were news leaks, as Winter had known there would be. There were dribs and drabs of the truth released to those few outlets the Recruiter trusted. And, as Winter had also expected, those leaks were downplayed and even suppressed by social media and the larger news organizations. Conspiracy theorists went to work in their place, compiling lists of Byrne associates who had died under mysterious circumstances. They were such long lists that some of the people on them were actually people Byrne had had murdered. But most of it was nonsense. The lists and the theories were swiftly banned as misinformation from Byrner and other social media, and anyone who posted them was locked out of his account. The larger news outlets covered them only as an oddity.

Nevertheless, over the months that followed, several events convinced Winter that his attempts to do justice on behalf of the dead had not been wholly unsuccessful.

The first of these events, the most dramatic and the most cruel, was Byrne's divorce. Only a month or so after that night in the lodge Molly left him, taking their children with her. The news media hinted that the marriage had broken up because Byrne had had an affair with an obscure but beautiful actress named Jessica Beamer. But Winter didn't believe it. Byrne idolized Molly. He would never have cheated on her. This Jessica Beamer had had nothing but bit parts before this. Now suddenly she landed a lead on a streaming series. Winter believed the part was her payment for letting the adultery rumors stand without comment.

All the evidence suggested there was more to the divorce than mere infidelity. For one thing, the settlement gave Molly what amounted to nearly half of Byrne's fortune. Since most of his money had been made before she married him, this was generous even by California standards. And yet Byrne didn't even try to contest it. Nor did he stop Molly from effectively taking custody of their children or full control of the Fairy Tale Fund. He merely issued a simpering, sentimental statement saying that he and Molly continued to have a "treasured friendship." Even had they known what they knew now, he said, they would've done it all again in the name of love. Molly herself said nothing except that the good work of the Fairy Tale Fund would continue.

Then, not long after the breakup was settled, Byrne surrendered control of his company. The algorithms and procedures that silenced his political opponents had appeared on several websites by then, but very few people understood them or took the time to read the explanations by the few who did. There were rumors of mismanagement and one or two accusations of misappropriated funds, but there was no legal action taken. There was simply another sentimental statement from Byrne. He said he was leaving the business because he needed time "to seek spiritual renewal," in order to "face the coming challenges of the new millennium." Shortly thereafter he surrendered his place on the board of the

Good World Project, and the project itself quietly ceased to exist. Which didn't make much of an impression on the public, most of whom had never known it existed in the first place.

In fact, to the average consumer of news, all of this made for little more than a moment's gossip. Billionaires get divorced. Company heads get ousted. Social media is awful. The rich, the powerful, the celebrated, and the well respected are, generally speaking, the worst people in any given country. Whatever low doings they get up to come as no surprise to the ordinary woman or man.

But to Winter the gossip told a deeper story. Byrne's empire had been destroyed, his life had collapsed, and all his power was gone, likely for good. So many wealthy and high-placed people were involved in his crimes that it was always likely he would escape exposure and prosecution. Yet clearly some of his co-conspirators—or someone—had put a choice before him: either the truth comes out and you go to prison or you leave quietly and let your wife leave quietly too.

Byrne had taken the latter option. A few months later a photograph of him made the rounds online. It was a blurry candid of Byrne on a secluded beach in Santa Catarina, Brazil. Dressed only in a pair of black swim trunks, the already slender billionaire appeared to have lost at least fifty pounds. His body was emaciated, bent, weak-looking. His face appeared dazed and haggard. His mouth was slack. His eyes were glazed and distant. As many online wits remarked he looked like he'd just been released from a concentration camp.

Winter was mildly disappointed to see Byrne escape the execution or life sentence that would have fallen on any more common serial killer. Still, he consoled himself that a fall from the heavens is a long fall. And while everyone must die and anyone might be put behind bars, it was a fate akin to damnation to lose the love of a woman like Molly Shea.

32

Winter saw her once. Molly. To his absolute amazement he got to speak with her one last time. It happened about nine months after that night in the lodge, on a stunningly beautiful autumn day.

In the coincidental way of these dramatic moments, Winter had been talking about her only moments before in one of his sessions with Margaret Whitaker. The photograph of Byrne on the beach had only recently been released, and it was she, Margaret, who brought the subject up.

Winter had just concluded another of his confessions about his career in the Division. As he sat in the client's chair, gazing into the room's tan middle distance, ruminating on his murderous past, Margaret said to him, "You know, with all these stories of yours, Cam, you're turning me into a conspiracy theorist."

Winter blinked out of his daze. "Really? I'd hate to think that."

"Well, you make me feel there's so much going on behind the news headlines that the average person doesn't know."

"Ah, well, yes. That much is true anyway. But they aren't conspiracies exactly. People do bad things to serve their own interests and then they lie about them to avoid exposure. Powerful people do very bad things and lie about them. And the flow of information is largely controlled by powerful people . . ."

"Who do very bad things . . ."

". . . and lie about them, exactly. That leaves conspiracy theorists free to weave their insane tales. Which really are insane, almost by definition."

"What do you mean? Why by definition?"

"Well . . . I spent the night once with a woman who was one of those—what do you call them?—congenital liars. Every single thing she told me about herself was untrue. And if I caught her in some contradiction or some obvious mistake, she would simply replace that untruth with another untruth. There was no bottom to it. It went on all night. Lies upon lies upon lies. And what I found was that, by the time morning came, a strange thing had happened to me."

"You began to believe her."

"Of course. I just began to accept whatever she said. Because I'm not insane. Only an insane person can live as if everything he hears is a lie."

"So the conspiracy theorists are insane because only an insane person thinks he's being lied to all the time. But they are, in fact, being lied to all the time."

"All the time. And because they're insane, their theories about the underlying truth beneath the lies are largely insane. They're insane but they're not entirely wrong. Not always anyway."

"What a frightening thought," said Margaret Whitaker.

"Just the way of the world, really. You know how they talk about the madness of crowds? Well, I wonder sometimes if the crowds are actually too sane—too sane to disbelieve all the lies they've been told by the powerful people who want to control them."

The two friends—and Cameron and Margaret had become friends now—smiled at one another over this. Then, after a moment of silence, Margaret spoke with slow care.

"You know, I saw a picture the other day of a man named Gerald Byrne, one of those tech billionaires, or at least he was."

Trained to watch her client's reactions closely she paused again. Winter drew in a deep breath through his nose. His whole body straightened in his chair. He was preparing himself for what came next, she thought. Which meant that her own conspiracy theories must have touched at least some version of the truth.

"Yes, I've heard of Gerald Byrne," he said. "What brings him to mind?"

"Oh, just talking about, you know, trying to get at the truth of things."

Winter lifted his chin, waiting.

"Anyway, this Byrne is a man about your age, but in this picture he looked like he was a hundred years old. He looked terrible, like he'd just been released from a prison camp or something."

"Yes. I've seen the picture."

"Apparently he's been through a difficult divorce and lost control of his company and no one quite understands why. So I did one of those things you do on the computer, where you start looking things up and one story leads to another and so on. The conspiracy theorists have all sorts of ideas about this Byrne person. They say all his enemies either died mysteriously or were ruined."

Winter's eyes and Margaret's eyes met directly, full of meaning. Winter said nothing.

Margaret said, "It reminded me of your stories about the Division."

"The Division? Oh. Yes. I see what you mean. The way people can be eliminated or destroyed."

"Yes. And that made me remember my little dog. My little wooden dog. How it was turned around a bit that one time, remember?"

"Yes, I do."

"You were very kind about it. Very reassuring. I appreciated that."

"Not at all."

There was another silence, their eyes still locked. And then, with one of those leaps of insight that made him love her, she said, "I was interested to read about Byrne's ex-wife. Molly her name was."

Winter said nothing but she could see his breathing grow slower.

"They called her Cinderella," she went on. "The Cinderella Girl, I think it was. Because she was just an ordinary person when they met, and now she's one of the wealthiest women in the country."

"The second wealthiest, I think."

"Really?"

"Mm. Maybe the third. I don't follow these things very closely."

"This Byrne had a very sad biography. A very difficult childhood. His mother committed suicide when he was very young," Margaret went on. Her gaze was still fixed on Winter and she could see—as she so often could—his own lonely childhood, right there in his eyes. She was suddenly, painfully aware of her love for him and she wished she could reach across the space between them and put her hand against his cheek.

"You know, I don't ascribe to any of that Freudian nonsense," she went on gently. "Men wanting to sleep with their mothers and all that. It's ridiculous. But I do think, when a boy is deprived of his mother, like Byrne was, I think he misses something in his life. Some feminine influence. I don't know how to describe it exactly."

"The yin of the pleroma," Winter murmured.

"My goodness, professor. How you do talk. What on earth does that mean?"

"The Eternal Feminine. The feminine aspect of the totality of God."

"Yes. Yes, exactly. Male and female he made us in his image."

"So they say."

"And since most women bear some portion of that—whatever you called it, the feminine principle—but no woman can thoroughly embody it, a man like Gerald Byrne is left looking for something that isn't quite real, something both more and less than a living woman. An idea instead of a human being. Unless he happens to start dating the Virgin Mary."

"Who'd be awfully difficult to impress, I imagine," Winter said softly.

Margaret smiled. "You see what I'm saying, though. If these sorts of feminine or masculine principles have any meaning at all, it's people who manifest them in the world. If someone is looking for love, he has to learn to love the person, then maybe he gets the principle to boot. It doesn't work if you try to do it the other way around."

Winter did see what she was saying, and he understood why she was saying it. He forced himself to sit quietly for a few moments, because he had the urge to make a reply he knew would be deeply stupid once it came out of his mouth. He wasn't sure what it would be exactly. But it would be something about how he wished he could reach not just across the space between them but across all the time, the years that separated them and put his hand against her cheek when she was young.

Instead, he said: "What a fascinating theory, Margaret."

"Stick around, boy-o. I've got a million of them."

He left her a few moments later. A few moments after that he saw Molly Shea.

33

He had left Margaret's office and was walking back to his apartment. His mind, as so often after a therapy session, was in a whirl of emotion and thoughts. Only slowly did the beauty of the day seep into his awareness. The sky was a rich midday blue. The air was chill with autumn and carried a wistful scent of dying leaves. Winter couldn't have said why, but he found his spirits were suddenly quite high and hopeful. The woman was a miracle worker, he thought. She had the ability to reduce him to the inner state of a child and at the same time make a new man of him. How did she do it?

He was not far from his apartment, thinking these things, when a black limousine of some sort slowly pulled up beside him. He noticed it and turned. The rear window slid down and there was Molly.

Winter could not have been more surprised if he had woken from a dream of her to find her standing at his bedside. It was as if the conversation he'd just had with Margaret had somehow conjured Molly's presence out of the empty air.

Her name was startled out of him. "Molly?"

"Professor Winter," she said. "Could I speak to you for a moment?"

"Of course. Of course."

He walked around the car and got into the backseat beside her. The chauffeur started the car rolling through the city streets.

"How nice to see you again," Winter said.

Physically, events had not transformed her as they had her emaciated ex-husband. She was her usual plump and sturdy self. But Winter could see at once that something had gone out of her. Some softness, some silliness—some femininity, he said to himself. Her hair was short now, waved. Her face was more serious, more sad. And there was something hard about her expression that had not been there before. Winter was sorry to see it, but who could blame her?

She sat silent as they drove. She looked out the window. He began to feel uncomfortable, just sitting there. After a few more moments, he said, "How are you?"

She glanced at him. Smiled sadly. Tilted her head. "I've wanted to talk to you for so long, and now I don't know exactly what I want to say," she told him.

"Take your time."

"It weighs on me that I called you that night."

"No, no, please. I set you free of it. You didn't know."

She smiled sadly again. Looked out the window again. Said something he couldn't hear.

"Excuse me?"

She turned back to him. "That's the question I ask myself every day. What did I know? I don't know why I feel I have to tell you this. I sometimes think I should hate you. I did hate you. But I think I only hated you because . . . because you woke me up from the dream I was living in. And now I have to ask myself for the rest of my life: what did I know?"

She laughed but it was not her old laugh. She shook her head. "All I wanted was a husband and a family to make a home for. And now instead of a husband I have all this . . . *money.*" She said it as if the word meant "useless trash." "I don't know why I'm telling you this. I don't know why I keep feeling that you're the one I have to tell."

She pinned him with her troubled gaze. "Why did you do it, professor? I don't mean that like it sounds, accusingly. I just really want to know. Why?"

He raised his eyebrows—a kind of shrug. "It's hard to explain. I have this strange habit of mind," he said. "Certain stories, mysteries, crimes, injustices seem to call to me, and I have to . . ."

". . . fix them."

"Solve them. Make them right. Yes."

"Well, then, you're not so different from Gerald, are you?"

"No. I suppose I'm not."

"Looking for some perfect thing, trying to fix the past."

"I suppose so."

"The two of you. Couldn't you just believe in God and leave it to him?"

"Apparently not."

"Gerald used to have these nightmares . . . Did I already tell you that?"

"You did, yes."

"I don't know why I feel the need to tell you any of it." She continued to look at him intensely. For a moment he thought she was going to cry, but she didn't. "Do you think I'm looking for you to give me absolution? Is that it?"

He had no answer to this. He would have happily granted her absolution on the spot, but he didn't feel it was his place. It would be fake if he did it. An act of mere politeness. And yet she was waiting for him to say something.

He said, "I have a friend, a sort of mentor. I told him about you. He said you were a woman of God and you would mourn your losses and then find meaning and move through suffering closer to the throne of heaven."

"Oh goody," said Molly drily. "Did he mention when that would happen? How long it would take? Because so far this just sucks."

She turned away from him to the window again. She looked out at the passing city streets. He felt bad for her. He felt bad she had lost her softness. More than that. She had lost her majesty, he thought.

"I'm sorry it's been so painful for you," he said.

Her sigh fogged the glass. "It's you men," she answered with a laugh. "You take it out of us. But then . . . I chose them! I'm the stupid one who chose them."

"Well. We're all playthings in the hands of love."

"I don't know why I'm telling you this. Why you, I mean."

In the silence that followed, Winter actually tried to consider the question. It was not an easy one. Because who was he after all? A lost man, goo-goo eyed over his superannuated therapist, pining for a little girl he'd known in childhood and even for the assassin who had pretended to be that girl grown up. Molly, at least, had lived her dream and given it all her devotion. And he was the one who had destroyed it. Why should she confess her sins to him?

But then all that confusion blew away like smoke and there in his mind was the simple, obvious answer to her question.

"It's because I know the truth," he told her.

She faced him, and he could see she knew he was right.

"You and I are really the only ones who do know," he went on. "And Gerald. And I suppose you want to know if, knowing the truth, I hate you or blame you or think ill of you somehow. And I don't, Molly. Truly. Not at all. It's not for me to forgive you. I don't have that power. But I don't blame you in the least. Gerald loved you, and he gave you a perfect life, and when you saw what that meant—what it really has to mean in this imperfect world—you walked away. Anyone who thinks they would have done better is lying to himself."

"You know who I think about?" she said. "I think about Gerald's father. He's the one who started all this in a way. A horrible, horrible man. Doing what he did. He was supposed to be a man of God! And he was just so utterly corrupt. He's the one who destroyed everything. He destroyed Gerald's mother. He destroyed Gerald's family. He destroyed Gerald's childhood, his faith. And look at him. He's fine. Married a rich girl. Became a powerful man, respected by everyone he knows. People love him. It's just . . ." She gestured helplessly.

"Hellishly unfair?" Winter said.

"Hellishly is right. In church, they used to preach that this world belongs to the devil. They don't preach that anymore. But they should. It's true. Nobody tells the truth about anything anymore, but that is the truth. This world belongs to the devil." She shuddered. "I sure hope your friend is right. About me and the throne of heaven, I mean."

"He certainly has a habit of being right about such things."

"I hope so." She took a deep breath and then another. "Well . . . I'm sorry to bother you."

"No, no."

"Where can I drop you?"

"This is fine," said Winter. "It's not far, and it's a lovely day."

"Bernard," she said to the chauffeur. The limo drew to the curb and stopped. Molly took Winter's hand. She smiled kindly, like a great lady. He supposed she would be a great lady now, with all that money. She leaned across the seat and kissed his cheek. She laughed. "Thank you for ruining my life," she said.

"Any time. You can understand why I'm welcome wherever I go."

She laughed again. Clasped his hand tighter. "Goodbye, professor."

He stepped out of the car and walked around to the sidewalk. He stood with his hands in his pants pockets and watched as the limo began to edge out into the city traffic. But it stopped where it was, slanted away from the curb. The window came down again. Molly looked out at him.

"What about you, professor?" she called through the street noise. "Do you have someone?"

"Someone . . . ?" he said.

"In your life. Someone to love."

His head went back. He gave a small laugh. "Ah. No. No, not really."

"You should," said Molly. "You really should."

"Really? You say that? Even now. With all your sorrows."

"Oh. Well." She smiled brightly, and with pleasure he saw for a second the woman she had been, still there inside her. "Sorrow is the price of love in a world where nothing lasts. Isn't it?"

He smiled back at her fondly. "Yes. Yes, I suppose it is."

"Without love and sorrow we're just objects in space," said Molly.

Winter was surprised by a surge of emotion. He pressed his lips together.

"Goodbye, professor," she said again.

He could only nod.

He felt sad as he watched the limo pull away, sad to see her go, and sad that she had lost that glorious thing she'd had, that feminine majesty. *You men take it out of us,* she had said.

He sighed to himself and thought: probably so. But then, we all fail one another so terribly, don't we? We cheat. We lie. We miss our connections on the paths of time. We search for God in one another's faces, and what beasts we are. What twisted beasts to search for God in. And who knows if he's even there?

With another sigh, Winter turned and continued walking home through the autumn weather.

That was the question, he thought. Who knows if he's even there?